MAGGIE SHAYNE

"... is better than chocolate. She satisfies every wicked craving."
—Suzanne Forster

PRAISE FOR MAGGIE SHAYNE'S NOVELS

## The Gingerbread Man

"[A] gripping story of small-town secrets. The suspense will keep you guessing. The characters will steal your heart."
—*New York Times* bestselling author Lisa Gardner

"Intricately woven . . . A moving mix of high suspense and romance, this haunting Halloween thriller will propel readers to bolt their doors at night."
—*Publishers Weekly*

## Destiny

"An altogether stunning book, *Destiny* lives up to the expectations created by *Eternity* and *Infinity* and then some."
—*Old Book Barn Gazette*

## Infinity

"[A] dark, enthralling brew of love, danger, and perilous fate."
—Jayne Ann Krentz

"A superb fantasy romance . . . The story line, especially the historical segment, is stupendous . . . Ms. Shayne augments her growing reputation for some of the best fantasies on the market today."
—*Painted Rock Reviews*

"A heartfelt and believable love story . . . Maggie Shayne's gift is that she creates believable characters who react very humanly to unbelievable situations."
—*All About Romance*

*continued . . .*

# Eternity

"A rich, sensual, and bewitching adventure of good vs. evil, with love as the prize."
                                                            —*Publishers Weekly*

"A hauntingly beautiful story of love that endures through time itself."
                                                            —Kay Hooper

"Ms. Shayne's talent knows no bounds when it comes to romantic fantasy; her latest is a hauntingly exquisite tale . . . lush . . . heart-stopping suspense, spellbinding romance, and enchanting characters. *Eternity* is to be treasured like the precious gem it is."
                                                            —*Rendezvous*

"[*Eternity*] is one of the best books of the decade as the magnificent Ms. Shayne demonstrates why she is ranked among the top writers of any genre."
                                                            —*Affaire de Coeur*

## MORE PRAISE FOR THE NOVELS OF MAGGIE SHAYNE

"Maggie Shayne is a reader's joy. Fast-paced, witty, delightful, and shamelessly romantic, her stories will be treasured long after the book is done. A remarkable talent destined for stardom!"
                                                            —Teresa Medeiros

"Ms. Shayne definitely knows how to keep you guessing with the many suspects and different twists this plot takes. Her characters come to life in a way that makes you feel as if you know every one of them . . . wonderful romantic suspense with edge-of-your-seat tension, steamy passion, and real emotions with which a reader can identify."
                                                            —*Rendezvous*

# Bewitched, Bothered and Bewildered

## Maggie Shayne

BERKLEY SENSATION, NEW YORK

THE BERKLEY PUBLISHING GROUP
Published by the Penguin Group
Penguin Group (USA) Inc.
375 Hudson Street, New York, New York 10014, USA
Penguin Group (Canada), 90 Eglinton Avenue East, Suite 700, Toronto, Ontario M4P 2Y3, Canada
(a division of Pearson Penguin Canada Inc.)
Penguin Books Ltd., 80 Strand, London WC2R 0RL, England
Penguin Group Ireland, 25 St. Stephen's Green, Dublin 2, Ireland (a division of Penguin Books Ltd.)
Penguin Group (Australia), 250 Camberwell Road, Camberwell, Victoria 3124, Australia
(a division of Pearson Australia Group Pty. Ltd.)
Penguin Books India Pvt. Ltd., 11 Community Centre, Panchsheel Park, New Delhi—110 017, India
Penguin Group (NZ), Cnr. Airborne and Rosedale Roads, Albany, Auckland 1310, New Zealand
(a division of Pearson New Zealand Ltd.)
Penguin Books (South Africa) (Pty.) Ltd., 24 Sturdee Avenue, Rosebank, Johannesburg 2196,
South Africa

Penguin Books Ltd., Registered Offices: 80 Strand, London WC2R 0RL, England

This is a work of fiction. Names, characters, places, and incidents either are the product of the author's imagination or are used fictitiously, and any resemblance to actual persons, living or dead, business establishments, events, or locales is entirely coincidental. The publisher does not have any control over and does not assume any responsibility for author or third-party websites or their content.

PRINTING HISTORY
Berkley Sensation trade paperback edition / December 2005

Library of Congress Cataloging-in-Publication Data

Shayne, Maggie.
    Bewitched, bothered and bewildered / Maggie Shayne.— Berkley Sensation trade pbk. ed.
        p. cm.
    Contents: Everything she does is magick—Musketeer by moonlight—The con and the crusader.
    ISBN 0-425-20576-2
    1. Occult fiction, American. 2. Supernatural—Fiction. 3. Love stories, American. I. Title.

PS3619.H399B493 2005
813'.6—dc22

                                                                    2005048146

PRINTED IN THE UNITED STATES OF AMERICA

10  9  8  7  6  5  4  3  2  1

# CONTENTS

# Bewitched, Bothered and Bewildered

# Everything She Does
# Is Magick

# Prologue

**Midnight, October 31, 1970**

*A* little Witch is born.

"*Her* name will be Aurora," Merriwether said firmly, staring down at the cradle she'd bought for her brand-new charge. The baby's mother, Merriwether's niece, had never embraced the secret ways of the Sortilege women. She'd rejected her heritage, turned her back on the ways of magick. Even claimed she didn't believe in it. Then she'd run away with a leather-bearing beast on a motorbike, shouting over her shoulder that her three aunts were completely insane, and ought to be committed because everyone knew there were no such things as Witches. Almost as an afterthought, she'd added that her aunts had best not be casting any spells to make her come back, or she'd hate them forever.

Nine months later, Melinda had the good sense to send her newborn daughter home to her three aunts, delivered to the front door by a social worker with the message that Melinda was "just not mother material."

Merriwether had known the child would end up in her care. She hadn't known *how* it would happen, but she'd never doubted it would, because she'd seen it in the stars. Aurora Sortilege was a special child, a child of destiny. And her aunts were here to see that she fulfilled it.

"Oh, yes, Aurora. It's perfect!" Fauna clapped her plump hands together near her rounded middle and gave a good belly laugh. Her face quivered with mirth, and her outrageous orange hair—frizzed from too many colorings and permanents—bobbed and bounced as if it were laughing, too. "It brings our little fairy tale full circle, don't you think?" she asked, still grinning.

"Our dear mother knew what she was doing when she named us after three benevolent—if fictional—fairies who care for a special little girl," Merriwether said, and she frowned a little at her younger sister's laughter. This was a serious matter—a great responsibility had been entrusted to them. But as she glanced at the child again, even her own stern expression softened. "Mother truly was gifted at divination."

Fauna smiled, and it dimpled her cheeks. "And so are we," she declared with a slap of her hand against one ample thigh. "Our Aurora will be blessed with an abundance of magick."

"Magick even more powerful than our own," Flora added in her gentle, timid voice. Her tiny frame bent over the cradle, she was tickling Aurora's chubby chin and eliciting a smile. "And a healing gift beyond measure."

"Oh, yes, indeed," Merriwether agreed. "But even then, it won't be as powerful as *her* daughter's will be."

"Only if we're successful." Flora frowned then, small face puckering, and paced away from the cradle in small, agitated steps. Leaning over the round pedestal table nearby, she peered into the misty depths of a crystal ball that reflected her face and snowy white puffs of hair. "Oh, so much hinges on this. What if we fail?"

"We won't," Merri assured her youngest sister in her firmest take-charge tone. "We can't. We all saw the prophecy at the same time. You in the crystal, I in the stars, and Fauna in the cards of the sacred Tarot. We've been entrusted by our ancestors with a great responsibility, sisters, and we cannot fail." She was putting on her drill-sergeant persona, and it fit, she knew, with her regal stature and steely gray hair. Her sisters called her imposing. But always with love in their voices. And *someone* had to be in charge, after all. As the oldest, it had simply always been her.

But when she looked down at the baby, she deliberately gentled her tone. "Aurora is going to become the mother of the greatest Witch our family has ever produced. But it can only happen if we follow the instructions we've been given to the letter."

"Yes," Fauna said. She, too, had come to the table, and she'd already begun shuffling her Tarot cards. She did that when she was nervous. Shuffled and shuffled. "The child has to be fathered by little Nathan McBride, Daniel's boy, from Mulberry Street. And you're a lucky one, little Aurora, 'cause that boy's gonna grow up to be a looker." She shook her head and stifled a chuckle. Then she frowned. "How we'll arrange that, I'll never know. Merciful Goddess, the McBrides don't even know about the traditional magick of their ancestors, or the power of their bloodlines. They don't practice the ancient ways. They live like . . . like *normal* folk." She grimaced after she said it, as if the words left a bad taste in her mouth.

"Not only that," Flora said, taking a hanky as snowy white as her hair from her pocket to polish her spotless crystal ball. "But he has to be a—a—a *virgin* when they . . . you know." She lowered her eyes and her cheeks flushed pink.

"We're all well aware of *that*, Flora," Merri said. "But there's just no help for it. We have to see to it that everything happens as it should." She glanced out the window above the baby's bed at the formation of the stars on this crystal-clear night, and frowned. "I've decided we should do this subtly, not come right out and tell Aurora the plan." She turned to the baby again. "Because if she's even half as rebellious as her mother . . . well, she'll be determined to do exactly the opposite of what we ask."

"You're right," Flora said, nodding slowly. "Though it's a shame we can't tell her the truth about her destiny." She blinked up at Merri. "But we will tell her the truth, eventually, won't we?" Merri nodded, and the worry in Flora's face eased.

"What I want to know is how we're supposed to keep that McBride boy from . . . er . . ." Fauna grinned, dimples deepening. "Expending his affections on some other girl?" She blew a carrot-colored curl off her forehead and kept on shuffling.

"Thunderbolts, Fauna, he's only two years old!" Merri glared at her.

The shuffling stopped. "Oh, but have you seen him? The lad's going to grow, and with those dark brown eyes and thick lashes, and those raven's-wing curls of his . . . well, let's just see what the cards say." She fanned the deck and pulled one card. "Knight of Swords."

"Oh, my," the other two said in unison.

"I think we'll have our work cut out for us, sisters," Flora said.

Merri sighed and shook her head. "Don't be ridiculous. Nathan McBride, even if he's the reincarnation of Don Juan himself, still won't stand a chance against three Sortilege Witches."

"So it's decided," Fauna said, nodding hard. "We keep him pure"—she grinned—"even if it kills him. For our Aurora."

The three Witches smiled knowingly, while the baby looked on with what seemed to be a worried frown creasing her forehead.

## October 31, 1973

$\mathcal{L}$ittle Nathan McBride scowled at the dark-haired toddler. He was already in kindergarten and he couldn't *wait* to learn how to read. He loved books and it frustrated him to no end that he couldn't decipher the words inside.

And now, here were those very weird old ladies from Raven Street, with their little kid who couldn't be more than three years old, and the brat was *reading*. Not whole sentences, of course. But words. That tall, mean-looking aunt of hers with the steel-gray hair would hold up a flash card with letters on it, and the kid would say "Cat!" or "Dog!" or "Bird!" And then everyone at the neighborhood Halloween party would burst into applause. Like she was some kinda genius or something.

Aurora. Whoever heard of a girl named Aurora, anyway?

Everyone was so busy fussing over her that they'd barely noticed the Batman costume he'd spent so much time picking out. Nope, they only had eyes for the brat-kid with the strange black eyes.

Nathan *hated* Aurora Sortilege. And he vowed he always would.

## October 31, 1980

$\mathcal{I}$t was Halloween. And more than that, it was Aurora's tenth birthday. And more than that—*this!* She could hardly believe it.

"Mr. McBride has invited you to go trick-or-treating with Nathan tonight," Aunt Merri said. And her words made Aurora's belly clench with excitement. Even *Aunt Merriwether* seemed excited. All of them did. "Do you think you'd like to accept?"

"Oh, yes! Yes!"

She hopped up and down, and could barely stand still while her three aunts helped her fuss with her Egyptian princess costume until she looked just perfect.

She'd had a wild crush on Nathan McBride for *weeks* now. But he was older, and he barely seemed to notice her. Tonight, he would, though. Maybe he liked her, too! Why else ask her along on tonight of all nights?

Tonight of all nights. . . . She blinked up at Aunt Merri. "I don't want to miss our Samhain celebration, Auntie."

"You'll be back in time, sweetheart. We'll wait for you. You just go and have a good time with young Nathan."

"If you're sure it's okay."

Aunt Merriwether nodded. "It's okay."

And so she went. She skipped all the way down Raven Street, turned right at the corner onto Mulberry, and only slowed down and felt her nervousness return when his house loomed just ahead of her. It was a nice house. Newer than her own. Hers was *ancient* in comparison. And Nathan's father was pretty important in this little town. He owned the drugstore, and a couple in other nearby towns, too. And she was just . . . just Aurora. She bit her lip.

Swallowing hard and whispering a tiny little invocation for courage, she marched up the walk and rang the front doorbell.

Nathan opened it. He was wearing blue jeans and a sweatshirt. His dark hair was long. He liked wearing it long because the big kids wore it that way. Aurora liked it, too. It was curly and soft-looking. She thought Nathan was the handsomest boy in the whole town.

"Where's your costume?" she asked him.

"Very funny. I'm almost thirteen, you know."

"You're not dressing up?"

"Course not, 'Rora."

She wished *she* hadn't dressed up. Suddenly she felt like a big baby in her beautiful princess outfit. "But how can you trick-or-treat without a costume?"

He shook his head, and stepped outside, pushing the door closed behind him. "I'm not trick-or-treating. I'm babysitting you while *you* trick-or-treat."

Her heart felt as if something sharp had just pierced it. "B-babysitting . . . ?"

"Hey, it wasn't my idea. Something those wacky aunts of yours cooked up with my dad. So are they really Witches like everyone says?"

She opened her mouth, but she couldn't seem to say anything to him. She was so shocked and so hurt she could barely breathe, let alone talk.

"Are you one, too?" Nathan gave her Egyptian princess gown a teasing tug. "So how come you didn't wear a pointy hat and carry a broom then? Do you think you'll get warts on your nose when you grow up? I heard all Witches get big ugly ones, sooner or later. And that they—"

She whirled and ran from him, tears burning paths down her cheeks.

"Hey! 'Rora, wait up! I was just kidding around."

"I hate you, Nathan McBride!" She never slowed her pace until she got back to her house. And she managed to wipe the tears away before she faced her aunts. She lied to them for the fist time in her life that night. Told them she was too sick to stay out. And that year she skipped Samhain, as well.

## October 31, 1986

It was Aurora Sortilege's sixteenth birthday, and her crazy aunts were having a Sweet Sixteen party for her. Up there at that crazy excuse for a house. The big old Gothic was older than this entire town, or so people said.

Nathan and Aurora had never gotten along. They tended to avoid each other like the plague. At school, if they were forced into it, they'd say hello and not much else. He didn't really care. He had a crowd of friends. She didn't have many at all. It was partly because everyone knew her aunts thought of themselves as Witches, and that made a lot of the parents nervous—some because they figured the three ladies must be nuts, and others because they figured the three ladies sacrificed children in naked moonlight rituals and worshipped demons.

Nathan had done a little reading on the subject. Just out of curiosity, of course. So he knew that none of that was true. And he really didn't believe in any of that Witch stuff anyway. But he still didn't like her.

The Witch thing was only part of the reason Aurora wasn't very popular. Mostly it was just because she was such a brainiac. Nathan was graduating this year. So was Aurora, two years ahead of schedule. And then he was heading off to college and she'd be shipping out to pre-med. She wanted to be a doctor. She'd make a good one, too. He remembered a time two years ago, when a great big red-winged hawk had swooped down in front of his car, right after he'd gotten his license. It crashed into the windshield and then rolled to the ground.

Aurora had been out walking and she'd seen the whole thing. Of course, she'd stomped over to the car screaming at him for being careless and stupid and a hundred other things. But then she'd knelt down on the road, and there had been actual *tears* in her eyes as she touched the unmoving bird. He'd walked over there to see if he could help. But he'd ended up just standing still and watching her as she'd started running her hands over the hawk, real slow, and talking under her breath. Her eyes were closed, he remembered that. All the sudden, the bird twitched. Then it came to flapping, shrieking life, and hauled tail out of there.

It didn't go far, he recalled. It landed heavily in a tree along the roadside, and it looked back at him and Aurora, and then it let out a piercing cry.

"You're welcome," Aurora had whispered. Man, he'd never forget that. He'd thought then she must be totally bonkers. Nathan had ignored her bright smile, and her whispered, *"I did it."* He'd told himself the bird was probably just stunned. He didn't believe all that Witch crap for a minute. And if Aurora was as smart as everyone thought, she wouldn't either.

Anyway, she'd had a nice touch with that bird, even if it had only been stunned. And she couldn't stand to see *anyone* hurting. So he thought she'd make a pretty decent doctor. Not that he cared. Hell, he wouldn't even be going to this birthday party except that . . . well, word around school was that no one else was going to show. And he kind of felt sorry for her. So he'd bought her a pair of fairly expensive earrings with emeralds on them. Tiny emeralds, but heck, he was making only three-fifty an hour part-time at the greasy spoon in town. And he was going over there to that house on Raven Street. He'd grit his teeth and ignore the way she always managed to irritate the hell out of him, and he'd wish her a happy birthday.

When he got there, though, and saw her sitting on the front steps crying her eyes out, something happened to him. He went all soft inside for some reason. He walked up the steps and sat there beside her.

"What's the matter, Aurora?"

She lifted her head, looking straight into his eyes with her black, shiny, wet ones. "You know. I can see that you know."

He shook his head in denial.

"No one's coming, that's what's the matter. And you knew it, Nathan. Why didn't you tell me?"

He blinked in surprise and glanced at his watch. It was still ten minutes before party time. How could she know already? Unless someone had said something. "It's early yet," he told her. "What makes you think . . . ?"

She sent him a look of exasperation. "I *know* things, Nathan. And I know this. And I know that you knew and you didn't tell me."

He lowered his head, unsure of what to say. Maybe she really did have some kind of . . . Nah. But when he looked up at her again, he noticed for the first time that Aurora was turning into one drop-dead beautiful girl. And he wondered why he had never noticed it before. She'd never cut her hair, so far as he knew. It hung to her waist like a black satin flag, smooth and shining. And her eyes had a very slight tilt to them that made them exotic, entrancing. And since they were as black as her hair, you couldn't tell the irises from the pupils. Just big black marbles. Onyx eyes. Deeper than just about any eyes he'd ever seen. Lashes like sable paintbrushes. Lips that used to seem too plump when she was little, now looked like they belonged on a cover model.

It surprised the heck out of him. But he suddenly realized that this girl, whom he'd spent most of his life disliking, was incredible. And unusual—and he supposed he found that just as attractive as everything else about her.

Did he . . . actually . . . *like* her?

He got to thinking about the possibility that maybe he did. Maybe he *more than* just *liked* her; the more he thought, the more he realized that it was true. He lifted his chin and looked at her, sitting there beside him on the top step, so heartbroken. He was going to do it. He was going to ask the little Witch for a date. He could hardly believe it.

He smiled to himself, because he sort of knew she'd always had a crush on him. It would make her day. Make up for the birthday party not happening and her favorite holiday being a wash, and everything else.

She got to her feet slowly while he was still thinking. "I can't believe I got all dressed up for nothing."

And she had gotten all dressed up. But not for nothing. She looked great in her denim skirt and silky sleeveless blouse. Pretty. Feminine. Delicate.

"Maybe not for nothing," he said.

She looked down at him, and for the first time, he saw hope in her eyes. "Why?" she asked. "Have you heard something?"

*Heard something?* He just shrugged. "What if some good looking senior came over here and asked you to go to the drive-in with him?" he said, as suavely as he could manage. And then he waited for her eyes to light up.

And they did. Widened and lit and shone, and she started to smile.

"You *have* heard something, haven't you? Is it him? Is it Bobby Ridgeway? Is he really going to ask me out? I had a feeling he was, but I didn't trust my own . . . oh my Goddess, here he *comes*!"

Nathan stood there feeling as if he'd just been dropped into a play where he didn't know the lines, while Bobby Ridgeway, the biggest jock in school, and until this very second one of Nathan's best buds, pulled up in his dad's station wagon and blew the horn.

"Hi, Bobby!" Aurora waved so hard that Nathan thought her hand would fall off, and went running down the steps to the car.

Nathan couldn't hear what they were saying after that. Just Bobby revving the Ford's motor once in a while and Aurora's deep, soft laughter. She didn't giggle. He'd never once heard Aurora giggle. A minute later she got in the passenger side and the wagon roared away.

Bobby Ridgeway was no dummy. Apparently he, too, had noticed that there was more to Aurora Sortilege than an overdeveloped brain and an Addams Family upbringing. Only *he'd* noticed a lot quicker than Nathan had.

The front door opened and Aurora's Aunt Fauna, five feet tall and three feet wide with blazing orange hair, stepped out looking heartbroken. "Oh, Nathan," she said—as if she knew. "I'm so sorry."

He wiped the stricken expression off his face and got up. "Hey, sorry for what? You oughta be happy. That niece of yours finally got a date. I was beginning to think it'd never happen." He turned to go, then turned back again and thrust the small, clumsily wrapped box into the woman's pudgy hand. "Give this to her when she gets back, will ya?"

"Of course I will. Thank you, Nathan. That was so thoughtful."

He shrugged and turned to leave. Thoughtful, heck. It was a pity gift, just like it would have been a pity date. He didn't even *like* Aurora. Never had.

Never would.


## June 1987

$\mathcal{A}$urora was valedictorian of the graduating class. She could have felt a little bad about that. Probably should have. After all, she was only sixteen, and was graduating early, and most of the other seniors thought one of them should have won the honor— that she should have been disqualified because she didn't really belong.

She'd never really belonged.

But she refused to feel guilty. Because the salutatorian—the sap who would have made valedictorian if not for Aurora—was none other than Nathan McBride. And he'd been a lousy jerk to her all year long. Sure, they'd never really gotten along, but he'd been worse than ever this year. It seemed to Aurora that it had begun about the time she'd started dating Bobby Ridgeway.

And she used to think Bobby and Nathan were friends!

Well, apparently not. But she didn't see why Nathan was taking it out on her. It had ended with Bobby, anyway. He'd pulled a hamstring at football practice in the middle of the season, and was going to have to miss an important game. So, being bound by oath and ancestral blood to help others whenever possible, Aurora had offered to work a healing for him.

He'd acted as if she'd claimed to have two heads. Said he didn't think all the talk about her being a Witch was anything more than gossip, or he'd have never asked her out. He called her a psycho and a weirdo and a dozen other names, and dumped her like a carton of sour milk. And as if that weren't bad enough, he went around telling everyone at school that Aurora really believed she was a Witch. As if it were impossible, for goodness' sake!

And then Mindy had tried to help. She really had. It wasn't her fault it backfired. Mindy had moved into town only last year, and she'd felt like an outsider, too, at first. Aurora, being who and what she was, had tried to make her feel welcome when everyone else had just ignored her. They'd become friends, and even when Mindy started hearing the gossip, she'd stuck by Aurora.

One day, Mindy heard some of the jerks scoffing about the Wallingford High Witch, and she jumped in their faces. Told them how Aurora had sped up the healing on her broken leg earlier that year, and how she'd been able to play soccer again before the end of the season, against the doctor's predictions and everyone's expectations.

But instead of helping, it only made matters worse. Everyone knew about her leg, and the unusually speedy recovery. But until then, no one knew the rest. And until then, everyone had ribbed and teased Aurora about the whole Witch thing, but no one had really believed it.

Now they did. And everything changed after that. When Aurora walked down the hall, conversations would stop, and wary eyes would watch her. Students, and even a few of the teachers, would step well out of her path to give her a wide berth. It was as if they were afraid of her.

Except for Mindy, of course.

*And* lousy rotten old Nathan McBride. *He* wasn't afraid of her, didn't believe in magick anyway, and probably wouldn't have been afraid of her even if he had. He laughed at the kids who acted skittish around Aurora and kept right on teasing her just the way he always had. "Hey, Broom-Hilda," he'd yell, because he was too dense to know the name was Brynhild and that she was a Valkyrie, not a Witch. "Get your broom outta your locker and fly it over here, will ya? I spilled something." Or " 'Rora, you'd best get your butt into that science lab and turn the eighth period class back into humans again before somebody dissects them!"

She *hated* that boy.

He'd always follow up by thumbing his nose at her, turning to his pale and wide-eyed companions, and saying, "See? I'm still in one piece. No warts, no locusts. I told you nothing would happen."

She figured he was probably tormenting her to prove she wasn't a Witch at all. Just a crazy teenager with delusions. And if she hadn't had the Witches' Rede drilled into her for most of her life, she might just have supplied him with whatever proof he required, the more painful the better.

But she couldn't do that. Wouldn't do it. She was a healer. She was going to medical school to become an even better one. If she went around causing harm, she might just lose the healing gift she'd been born with, and that would break her heart.

At the graduation ceremony, she delivered a short speech no one really wanted to hear, about kindness and tolerance and openmindedness and freedom. And she wore a tiny pair of emerald earrings.

And when it was over, and everyone threw their hats in the air, someone turned to hug her impulsively, and she impulsively hugged back. And then she realized it was Nathan, and backed away with a gasp.

He blinked and looked as surprised as she was. Then his gaze shifted downward just slightly, and he smiled. "You wore them," he said.

The crowds surged around them, tugging them apart. She was surrounded by her loving aunts, and he was being slapped on the back by his father and a bunch of relatives from out of town.

And that was the last time she saw Nathan McBride for a very long time.

# Chapter 1

October 1997

Nathan McBride stared across the fancy restaurant's most secluded table into Elsie Kincaid's big blue eyes. The taper candle set her blonde hair alight with its golden gleam, and cast dark shadows into the depths of her cleavage. And he did mean *depths*. It was like Davy Jones's locker down there, and he was more than ready to go diving. The way she kept leaning over the table suggested she was ready, too.

And so what if those baby blues were a little vacant? It wasn't as if he were looking for a prospective brain surgeon here. He simply wanted to get laid. Period.

He felt a little guilty for that rather unenlightened thought, but damn, frustration would turn a red-blooded man into a chauvinistic beast pretty fast. He ought to know. He'd been frustrated for well over a decade now.

He pushed his plate aside, reached across the table, took her hand in both of his. "You ready to order dessert?" he asked her softly.

"Oh, Nate, I think you *know* what I'd like for dessert."

He gritted his teeth and managed not to grimace when she called him "Nate," which he detested. It wasn't hard to ignore that minor irritant when her foot, minus its spike-heeled shoe, began running up the inside of his leg under the table.

*Hot damn, this is it.*

"So, um, can I take you back to my . . ." He bit his lip. "Your place?" No more taking chances by bringing a woman back to his place. He was beginning to think it was haunted. There was the night with that blue-eyed blonde, Suzanne, when the heating ducts decided to spew black smoke. And the time with that other blue-eyed blonde, Rebecca, when the air conditioner mysteriously caught fire. And don't forget the blue-eyed blonde, Anne Marie, and the SWAT team with the wrong address.

Nope. Not with . . . er . . . Elsie. Yeah. Elsie. With a chest to match the name, he thought. Then he realized he was turning into a real pig.

"Sure," she said. "My place is great." She slinked out of the chair and across the floor for his viewing pleasure, pausing at the exit to send a wink over her shoulder at him. She was very good at slinking. He fumbled for his wallet, dropped it twice, and fished out a handful of bills to pay for their meal. Then he got up and wandered out after her.

And the whole time, he was feeling very nervous. Glancing over his shoulder. Wondering what could possibly go wrong *this* time.

She sat behind the wheel of his car, the Jag he'd spent a small fortune on because no man could drive a Jag and not have constant bouts of wild sex, right?

Wrong, as it turned out, but it had been worth a shot.

Elsie called out the window to him. "Can I drive it, Nate, sweetie? I'd be soooo grateful."

"Oh, yeah," he said, and stopped near the door to hand her the keys. She started the engine, and it gave its distinctive Jaguar roar when she revved it. Nathan smiled, about to turn and walk around to the passenger side.

He only vaguely heard the change in the engine's sound when she slipped the shift into gear. The way the tires spun when she popped the clutch was a whole lot louder, causing him to spin around in surprise. And of course, he was paying complete attention when the sideview mirror of his car plowed into him like a wrecking ball intent on castration.

Elsie screamed before Nathan ever hit the pavement. Then he landed like a ton of bricks. He heard those heels clicking toward him, heard her babbling about her foot slipping, saw her cleavage in his face as she bent over him and figured that was about as close as he'd ever get to it. He was going to die a virgin.

Then he passed out.

"Ooops!" Fauna said.

She and her sisters stood around the crystal ball, looking on, wide-eyed.

"Oh dear!" gasped Flora. "Did we kill him?"

"No, but we might have damaged something vital!" Fauna shouted. "Did you see where that bubblehead hit him?"

"He'll be all right." Merriwether stroked the crystal ball with her palm. "Aurora is on E.R. duty tonight. Now that she's finally come home, it's high time we see to the business of getting those two together."

"And not a moment too soon. I'm exhausted." Fauna fanned herself. "I vow, Merriwether, I've never seen a man so determined to get—"

"*Fauna!*" Flora's shocked voice and red cheeks stopped her sister's descriptive sentence.

Merri simply shook her head at the both of them. "You're overstating it, Fauna. Any man would be acting just the same."

"But he tries every night!"

"And every night we have to bring disaster crashing down on his head. You'd think he'd give up after a while, wouldn't you?" Flora asked softly, shaking her head and looking truly sorry for all the havoc they'd been forced to wreak on Nathan McBride's life.

"He isn't thinking with his brain, sisters," Fauna quipped with an impish grin.

"He just doesn't realize that he's been waiting for her all along. Er, with a little help from us. But once he does . . ." Flora's clasped hands pressed to her cheek, her lashes fluttering. "Oh, I wish I could be there to see it when their eyes meet across the room for the first time, and Cupid's arrow hits them right in their tender little hearts."

Fauna stifled a laugh, and snorted. "I'll admit it would be good to see that man hit with *something* besides his own car!" She and Flora burst into laughter at that, and while Merri sniffed indignantly at their irreverence, she had to battle a grin herself.

"*Dr.* Sortilege to E.R.," the hushed voice on the P.A. system repeated. Aurora hurriedly gulped the rest of her herbal tea and got up from the first break she'd had all night to rush down the hall to the emergency room, her senses pricking to full alertness and telling her all she needed to know.

It was not a life-threatening injury coming in. It was minor, but pretty painful to the victim. Her brain told her those things before she ever set foot inside the treatment room, just as it told her when things were not so good. It was nice, this gift she'd inherited from her ancestors. It gave her time to prepare, and more often than not, helped her make her patients well again.

She'd had the powers for too long to consider them odd. They were just a gift of heredity, like her jet-black hair and ebony eyes. Then again, she didn't broadcast the fact that she was a Witch, either. While she was at work, the gold Pentacle rested *under* her white coat. But it didn't matter. Everyone in this town knew about those strange Sortilege women in the old house on the hill. She'd thought they might have forgotten while she'd been away, but no such luck. But for some reason, the whispers and gossip no longer bothered her. Maybe because she was an adult now, sure of herself, who she was *and* what she was. Confident and proud of both. And maybe because of that change in attitude—or maybe because they'd done some growing up, too—the gossips were not as malicious or mean-spirited as they had been in high school.

Some of the locals looked at her oddly. Some were nervous around her, and simply avoided her. Some came to her asking for love potions or lottery numbers. But most of the longtime residents just shrugged off her family's weirdness. They'd had generations to get used to it, after all.

She stepped into the treatment room, quickly scanning the chart the nurse handed her. "Hello, Mr. . . ." Her eyes found the name. "McBride?"

She blinked, and lifted her gaze to the man on the bed.

His eyes were closed as he lay there, hurting pretty badly, not looking back at her. But it was him. And she felt something. Some jolt. A psychic buzz. She swallowed hard and shook herself.

"Call me Nathan," he told her through gritted teeth. He turned his head toward her and opened his eyes, but they focused on the front of her lab coat instead of her face. His eyes widened with interest then, and his gaze slid down her body, over her legs to her toes, and back up again. "Call me anything you want, as a matter of fact."

"Nathan McBride?" She lifted her brows. "You're just as sleazy as you always were, I see."

He frowned, bringing his eyes up to meet hers at last. And then she saw the recognition in them. He glanced at the name tag pinned to her white coat. "Dr. Sortilege. Holy crap, Broom-Hilda's back."

"That's right," she said, and she lifted her chin and forced a smile. If no one else's opinions mattered to her anymore, then why did his lighthearted barb sting? "The little girl who used to play tag-a-long. You must remember. You said I was a pest, and that my aunts were weirdos and that I would probably grow up with warts on my nose."

Her patient's face went a shade whiter, and he licked his lips nervously. "You . . . have a real good memory, Aurora." He tried for a smile. "Do you hold a grudge as long?"

"Of course not," she said with a sweet smile, and then turned to a stainless steel tray full of instruments at the ready, picked up the longest, sharpest scalpel on it, and tested its edge with her thumb. "Nurse, bring in the cranial drill, will you?"

"Hey, wait a min—"

She looked at her patient and winked. The nurse, Meg, a friend of hers, burst out laughing while Nathan McBride, former jerk of the universe, sat in the bed staring from one of them to the other. "You ladies are brutal."

"No more than you were ten years ago," Aurora quipped. She handed the scalpel to Meg. "Get this sterilized, will you?"

Meg nodded and left the room. Aurora managed to stop smiling and leaned over the bed. "I guess you're hurting enough right now without me adding to it."

"Does it show?" he asked wryly. "And here I'm trying to impress you by being too manly to let a little pain bother me."

"You can't hide it from me, anyway, so don't waste the effort."

"Yeah, I forgot. You're a Witch."

"And a doctor," she reminded him, lest he forget.

"A Witch doctor? God help me."

"Watch yourself, Nathan, or you'll be sitting on a lily pad eating flies."

"Very funny." He lay back on the pillow, then eyed her. "You *were* kidding, right?"

" 'An it harm none, do what ye will,' " she quoted. "The most important line in the Witches' Rede."

"Lucky for me."

"You're damn right, it is."

He frowned at her, but she didn't elaborate. "So let's see if I have this straight," she went on. "Your date backed your Jaguar into your groin, is that about right?" She leaned over him and lifted his shirt away from his belly. He hadn't gone to pot. He had washboard abs that sent little tingles of awareness up into her fingers when she touched him there. Ignoring the shivers, she probed his abdomen gently. "Is this tender?"

"Yeah. A little bit."

She took her hand away, and held it, palm down, a fraction of an inch above his groin, and she closed her eyes.

"You preparing to grab me?" He sounded a little nervous.

She smiled slightly. "Shhhhh. Relax for a second."

He did. She felt the pain, the bruising, but nodded, reassured that the damage wasn't serious. She'd confirm her diagnosis in a more scientific manner, of course. But she always felt better knowing as soon as possible.

Opening her eyes again, she asked, "You hit your head when you landed?"

He nodded.

Aurora pushed his dark hair aside and looked at the bump on his head. She held her receptive hand over it and knew it was throbbing, but not dangerous. Mild concussion at the worst. She'd confirm that, as well, with a precautionary X ray. "You can feel better knowing there's nothing seriously wrong," she said. "Let's just be as thorough as possible, though. Don't want you suing me." And she pulled on a pair of latex gloves, then slipped her fingers inside the waistband of his jeans and began undoing them.

His hand landed atop hers instantly. "Hold on a minute!"

She couldn't pull her hand away, so she left it there. "Problem?"

"Yeah, there's a problem. What do you think you're doing?"

She smiled. "I always heard that men who drive Jaguars are try-ing to make up for having small genitals," she said sweetly. "I just wanted to check." His jaw dropped. She shook her head and rolled her eyes. "I'm examining you. I'm a doctor, Nathan. What do you *think* I'm doing?"

"I *think* I'd like a doctor with a little less sarcasm, and a little more testosterone. A *male* doctor, if you don't mind. And could you make him a few years older than Doogie Howser?"

She lifted her brows. "So it *is* true? About the small—"

"Dammit, Aurora, get me a male doctor or I'm outta here."

"You're as big a jerk now as you were ten years ago, McBride," she snapped. "And I hope your balls swell up and fall off."

"What happened to your phony line about harming none, *En-dora?*"

She smirked at his name-calling. "Hey, I didn't say I'd cause it, just that I'd *like* it." She peeled off her latex gloves and tossed them onto his chest. "And before I go, I'll tell you what Dr. Stewart is going to tell you after a thorough exam and a few hundred dollars' worth of X rays. You probably have a mild concussion, which is amazing consid-ering how hard that rock you call a head must be. Your family jewels will be sore for a day or so, but no damage was done. And you have a big purple bruise on your right elbow. That's going to bother you more than anything else, because you'll wince every time you bend the arm." She spun on her heel to head out the door, then stopped in her tracks and turned to face him again. "And one more thing— something Dr. Stewart *won't* tell you. You're still a virgin."

He gasped. He sputtered. He stared at her as if she'd grown an-other head.

"Remember all this next time you feel like calling my abilities as a doctor—or as a Witch—into question, Nathan McBride."

\* \* \*

D̲r̲. Stewart examined him thoroughly and ordered a complete set of X rays. When all was said and done, he told Nathan that he had a mild concussion. That his groin was going to be sore but no serious damage had been done. And that the bruise to his right elbow would probably give him more trouble than any of the other injuries.

He *didn't* tell him that he was still a virgin, but Nathan didn't figure that sort of thing showed up in an X ray.

But Aurora had known. And how the hell did a skeptic like him explain that? How could she know something he'd never told another living soul?

Damn.

He felt invaded. Embarrassed. As if he had to explain or defend himself to her. It insulted his pride that she knew, that she must be thinking what she . . . must be thinking. And for God's sake, when had he ever given a damn *what* Aurora thought? Besides, it wasn't as if he'd *chosen* to be celibate. It was just that every time he got anywhere near scoring with a woman, some sort of disaster happened. It had been this way since college, and he was beginning to think it would stay this way for his entire life.

Hell, maybe he ought to join the priesthood.

It was as if he were cursed.

*Cursed?*

What if . . . She'd always hated his guts. So suppose she'd . . .

Nah.

He sighed and fell back on the bed. Dr. Stewart came in with release forms for him to sign, and Nathan took the pen and scratched his name across the bottom. "Tell me something, Doc, do you believe in curses?"

Dr. Stewart smiled. "I know you made her mad, son, but Aurora Sortilege would never go putting any curse on anybody. Wouldn't hurt a fly, that one. Don't be listening to gossip."

"That's easy for you to say." He shook his head. What he was thinking was really silly, because he didn't believe in that kind of crap.

"If someone put a hex on you, son, it wasn't Aurora." He winked then. "But I'd bet my last dollar she could help you get rid of it."

Nathan gaped. "You telling me you *believe* in all that . . . that *Witch* stuff?"

Dr. Stewart drew a thoughtful breath, frowning hard. Then he sighed and sat down in the chair beside the bed, crossing one leg over the other. "Yesterday, Aurora and I were sitting in the doctors' lounge having coffee. All of the sudden, for no apparent reason, she dropped her cup on the floor." He shook his head. "Coffee all over the place. She got up and ran out of there like her chair was on fire. Next thing I knew she was pushing a crash cart down the hall. She stopped outside one of the patients' rooms . . . and about a second later, the man inside went into full arrest."

Nathan scanned the doctor's face to see if he was kidding. Didn't look like he was. "Did you ask her about it?"

"She said she heard the alarm going off on the man's heart monitor, but she didn't. There wasn't any alarm. We found out later that one of the nurses had left it unplugged. Damn thing never would have gone off."

*Sure, and it's almost Halloween and I'll bet it's this guy's favorite holiday—next to April Fool's Day, that is.*

"It wasn't the first time something like that's happened, either."

"Then you *do* believe she's some kind of a Witch?"

"It's uncanny, boy. I'll tell you that much."

The man didn't seem like the practical-joking type. And Nathan got to thinking about some of the uncanny things *he'd* seen Aurora do, from the time she'd been pint-sized to a peanut.

"So . . . so if there *were* some kind of curse on me . . ."

"Or even if it's just bad luck," Dr. Stewart continued, "Aurora would be the person to talk to about it. No doubt in my mind about that."

"Yeah," Nathan said. "Unless she happens to hate my guts." *Or unless she's the one who cursed me in the first place.* The possibility didn't seem quite so farfetched anymore.

Dr. Stewart chuckled deep in his gut as he got up and walked out of the room, shaking his head.

Well, Nathan thought, he really had nothing to lose. If he didn't figure out why the fates seemed to be conspiring to keep him from ever having sex in his life, he was going to lose his mind. And the embarrassing part—the part where he actually had to admit that he was still a virgin at twenty-nine—was already over. Aurora already knew. So maybe he *should* try to get her to help him.

And maybe he should just stick hot needles into his eyes. First he had to decide which would be more unpleasant.

# Chapter 2

*Aurora* ducked her head to miss the wind chimes that hung from every possible place on the front porch and kept the house sounding like an ice-waterfall all the time, and headed through the front door.

Aunt Flora looked up from where she'd been concentrating hard on two pink candles with heart shapes carved into their bases and rose petals scattered around them. And her athame was still in her hand.

"Sorry," Aurora whispered, pausing in her tracks. "Am I interrupting a ritual?"

"No!" Aunt Flora said, too quickly. Almost as if she had something to hide.

"Now, Auntie, it looks like a love spell to me." Aurora crooked a brow. "Hey, you aren't trying to conjure up some prince to come steal you away from us, are you?"

"Of course not, dear! Why, I would never. Oh, no, absolutely not, darling." She cleared her throat, muttered a quick, "As I will it, so mote it be," half under her breath, and snuffed her candles.

Aurora got a little queasy feeling in the pit of her stomach, one that told her she was being kept in the dark about something. Before she could question Aunt Flora, however, Aunt Fauna came in from the back door, a basketful of freshly cut herbs and various roots over her arm. "Ohhh, you're home!" she exclaimed. "Merriwether, she's home!"

Aunt Merri's steps came from the second floor as she hurried to the top of the stairs. "Wait until you see what I bought you today, Aurora!" She waved the little box she held in her hand as she trotted down the stairs. Aurora winced, and quickly sent a protective wish out to her, to keep her from falling and breaking something. "I saw it and I just knew—"

"Oh, wait until you see it!"

"You'll never take it off!"

Her aunts were acting decidedly suspicious tonight. Aurora's warning bells were going off. Of course, she loved them with every cell in her body, and knew they'd never dream of harming her. But meddling was certainly not beyond them.

"Thank you, Aunt Merri," she said, taking the box warily and opening the lid. "Oh. My. That *is* beautiful." Aurora lifted the necklace from the box—a gold chain with a rose quartz stone suspended from it, and the Runic symbol for love etched onto the surface. "But, Aunt Merri, why this particular stone?"

"It spoke to me," Merri said. "Just felt right, you know. One of those impulse buys."

Aurora frowned. "You've never done anything impulsive in your life, Aunt Merri. Now why don't you girls tell me just what's going on here? Hmmm?"

They all shook their heads, muttering denials, and averting their eyes. Aurora's sense of foreboding grew stronger.

"Tell us about your day, dear."

"Oh, yes, do! Did you meet anyone interesting today?"

"Anyone new?"

She tilted her head, knew they were changing the subject, and decided to let it slide. For now. "The only new patient wasn't really new. The little brat who used to pick on me when I was younger. He grew into a bigger brat, and a chauvinist pig to boot."

"Why, whoever can you mean?" Flora asked faintly.

"Certainly not that sweet little McBride boy?" Fauna said, as Merri elbowed her in the ribs.

"Now how on earth could you know . . . ?"

"The cards, dear! The cards."

"I didn't know there was a Nathan McBride card in your deck, Aunt Fauna. Unless you're referring to The Fool."

"Oh, dear," Fauna said. "Then you did see the McBride boy today?"

"Only long enough to wish I hadn't," she said. "I swear I've never known a bigger jerk in my life. Demanded a male doctor. Of all the nerve . . ."

"Don't be too hard on him, Aurora," Aunt Merriwether advised. "Maybe he was just embarrassed."

"Or shy," Flora put in.

"Or nervous," Fauna added.

"Or an idiot," Aurora declared. "If I ever see him again, I think I'll . . . What? Why are you all looking at me like that?"

"Like what, dear?"

"Like you've done something I'm going to hate, is like what."

"Well . . . well, you see, we were under the impression that . . ." Fauna began.

"That you and Nathan McBride were old friends," Flora finished for her.

"So when his father called to say he'd heard you were back in town, and to ask how you were doing . . ." Merri's voice faltered. "We . . . well, that is, we . . ."

"You what?"

Merri swallowed, lifted her chin, and said with authority, "Invited him to dinner."

"Nathan and his father, that is," Fauna added quickly. "You know, his father, Daniel, he's always been kind to us. Always willing to order even the most obscure herbs, if we asked, and never once pried into what we could want with them."

"He's retired now, you know. Turned the chain over to Nathan," Flora said.

"Chain?" When Aurora had left, there had only been a handful of small drugstores.

"It's a rather impressive chain of pharmacies now, dear," Aunt Merri clarified. "Nathan has a head for business. And you mustn't be upset about this dinner. We just thought it would be nice to . . ."

"To be sociable," Fauna finished. Then she sighed and wiped her neon hair from her brow as if exhausted.

"When?"

"Why, tomorrow night, dear."

"Fine. I just won't be here then. I'll make something up and . . ."

"Oh, no you won't," Merri said, and for once her voice sounded a bit harsh, and even a little disapproving. "That would be not only deceitful, but rude, and we've raised you better than that."

"Oh, that we have," said the usually timid and soft-spoken Flora, shaking a forefinger. " 'Ever mind the Rule of Three. Three times what thou givest, returns to thee.' "

Aurora pressed her fingertips to her temples and closed her eyes. "All right, all right. I'll suffer through dinner with the idiot. But if you expect me to enjoy it, you'd better think again."

"Oh, darling, that's better. And of course you'll enjoy it. I'm sure Nathan's become a wonderful man." Merri smiled.

"No one's at his best when he ends up in an emergency room," Flora said sympathetically.

"You might be very pleasantly surprised, dear," Fauna put in.

"I'll be surprised if he has the nerve to show up," she retorted; then she made her way upstairs to her own suite of rooms to sit and ponder the possible reasons for such a terrible scourge appearing in her life right now, just when everything had been going so smoothly.

The place scared the living hell out of him.

First, it was old, and creepier than even he remembered. Then again, he'd never come all the way inside before. And the house was older now than it had been last time he'd come over here. But only by a decade.

It was Gothic in style, with tall narrow windows so ancient that the glass was thicker at the bottom of the panes than at the top. The house had been freshly painted, sure, and kept in good repair. But a weed patch that his father assured him was an herb garden took up half of the side lawn, and a dense flower garden, with a path that led to its center and enough trees and shrubs to keep that center hidden, took up most of the back. He'd always wondered what was hiding inside the depths of that garden. Then there were those wall-to-wall wind chimes lining the front porch, tinkling constantly. The place gave him the chills. He kept expecting bats to come flying out of a dormer window.

His dad had come down with a mysterious, hacking cough just before it was time to leave, and insisted it was probably his allergies acting up. He'd said Nathan had to go or the three old ladies would be insulted, and goodness only knew what would happen then.

Nathan didn't particularly want to think about what would happen then. He grinned self-consciously and reminded himself that he didn't believe in that stuff.

He rang the doorbell and it chimed with a deep and resonant tone. He grinned harder as he imagined Lurch coming to answer it.

But instead a tall, regal woman with steel-gray hair and piercing black eyes opened the door, and Nathan's smile died. "Hello, Nathan," she greeted him. "You probably don't remember me. I'm Merriwether. Do come in."

"Hello, Nathan," said another voice, this one coming from a body no bigger than a minute. She was four-eleven if he'd ever seen it, and weighed perhaps ninety pounds dripping wet. She had hair as soft and white as cotton, and the face of everybody's cookie-baking grandma. "It's so good to see you again, young man. I'm Flora, remember?"

"And I'm Fauna," called another, this one short as well, but as round as a pumpkin and with hair about the same color. This one he remembered.

"Good to see you again," he managed. "I'm sorry my father couldn't make it. He said to tell you how badly he feels for missing this." As he spoke and listened to their pat replies about being sorry that his father couldn't make it, Nathan looked past them. But *she* was nowhere in sight. There was plenty to look at, though. It smelled fantastic in here, and he spotted the source—incense burning in brass pots that looked Oriental and ancient. There were candles glowing everywhere. Mostly pink and red, he noted, wondering if the colors were significant in any way. Soft music was playing, sounding whimsical and Gaelic to him. Every window had a crystal prism suspended in front of it, and every shelf was lined with other stones—amethyst clusters and giant glittering geodes big enough for a small child to crawl inside. A tiny table sat in the window to the north, and there was a black iron cauldron sitting in its center, and various other items arranged around it: candlesticks, statuettes of mythical figures of some sort, wineglasses, an ornate silver hand mirror.

"And what is it that kept your father away, Nathan?" the tall one—Merriwether, he thought—asked.

"I think it's an allergy or something," he said, still distracted—

still searching the place for Aurora, and wondering why he was. He didn't even like her. Didn't even like her type. He liked blue-eyed blondes with more bustline than brain. Not willowy raven-haired Witches with black eyes that could burn holes in solid rock. He still didn't see her. But there was a round table in the room's center with an elaborately decorated deck of oversized cards on it, and what he thought was a crystal ball in the center. Its base looked like pewter, and was made in the shape of a gnarled, clawed hand, long fingers grasping the crystal ball and holding it up.

A cold chill went up his nape.

"Oh, your father's ill?" tiny Flora asked with concern.

"Yes. Just allergies. Nothing serious. He's . . ." Nathan's voice trailed off. Aurora appeared at the top of the stairs, and he went utterly still. She was . . . man, she was mesmerizing. Okay, so maybe he *did* like dark, spooky women. Maybe he'd just never realized it before. She just . . . she hadn't looked like this at the hospital, in that lab coat with her hair tied back and . . .

But now . . .

She came down the stairs in a black dress that hugged her arms from her wrists to her shoulders, dipped to cling to her breasts and her waist, snugged its way over her hips, and then turned into free-flowing rivers of satin that swayed around her legs when she moved. Her hair was long, very long, and gleaming in the candlelight like magic. And her eyes, they were almond shaped and more exotic than ever, lined and shadowed and as black as polished onyx.

For the life of him, Nathan couldn't figure out why she would take pains to look this good for a man she disliked as much as she disliked him. Why? He wondered if maybe Bobby Ridgeway was coming over later.

Why? For Goddess' sake, why did she go and dress up in her full-moon best for a man she didn't even like?

To punish him, that's why, she thought forcibly. To show him just what he's missing by brushing me off as too weird or too intelligent, too female or too young for his tastes. Let him see what he's missing and live the rest of his life writhing in agony over his foolish pride back at the hospital. And before, when she'd been younger, and he'd shunned her so often.

She told herself it meant nothing, that she had forgotten all about it long ago. But it was a lie. She'd adored him when she'd been a child, and he'd tossed her hero worship back into her face. Well, let him just take a good look now at what he'd rejected back then.

And if that's what she wanted, it was working, because he couldn't seem to take his eyes off her.

"Aurora," he said in a choked voice.

"Hello, Nathan. How is your . . . elbow?"

"Still pretty sore," he said. "But amazingly enough, everything else seems to be back in working order."

"Who could have guessed?" she asked sweetly.

He lowered his head. "You could. And you did, and I was an idiot. Okay?"

She blinked twice, standing at the bottom of the staircase. "Was that an apology?"

"Maybe," he admitted, coming forward, crossing the room until he stood a foot from her, facing her. "Let's not forget, I wasn't the only one who was obnoxious in that emergency room."

"So, you're expecting an apology from me?"

He let his gaze dip lower, slowly, and brought it up to her eyes again. "I'll tell you what, Aurora. That dress is apology enough for me. What do you say we call it even?" He said it softly, for her ears alone.

She felt her face drain of color. "This dress is no apology to you, Nathan. I wore it because I'm too old to stick out my tongue and thumb my nose at you. But you're obviously too dense to get the message."

"The only message I'm getting from that number, honey, is 'come and get it.'"

"The only message this number is sending out, *honey*, is 'you can't have it.'"

"Hey, did I say I wanted it?"

"Your pants said it for you." She sent a meaningful glance at the changing shape behind his zipper and lifted her brows, daring him to deny it. "You were right. Everything seems to be back in working order."

It seemed he'd run out of comebacks.

She smirked, but only for a moment. It was when she saw her three aunts grabbing for their coats, and the little emergency tote-bag they kept near the door, that she felt her smugness turn to panic.

"Where do you three think you're going?" she asked, trying not to sound desperate.

"To see Daniel, dear," Merri announced calmly.

"Nathan's father, Aurora."

"He's ill. It's the least we can do."

"Yes, I have the best remedies for allergies like this," Flora added, running into the hallway where bundles of herbs hung upside-down to dry, and snatching a sprig of this and a pinch of that to take along.

"But . . . but . . . Aunt Flora, the man *owns* his own drugstores!"

Aunt Flora put a hand to her mouth and tittered delicately. "You're such a joker, Aurora. As if a drugstore compares to a Witch when it comes to remedies."

Aurora gave her head a shake. "Well then . . . what about dinner?"

"You'll have to play hostess tonight, dear," Aunt Merri chided. "It's your duty. You do right by our guest, and don't embarrass us."

"Everything's ready, Aurora," Fauna called. "It's all on the warming rack. Just take it out and eat."

"Enjoy!" Flora sang out as she headed through the door.

And that was that.

"Well," Aurora said, hands on her hips. She stared at the door they'd just exited for a long moment, then turned to face Nathan again. "I hate to tell you this, but I think we're being . . . fixed up."

"I thought my father's cough sounded a little overblown," he said wryly. "He must be in on it with them."

Aurora stared at him, eyes narrowing. "Was this your idea, Nathan McBride?"

"I like blue-eyed blondes. Glenda the Good Witch is my style. Morticia Addams does nothing for me."

She looked at his crotch. "Oh, I can see that. Shall we put it to the test? You want me to speak French and see what happens?"

"Go ride a broom, why don't you?"

"We don't *ride* our brooms, you idiot."

"Hey, don't tell me what you *do* use them for. I don't think my heart can take it."

"I don't think your zipper can."

He sighed, looked at the floor, and shook his head. "Dammit, Aurora, I can't believe I came here thinking I could ask you for help when you're every bit as defensive and touchy as you ever were."

"You try growing up with half the local ignoramuses thinking you're some kind of satanic nutcase and see how defensive and touchy *you*—" She blinked and stared at him. "What do you mean, you came here to ask for my help?"

"I never, ever thought you were satanic."

"I don't even believe in the devil," she told him.

"Well that's a relief. I was beginning to think you thought I was him."

"The way you teased me, back then . . ." she began. "I thought you were as superstitious and bigoted as . . ." She gave her head a shake and cut herself off.

"I was a kid. Kids are idiots sometimes. Hell, Aurora, I teased *all* my friends." He frowned a little, and tilted his head. "I should have thought harder, though. I guess you took about all the teasing you could handle. My adding to it didn't help a bit, did it?"

"I don't see how anyone could think it would *help* at all." She blew air through her teeth. "Not that it bothered me in the least."

"Only enough so you're still angry about it."

"Do you want to eat, or what?"

"No. I want to tell you something."

She lifted her head, met his eyes, and thought he looked sincere. "What?"

"I think . . . I might have . . ." He closed his eyes briefly and clenched his jaw. "This is going to sound insane."

Frowning, she scanned his face. "Is this something physical? What do you think you have, Nathan?" The doctor in her was at full alert as she searched his face, mentally noting the healthy color of his skin, and the clarity of his eyes. Brown eyes, velvety brown, with darker stripes. Eyes that were looking into hers right now with . . .

She blinked and looked away.

He lowered his head. "Yeah, it's physical all right, but not the way you think. I think I might have some kind of curse clinging to me, Aurora. Does that sound crazy?"

She took a step away from him, watching his face, wary of a trick to make her look foolish. "A curse? I didn't think you believed in that sort of thing."

"I don't . . . do you?"

"Of course."

"So . . . did you?"

She frowned up at him. "Did I wh—" She opened her eyes wider and lifted her brows. "You want to know if I hexed you, Nathan?"

He only nodded.

She closed her eyes to hide the flash of pain she felt. Unexpected, unreasonable, but real. "I always thought . . ." Biting her lip, she shook her head and turned away.

"Aurora?" He touched her shoulder, bringing her gently around to face him again. "You always thought . . . what?"

"That you were the only one who wasn't afraid of me, Nathan. The only one who didn't seem to think that being a Witch made me some kind of monster." She shook her head. "I guess I was wrong."

His brows furrowed when she felt the barest hint of moisture burning in her eyes. He leaned closer, staring at it there, as if he couldn't quite believe it.

"For the record, Nathan, I would cut off my hand before I'd hurt anyone. I don't even kill spiders, for Goddess' sake."

He looked slightly ashamed. But he offered no apology. "Hell, if you had a Witch who hated your guts living around the corner, combined with the kind of luck I've had lately, you'd probably think—"

"I'd think of asking for some help," she said. She walked past him into the dining room and sat down at the little round table with the crystal ball and the cards. "So what makes you think it's a curse? Maybe the things that have been happening to you are for the best, did you ever think of that? A lot of people think they're having bad luck . . . missing planes or appointments or having their cars break down—when in fact, the delays and such are really protecting them from disasters."

"Yeah, well this delay isn't saving me from anything but pleasure."

"Really?" She lifted her brows. "So you really believe it's a curse?"

He came closer, but didn't sit. "The evidence sort of makes it hard not to believe it."

"What evidence?" she asked him.

He sighed and met her eyes. "I can't get laid to save my life."

Aurora bit her lip. She gritted her teeth. She held her breath. Nothing worked. She burst out laughing uncontrollably. And she regretted it instantly when his face darkened with furious anger, and he whirled around and slammed out of the house without a backward glance.

Her laughter died slowly as she stared after him. And then she titled her head to one side, frowning. "My Goddess," she whispered. "He was serious." She went after him, called his name out into the night, but he was already slamming his car door and roaring the engine.

She thought about making it stall so she could go and apologize. But messing with his car wasn't a good idea, and it might be considered manipulative magick, not letting him leave when he clearly wanted to. A Witch mustn't mess with another person's free will. No manipulation. Then again, she wasn't supposed to hurt anyone either. And she had a hollow feeling that maybe she just had . . . badly.

# Chapter 3

"Aurora Rose Sortilege, what *did* you do?" Aunt Merriwether looked very upset as she stood there with her hands on her hips, glaring.

"I didn't mean it," she said, and she knew she sounded like a six-year-old. "He was so obnoxious. He made me angry, and then he told me something and I thought . . . well, I didn't think, but I . . . well, I laughed at him." She drew a breath, cringing beneath the shocked expressions on her aunts' faces. "I know I shouldn't have done it, but it just came out. And then I realized he was sincerely asking for help, but by then it was too late. He was furious, and stormed out of here like the hotheaded childish brat he is."

"And I can't say that I blame him," Merriwether retorted.

"Oh, Aurora, men have such easily wounded pride, you know. You shouldn't have laughed." Fauna wrung her hands as if this were the most horrible of circumstances.

"Look, don't worry about it. I never liked him and he never liked me and we'll probably never see each other again, so—"

"I'm afraid that won't do, sweetheart." Flora said sadly. She looked at the others. "I think it's time we told her."

"I *knew* it! What have you three been keeping from me?"

Tiny, delicate-looking Flora faced her, while the other two waved their hands wildly as if to tell her to keep quiet. "Darling, there's a secret the Sortilege Witches keep—the secret of our powers. The reason our magick is so much stronger than that of most other practitioners of The Craft."

Merriwether and Fauna stopped gesturing and frowned, as if they had no more clue what she was getting at than Aurora did.

"I thought . . ." Aurora said in confusion. "I thought it was just the bloodline. The power of our ancestors, and all that . . ."

"No dear. There's more to it than that. A secret you must vow never to tell . . . unless it becomes absolutely necessary. I never would have told it to you, dear, except perhaps on my deathbed. But now you must know."

Aurora leaned forward, brows lifting high. This sounded so . . . so dire.

"Every Sortilege Witch is destined to lose her powers, her gifts, her magick—on the day she turns twenty-seven, my child."

Aurora drew back as if her petite aunt had slapped her. She'd be twenty-seven in a little over twenty-four hours. At midnight on Halloween! *Tomorrow!* "No!"

"Oh, yes. I'm afraid it's true."

"My . . . my *healing*!"

"Well, you can still practice medicine, dear, but—"

"No. This can't be, Aunt Flora, please!" Panic was making her heart beat wildly in her chest. She couldn't lose her healing gift. Suppose some injured child was brought in, like the one last month with the ruptured spleen, who'd been wheeled past her in the hall after the physician on call had missed the diagnosis. He'd have died if her special sense hadn't told her . . .

"What can I do?" She gripped her aunt's shoulders, and searched her face. "There's something. Yes, there must be! You still have your magick. All of you do!"

She turned to Merriwether and Fauna, but they only shook their heads and nodded at Flora to go on.

"Yes, child. There's one way you can keep your magick. But I'm afraid you're not going to like it very much."

"I don't care! I'll do anything. Tell me."

Flora cleared her throat. "You have to have . . . er . . . *relations* . . . with a man before your twenty-seventh birthday, dear. And . . . the . . . the man, has to be . . . pure."

"Pure?"

"Unsullied," Fauna said helpfully.

"Oh for heaven's sakes," Merri put in. "A virgin. The man has to be a virgin. *Now* do you understand why we're so upset with you for driving Nathan off the way you did?"

Aurora stood still, gave her head a shake, but they were all still there, still looking at her expectantly.

"That has to be the most ridiculous bunch of . . ." She stared, wide-eyed, from one of them to the other. "But . . . you have to be joking. I mean, it makes no sense. I've never heard of anything so . . . so bizarre!"

"We're not joking, darling," Flora denied gently. "So I suggest you begin making amends with that young man. And the sooner . . . the better."

The reality of it hit her then. They were telling her she had two choices—lose her powers, or sleep with Nathan McBride.

"Wait," she said, racking her brain. "There must be some other male in town who's still a virgin."

"Of course, dear. Over at the high school, perhaps, but they'd arrest you for that."

"*Aunt Merri!* I didn't mean—" She pushed her hands through

her hair and began pacing. What was she going to do? What in the world was she going to do? "There has to be another virgin! Anyone but him!"

"Even in our day, we had trouble finding them, child," Merriwether explained. "It's long been tradition for . . . yes, for the older women of the family to see to it that one young man remained . . . chaste, so that when the time came . . ."

Aurora's eyes widened until she felt they would burst. "It was *you*? You three are the ones who hexed Nathan?"

"We didn't *hex* him, dear. We just . . . interfered a bit. A little binding spell. A little spying in the crystal. A little . . ."

"Aunt Merri, you ran him over with his own car! I wouldn't call that little!"

"*That* was an *accident*! We'd never hurt the boy . . . well, not deliberately."

Aurora pressed her fingers to her temples and closed her eyes. "I'm going to my rooms," she said. "I have to meditate."

"Flora, that was positively ingenious," Merri exclaimed, hugging her small sister hard. "How did you ever come up with it?"

"Well, she was going to blow the whole thing. We couldn't let that happen, could we?"

Fauna shook her head. "It was awfully mean, though. And where did you come up with that deadline? By her birthday?"

"If we don't hurry, that young man will kill himself trying to get past our spells to get . . . well, you know."

"Halloween's a good date anyway," Merri said practically. "It's going to work out perfectly. You picked the one thing she would never risk losing—her healing gift. It was brilliant."

"But poor Aurora. This isn't going to be easy for her. And I hate that we had to lie to her like that," Flora fretted.

"We'll tell her the truth later. She'll understand. And she won't mind, once she falls in love with Nathan."

Fauna, though, was still shaking her head. She paced to the table, picked up her favorite Tarot deck, and drew a single card. "Two of Swords. Ladies, you're forgetting. Our divinations told us Nathan was to be the father of Aurora's little girl. But not that they'd ever fall in love. There's a good chance they won't."

"Not fall in love?" Flora asked in dismay.

"Have a child and not be together?" Merri added.

"It's possible."

Merri wrung her hands and began to pace. "Oh, my. Oh, dear. We *can't* have that."

$\mathcal{A}$urora didn't sleep all night. She couldn't even lie still. Mostly, she paced as various scenarios played out in her mind. This couldn't be true. It was too ludicrous to be true. Her aunts must be playing some horribly cruel trick on her. But why? They were eccentric, yes. And meddlesome. But this . . .

Maybe this was just a matchmaking scheme gone too far. Maybe they were just trying to set her up with the man they perceived to be perfect for her.

Perfect for her? Nathan McBride?

She groaned softly and paced some more. She supposed it was possible they were matchmaking.

But what if they weren't? What if she really would lose her healing gift?

Closing her eyes, Aurora realized she couldn't risk that. Even sleeping with Nathan would be better than that. And besides, she'd only have to do it once. Right? Just one night with Nathan, and she could relax. She grimaced and shuddered a little. One night with Nathan. Maybe if she got really drunk first . . .

For just a moment, she pictured Nathan trying to rid himself of his virginity all these years, with her aunts constantly interfering. The thought made her smile, and then made her laugh softly. Poor Nathan. No wonder he thought he was cursed.

But this wasn't funny, and her laughter turned sour. She didn't have any choice here. She was going to have to make nice with Nathan. She was going to have to . . . she bit her lip and made a face . . . seduce him. Oh, Goddess, if this did turn out to be a trick she was going to strangle those aunts of hers!

Meanwhile, though, she was just going to have to straighten her spine, grit her teeth, and get through this thing. She was strong. She was a Sortilege Witch, for goodness' sake. She could do it.

Unless, of course, Nathan wasn't willing.

Nathan, twenty-nine and still a virgin. So frustrated he'd actually made himself come to her for help. Mercy, he'd be more than willing.

# Chapter 4

$\mathcal{I}$t was Halloween, and Nathan had decided to take the day off and sleep in for a change. Hell, he'd earned it. Last night's humiliation had taken quite a lot out of him. Not to mention that he was still a bit sore—mostly that elbow, though. The rest of him was already back to normal. Not that it mattered, he supposed. The parts of him that were better would probably never see much use, anyway.

He'd like to strangle Aurora Sortilege. Coldhearted snake of a woman.

He was plodding through the apartment in his boxers, heading for his first cup of coffee, when the doorbell sounded. Pushing both hands through his hair, he stopped in midplod and turned. Probably his father. He'd promised to do some work at the house today, hadn't he? He was going to mow the lawn and take a look at that sticky window in the back.

He strode to the door and yanked it open, only to see Aurora standing on the other side. She looked at him. Huge ebony eyes, wide and a little uncertain. Satiny hair framing her face.

He took a single step backward and started to close the door.

"Hold on! I brought a peace offering!" She held up a big white bakery box, and he caught a whiff of fresh doughnuts. Blueberry filling, if he wasn't mistaken. His favorite. He wondered for a minute if she knew that because he'd told her, or because she'd been reading his mind.

Hell, no. If she could read his mind, she wouldn't be here without an armed bodyguard.

He pulled the door wider again. "What's this about, Aurora? What are you up to?"

This time her almond gaze slid from his, traveling slowly downward, and he squirmed a little, realizing he was standing there in nothing but a pair of boxers. Her eyes widened and she jerked them up again. "Maybe this was a bad idea." It was her turn to take a step backward.

He reached out fast, not quite sure why he did it, but sure enough, his hand was wrapped around her wrist and she was looking slightly alarmed.

He shook his head and let go. "Come on in, Aurora. Rest assured, if I get the slightest urge to try anything, my apartment will catch fire. You're perfectly safe with me."

She lowered her gaze quickly. Guiltily? What the hell . . . ?

Sighing in resignation, she came in. He closed the door. "There's fresh coffee in the kitchen," he told her as her eyes once again slipped lower. "I suppose I'd better put some clothes on. You sure as hell aren't here to see me naked."

As he turned to go, she muttered something that sounded like, "A lot you know," and he spun around frowning at her, and asked, "What's that?"

"Nothing," she told him quickly. "Go ahead. Get dressed."

There was something different about her, he realized while he was searching her face. Something more than just the fact that she seemed nervous and less hostile than usual. And then it hit him. She was wearing more makeup than he'd seen her wear before. Subtle, but there, shadowing those black eyes with mystery. Clusters of silver moons and golden stars dangled from her ears, and he thought he caught a whiff of exotic perfume mingling with the coffee and doughnut aromas. He looked her over more thoroughly than he had before, his curiosity piqued. She wasn't dressed for the hospital. Short black skirt and a semisheer blouse to match. He could see the dark sports bra she wore underneath. The nylons were black, too. And the shoes were open toed, with heels four inches high.

What the hell was she doing here, dressed like that?

He took a step toward her, forgetting for a second that she was the woman he'd been fantasizing about murdering, and entertaining a few more pleasant fantasies instead.

Her eyes met his and widened. "I th-thought you wanted to get dressed," she stammered.

He stopped, the fantasy shattered. Who was he kidding? It wasn't going to happen. Hell, as much as he disliked her, he didn't think he wanted it to. No matter how deprived he was. He shook his head and turned to go into his bedroom.

When he came back, he found her in the kitchen, sitting at his small round table, staring into space with an unfocused look on her face, and stirring her coffee into a small caramel-colored whirlpool. The box of doughnuts sat in the middle of the table, unopened.

Nathan walked past her, poured himself a cup, and sat down opposite her. She seemed to pull herself together, and looked at him. "You didn't shave."

"Didn't know it was required," he responded. "I never shave on my day off."

"Oh."

He ran one hand over his stubble. Hell, some women found the unshaven look sexy. Or . . . so he'd thought. It looked to him like it just made this one nervous. More nervous than she'd already been.

"So are you going to tell me what you're doing here dressed to kill, Aurora, or am I supposed to guess?"

She started, and glanced down at her attire. "What's wrong with the way I'm dressed?"

"Nothing."

"Then why—"

"What are you doing in my kitchen, Aurora?"

She licked her lips. Drew a breath. Stirred faster. "I wanted to apologize. For last night."

Aurora? Apologize? To *him*?

"I shouldn't have laughed at you. I just . . . I didn't realize you were serious, you know? You're always teasing me. I half expected you to follow it up with some lewd proposition or smart remark."

He didn't say anything—just sat there, watching her, waiting for her to cut to the chase.

"I wasn't laughing *at* you, Nathan, I was laughing with you. I thought you were joking—about the curse, not the . . . other thing. I mean, I know you. I figured if you'd been celibate all this time it was because you had a good reason to want to be. I mean, come on. *Look* at you. Any woman would want . . ." She clamped her jaw as if to stop herself, and her eyes widened.

Nathan felt himself smile, just a little. So she did like the unshaven look after all, did she?

"That's not the part I have trouble with." He took a long, slow sip of the hot coffee, then lowered the cup. "Them wanting me, I mean. But something always happens. Just like this last episode with what's-her-name . . ." He stopped talking and shook his head. "Why the hell am I even discussing this with you?"

"Because I can help you," she said. He met her eyes. She looked away, reaching for a doughnut he had a feeling she didn't want.

"I doubt that." He watched her face. "I don't know why I

thought of asking you in the first place, Aurora. You know damned well I don't believe in your hocus-pocus bullshit."

Her eyes narrowed, and anger reddened her cheeks. Her head came up fast, and her lips parted to deliver the scathing comeback he fully expected.

But it never came. She caught herself, drew a breath, closed her mouth.

"You can at least let me try."

Nathan leaned back in his chair, frowning at her. Now this was one hell of an interesting turn of events. Since when did she resist an opportunity to slam him? "How?"

"Well . . . this woman who ran over you . . . you don't even remember her name."

"So?" He reached for his coffee, took another sip.

"So . . . have they all been like that? Women you barely knew, just wanted to sleep with?"

He pursed his lips and thought about it. "Yeah, pretty much."

She shrugged, a delicate lift of one shoulder. "So maybe that's the problem. Maybe you're subconsciously sabotaging yourself because you know you don't really want to sleep with a stranger."

His frown grew. "You sound more like a shrink than a Witch."

She tilted her head. "Maybe you'd be okay if your first time could be with someone . . . someone you know. Someone . . . you've known for a long time."

"Yeah, right. Like who?" He took a big gulp of coffee this time. Bitter and black and strong, just the way he liked it.

"Like me."

The coffee spewed from his mouth like a geyser, showering the table, the doughnuts, and the front of that sexy blouse she was wearing. The cup fell to the floor, spilling what was left. And Nathan bent over the table choking on the small amount he'd managed to swallow.

Aurora came around the table to pound on his back, which any doctor should know was totally illogical, but was the instinctive reaction anyway.

He drew a few wheezing breaths and managed to sit up straight again, as he lifted his head and stared into her eyes. She was joking. She must have been joking.

She stared back at him, dead serious.

"Hell, you're not joking, are you?"

"I . . ." She took her hand off his back, and shrugged. "I was just trying to help. If it seems so ludicrous to you, then just forget it."

She turned around and headed for the door.

He leaped out of his chair as what might be his only chance at sex seemed about to flee. "Wait a minute! Hold on, for crying out loud."

She stopped, her back to him. And he stopped, too, looking her up and down from behind, liking what he saw, and shaking his head. This was too strange.

"You took me by surprise, that's all. Look, if you're willing . . . well, hell, Aurora, I'd be nuts to say no."

He saw her stiffen her back, square her shoulders, and slowly turn to face him, looking like Joan of Arc turning to face the stake. "All right then."

"All right then?"

She nodded, her face grim, and lifted trembling hands to the tiny buttons at the front of her blouse. "Let's get this over with."

Nathan stood there, feeling as if she'd just dumped ice water on him. "I can tell you're really looking forward to this."

"Don't get any ideas, Nathan. This is nothing personal." She unbuttoned another button. And then another. Crisp and efficient, she removed the blouse and stood there in a sports bra and a miniskirt, looking like every man's fantasy.

"So you don't really want me," he said flatly.

"Of course not."

"You're just doing this as a favor."

"Naturally." She reached behind her to unzip the skirt, pushed it down over her hips, and stepped out of it when it slid to the floor. The nylons were not panty hose—they were stockings, black and silky and held up by lacy red garters. The panties she wore were red, too, and skimpy. And her belly was smooth and tight, and her breasts round and firm behind that black scrap of spandex that covered them. He wished he liked her at least a little bit.

He swallowed hard. It looked as if she'd come here for the sole purpose of bedding him. It made him nervous as hell. "And what do you get out of this?"

She shrugged again. "Nothing you need to know about. Are you going to stand there gawking or get naked?"

Good question. Nathan wasn't sure he wanted a woman who didn't want him back. But . . . what if she did? "Come here, Aurora."

He saw the alarm flash in her eyes, followed by resignation and stoic resolve. She stepped closer, then still closer, like the village virgin stepping up to the mouth of the volcano.

Nathan slipped his hands around her waist and pulled her against him. She was warm, trembling slightly. He bent his head and touched her lips with his. She gasped and drew away.

He pulled her close again. "Come on, Aurora. If you're afraid to even kiss me, how do you expect to do anything else?"

"I'm . . . n-not afraid."

"No?"

She shook her head.

"Prove it then. Kiss me like you mean it. Maybe even pretend to enjoy it." He didn't give her time to answer. He kissed her again.

It was slow, her reaction. Her lips relaxed bit by bit as he worked them, and even parted a little. Her arms went around him, palms pressed flat to his back, softly. Nathan touched her lips with his tongue, traced their shape lightly, then slid between them.

And she shivered.

A delicious little shiver. It made him shiver a little himself.

He cupped her bottom with his hands and pulled her hard to

him, arched his hips so that he pressed tight into her, bent her backward, and proceeded to kiss the living hell out of her.

And surprise of surprises, she started kissing him right back. He felt her hands moving upward, threading into his hair—felt her body press against his. She tipped her head back and opened her mouth to him, and her tongue danced with his and tangled and fought.

He lifted his head slowly, staring down into her face. "I can't believe it," he said softly. Her eyes were glittering, her face flushed, her lips parted as short, shallow little breaths rushed in and out between them. "You want me. You little fraud, you've wanted me all along."

"In your dreams," she whispered in a voice so sexy it sounded like an endearment.

He let his arms fall to his sides and stepped away from her. "You're a liar."

"I—" She followed him with her eyes as he bent to pick up her blouse, then her skirt, and turned to hold them out to her. "What . . . ?"

"Put your clothes on, Aurora. I don't accept pity sex, so if that's what this is, you can forget it." It wasn't, though. He knew damn well it wasn't. He wasn't sure how he felt about that, but he wasn't going to do her unless she admitted it.

"But—"

"But nothing. I know you want me. And if you're honest with yourself, you know it, too. So why don't you just come back when you're ready to admit that, and then we'll see."

Her eyes rounded, gleaming with a slow burning anger and maybe just a hint of the humiliation he'd felt last night when she'd laughed in his face. Good.

"You arrogant, egotistical, *stupid*—"

"Yeah, yeah."

She pulled on her blouse in angry, jerky movements, and yanked the skirt up in much the same way. "You're going to regret this, Nathan McBride!"

She spun and slammed out of the apartment.

"Hell, Aurora," he whispered after she'd gone. "I already do."

# Chapter 5

*Aurora* couldn't believe it. She was humiliated. She was disgusted. She was . . .

She was turned on.

By Nathan McBride, for Goddess' sake!

It wasn't as if she were some blushing, clueless virgin being assuaged by unfamiliar urges, either. She'd had men before. In college, in med school. Not many, but enough to know her way around.

So why had a single kiss from the man she'd spent her entire life detesting sent her senses spinning out of control? Why did it feel as if he'd made love to her more thoroughly than any man ever had, when all he'd done was kiss her?

Why had he turned her down?

"I'm pathetic," she whispered.

She'd made a fool of herself with Nathan just now, and she kicked herself for it all the way home. But as she walked up the front steps in the early-morning breeze, she knew that wasn't the worst of it. The worst was that she still had to make him sleep with her. Somehow. She had to. And she had to do it before this day ended. Because today was Halloween. At midnight tonight she turned twenty-seven. There was no getting around it. She had to sleep with him.

But if that meant admitting to the creep that she might have decided it wouldn't be a totally revolting experience, it would never happen. She'd die before she'd do that.

She stood there, not wanting to walk in and face her aunts, debating whether she could get away with sneaking off for the day, when the front door burst open. Aunt Merri stood there, her face chalk-white, her eyes wide.

"Aurora! Thank goodness! We've been calling . . ." Her voice trailed off and she blinked at moisture gathering in her eyes.

Something terrible was happening. She knew it with every cell in her, and not just because of her aunt's stricken face.

*Flora. It's Aunt Flora.*

"Where is she? What happened?" Aurora followed quickly as Merriwether turned to hurry back inside.

Aunt Flora lay on the sofa, looking for all the world as if she were sound asleep. It was only Aurora's keen healing sense that told her otherwise.

"We can't wake her up," Fauna whispered, looking up into Aurora's eyes, her own red-rimmed and puffy. "She just came in here, lay down, and closed her eyes. And now we can't wake her up."

Aurora stared down at her beloved, fragile aunt, lying so still, and her heart tripped over itself in her chest. Vaguely she heard squealing tires as a car skidded to a stop out front, and then heavy steps thudded into the living room.

"Aurora?"

She turned. Nathan stood braced in the doorway, looking worried. "How did you—" she began.

"I called him, looking for you," Aunt Merri interrupted. "But you'd already left."

"Never mind that," Fauna said, and her voice was a plea. "Aurora, what's wrong with her? What—"

"I don't know." Her hands trembling, Aurora reached to her tiny aunt's throat to feel her pulse, soft and too slow. Her breaths were slow, too. And shallow. Her skin was clammy to the touch. Her Aunt Flora . . . her precious Flora. So fragile, even in the best of health. "I . . . I can't . . ." Aurora battled tears, but they came anyway.

And then she felt Nathan's hands on her shoulders, a gentle squeeze. "Merriwether, call the hospital and tell them we're bringing her in. Fauna, will you get us a blanket? It's still chilly outside."

The two nodded and scurried to obey the calm orders he gave. And his hands were still on Aurora's shoulders, so he must feel her sobs.

"You can help her, Aurora. You're letting your emotions cloud your judgment."

"What do you know about my emotions, Nathan?"

"Nothing. But I know what I saw when I was sixteen and hit that red-tailed hawk with my Mustang. You remember?"

She closed her eyes. How could she forget? It had been the first time she'd actually tapped into this power she'd been born with. She opened her eyes and looked at Nathan. "You don't believe in my . . . 'hocus-pocus bullshit.' Isn't that what you called it?"

"So maybe I lied." He was kneeling now, beside the sofa, hands still on her shoulders. "And maybe it doesn't matter what I believe. It's what you believe that counts, here. So pull yourself together, Aurora. Your aunt needs you right now."

Something passed into her. Some calming, strengthening energy flowed, and she was too in touch with the vibrations around her not to be fully aware of it. The warm force moved from Nathan's hands, into her body where he touched her, and it filled her.

His own power. The power he didn't even know he had. Still alive in his blood and somehow infusing her with courage. She closed her eyes, and he started to move his hands away from her. But she caught them with her own and held them to her shoulders, and felt the energy building until she brimmed with it. She'd drawn in before the powers of Mother Earth and Father Sky and even the energies of the moon to empower her magick. But never the essence of another human being. . . .

She pulled the power into her, centering it, feeling the pulsing golden glow of it in her solar plexus. And then she took Nathan's hands away and turned to her aunt. She lifted her hands, palms down, and moved them slowly, hovering a hair's breadth above Flora's small body, head to toe, feeling her aura, searching for the invader that was making her aunt so ill.

And finding it. A red throb, pulsing against her palm from Flora's left ankle.

Quickly, Aurora grasped Flora's ankle, pushing up the leg of her pants, bending closer.

"Aurora?" Nathan asked.

"Snake bite," she whispered, and she spotted the tiny marks and the red swelling around them.

"But . . . we don't have any venomous snakes around here. Are you sure it's—"

"Rattlers. We have rattlers. Not many, but every once in a while . . ." Her senses told her she was right. "Aunt Merri," she called, louder now, and her aunt poked her head in from the kitchen, the phone still held to her ear. "Tell them to get some an-tivenin. It was a rattlesnake. And then come to the hospital. We have to hurry." As she spoke she was yanking the silk scarf from Flora's head and twisting it around the leg, above the bite.

"Get her to the car, Nathan," she said softly. "You drive."

*He* didn't believe it. Okay, he'd told her he did, but he'd only said it . . . hell, he didn't know why he'd said it. To snap her out of her momentary panic, he supposed. To give her some kind of strength so she'd do what needed doing.

And oddly enough, it had worked. When he'd picked up the phone after she'd stormed out of his apartment—when he'd heard her aunt's frightened voice on the other end—he'd had this feeling that he should come over here. That Aurora . . . needed him. Stupid. Ridiculous, really.

But then he'd touched her, and it was almost as if she really had. As if his hands on her shoulders, his being there with her, had helped her somehow. As if she were drawing something from him . . .

He shook his head and paced the waiting room some more. He'd driven like a maniac to get here while she'd worked on the snake bite in the backseat. He'd slowed down once—only once, and she'd snapped at him for it.

"The light's red, Aurora—I have to—"

She'd glanced over his shoulder, waved a hand toward the light. Green. It had turned red two seconds ago, but when she did—whatever the hell she'd done—it turned green. "Don't worry about the lights," she'd told him. "Just drive."

He hadn't hit another red light all the way to the hospital. Just roared right up to the red ones without even slowing down, and every last one turned green before he got to it.

He frowned slightly, glancing toward the doors to the treatment room where Aurora and her aunt Flora were. "Weird," he muttered.

Merriwether and Fauna came running in, rushing up to him, wide eyes full of questions. He opened his mouth to tell them he didn't know anything yet, wishing he could say something more reassuring, but before he spoke, the doors opened. Aurora stepped out, leaned back against the door she had closed behind her, and met their eyes one by one. She nodded and smiled tiredly to reassure them of dainty Flora's well-being.

God, she looked wiped out.

"She's going to be okay," she said. "You can go in. . . ."

She never finished. Her two aunts rushed her, nudging her gently aside and hurrying in to see their sister, the doors banging closed behind them.

Nathan took a step toward Aurora. "What about you?" he asked her gruffly. "You going to be okay?"

She smiled weakly, nodded once, and sank toward the floor as if her legs had just melted beneath her. Nathan lunged, grabbing her before she landed and pulling her into his arms to keep her upright. She only leaned against him as if she were made of water, so he turned her and scooped her up, carried her into the first empty room he came to, and lowered her to the bed there.

She didn't pass out. She was conscious, shaking her head, blinking. "I'm okay. Really, I'm—"

"The hell you are." He kept her from sitting up by gently pressing her down to the pillows. "Just lie down for a minute and tell me what happened."

She did lie down; she closed her eyes, then closed them tighter, and a tear slipped from beneath them to run slowly down her cheek. "I almost lost her. For the love of the Universe, Nathan, I almost lost her."

The tears came then, fast and furious, and she sobbed so hard it broke his heart to see it. He sat on the edge of the bed, gathered her small body close to his, held her hard against him, and felt her trembling in his arms. "But you didn't. She's okay, Aurora. You saved her life. I've never seen anything like what you did today."

Her arms crept around him and she clung there, crying. "But if . . . if I hadn't known what was wrong . . ."

"You did know," he said softly. "I don't know how, but you did. And she's going to be okay now."

"I know," she whispered. "I know, but . . ."

He straightened away from her, but she clung. "Hold me, Nathan. I need you."

He held her. He couldn't believe what she'd just said, but he'd heard it, loud and clear. She needed him. Holy crap. She was so soft, so vulnerable, so tortured right now. And Nathan was overwhelmed with the need to make it better.

God, how had he ever thought he disliked Aurora Sortilege? Right now, he didn't think he'd ever want to hold anyone else.

*I need you.*

"I'm here for you, then," he told her. "Aurora, I'm right here, okay?" He stroked her hair. "Anything you need, you just say the word and I'll do it."

She sniffed, sat up a little straighter, wiped at her eyes, and stared into his. "I hope you mean that." Her voice was hoarse.

He smiled gently at her, as he reached up to brush his thumb over her tear-stained cheeks. "Hell, Aurora, it surprises me as much as you, but I do. I mean it."

"You don't even like me."

He shrugged. "You were never my number one fan, either, as I recall." She lowered her gaze. He hooked his forefinger under her chin, lifting her head until she looked at him again. "But what if we forget all that?"

She frowned, searching his face. "Can we? Can we really do that?"

"Hell, Aurora, I think we already have." He smoothed her hair away from her face. "I like you now."

She closed her eyes, almost as if she felt guilty. "You saved Aunt Flora's life," she said softly.

"All I did was drive. You're the one who—"

"No." She opened her eyes and looked right into his. "You did it, Nathan. I was standing there falling apart, and you . . . you helped me. You knew it. You felt it, too, didn't you?"

Nathan battled a shiver. "I felt . . . something. I still don't know what it was."

Aurora nodded, but said nothing. After a moment, she pushed herself up straighter. "I should go, see about Aunt Flora, talk to—"

"I want to see you, Aurora." He blurted it without even realizing he was going to. And then he added, "Tonight."

She bit her lower lip. "I don't know . . ."

"Because you still don't like me?" he asked, only half kidding.

"No," she whispered, and she reached out and touched his face. "Because I do."

# Chapter 6

*Aurora* paced the house, wringing her hands. This whole thing would have been easier if she'd kept on hating Nathan. But now . . .

Now, she liked him. And maybe she always had. And maybe it was a little more than *like* that she felt for him, and had been all along.

And so she was going to use him. Sleep with him for the sole purpose of preserving her powers. She felt like a slug.

But what choice did she have? Suppose something like this happened after tonight, after she lost the gift? Suppose she was unable to help one of her precious aunts when they needed her? Or one of her patients?

Oh, what was she going to do?

She couldn't eat. Aunt Flora was spending the night in the hospital, just as a precaution. Aunt Merri and Aunt Fauna refused to leave her side. They insisted on spending the night with their youngest sister. Aurora wasn't worried about them, not even Flora. She was fine. The three of them were probably organizing a senior slumber party and ordering pizza by now.

Tonight was Halloween. At midnight she would turn twenty-seven. She had to make a decision, and make it fast.

Looking skyward, Aurora whispered, "I need help. I don't know what to do."

And like the whisper of a breeze, she heard, "Yes, you do."

"Yes," she said softly. "I do."

An hour later, Aurora sat outside bathed in moonlight. The circular spot in the center of her aunts' flower and shrub garden was sacred ground. They'd made it so, and so it was, surrounded by blossoms— this late in the fall, mostly oranges and yellows, sunflowers, marigolds, and daisies. She reclined on the grassy ground in the center, where a large flat stone of dark granite held court. She lit the candles she'd placed on the stone, then the incense. And then she rose and lifted her arms out to the sides, head tipped back. Slowly, she drew her arms in again, crossing them over her chest, lowering her head.

Aurora stood still for a moment, feeling her energies gathering, ready to do her bidding. She opened her palms, cupped in front of her, and visualized a tiny ball of pulsing white light swirling in her hands. A ball of purity and goodness and power. A ball where only positive forces could exist, and where time and space did not. A meeting place between the worlds. When she could *feel* it there, when she could *see* her ball of light, she parted her hands and let it fall to the ground. And when it hit, it exploded. The bubble of white light expanded on impact, filling the tiny spot in the center of the garden, and surrounding Aurora completely. Above and below, continuing beneath the earth's surface. Around and about, creating a place of magick.

This done, Aurora sat down. "And now," she whispered, "Ancient and Shining Ones, tell me what I must do."

\* \* \*

*Nathan* got no answer at the front door. He hadn't really expected to at this time of the night, but he couldn't sleep. He was worried. Not about Flora. That eccentric old Witch would be just fine. He hadn't left the hospital until he'd been assured of that. He wasn't even all that worried about Aurora, though he had been for a short while. Falling apart in his arms wasn't exactly typical behavior on her part. Then again, neither was offering to sleep with him.

Couldn't quite get that part off his mind, could he?

Figured. He was nothing if not obsessed.

Well, he'd tried the door, and she hadn't answered, so either she was sound asleep or she didn't want to see him. He turned to go, then paused as a stray breeze carried a whiff of something smoky and exotic to his nose. He inhaled, frowned. There. A thin tendril of smoke, and it almost seemed to crook like a finger, beckoning him to follow. Dumb idea, of course, but as it receded around the corner of the old house, he followed it anyway.

And then he came to a stop in the backyard. Because there was a glow coming from the hidden center of that mysterious flower garden. A flickering dancing glow, as if of candles . . . and something else.

He walked closer, slowly, and for some reason he couldn't even begin to understand, he followed the path that had frightened him as a kid—followed its twisting, snakelike course, to a place at the center, a clearing amid the greenery, in the shape of a perfect circle. And he stood there, frowning at the sight of Aurora in its center. She wore some sort of robe, hooded and black and gleaming like satin. She'd been sitting when he'd first spotted her, but she was standing now, moving in graceful patterns that seemed almost like a dance. The moonlight beamed down on her. But the light was more than that, as well. It seemed to surround her—a shimmering, surreal kind of opalescence bathing her like the glow of a spotlight. Or was it radiating outward from somewhere inside her?

She went still, head tilted as if she were listening to something. Or someone. And then she turned, and she saw him there.

He held those black eyes of hers, unable to look away. And he could have sworn someone gave him a shove from behind to get his feet moving. He walked up to the very end of the path through the flowers, and stopped at the edge of that circle of light that surrounded her, not quite sure why, not even sure it was real.

She smiled very softly, as if she approved of something he'd done. She didn't say a word, just came forward and knelt down, pointing her finger at the ground near his right foot. She rose, tracing an arch in the air, up one side of him, over his head, and down the other. And damned if it didn't seem to him that the odd glow, the one that couldn't be real, vanished in the spot she'd outlined. It was like a . . . a doorway.

She took a step backward, still not speaking. He swallowed hard, not quite sure what he was getting himself into. A little bit afraid.

This time he was *sure* someone shoved him. A hard hand seemed to slam into his back, and he lurched through the imaginary doorway, swinging his head around to see who was back there. But there was no one. And the hairs on his nape were beginning to stand upright and bristle with electricity.

Aurora seemed unperturbed, though. She moved past him to the spot he'd just come through, knelt again, and drew with her finger . . . a line this time, right to left, along the bottom of that doorway that wasn't really a doorway.

And the glow filled the area once again. Nathan blinked and rubbed at his eyes, but it wasn't going away. This spot, this one circular area, looked different from everything else around it. And it *felt* different, too. Warmer. Even a hint stuffy. Like he was inside instead of out.

Dumb.

"Take off your shoes, Nathan," she whispered, and her voice was soft and deep. "This is sacred ground."

Sacred ground. Right. Okay, he'd definitely entered the Twilight Zone. But he took off the shoes, all the same, and peeled off his socks, too, just for good measure. He tossed them without thinking, expecting them to sail right on out of this unearthly glow and into the darkness of the garden beyond. But they didn't. It was as if they hit a wall and bounced back, falling soundlessly to the ground.

He stared at them. But Aurora was moving again, and that drew his attention back to her. And then he was pretty sure that his heart stopped for a second. Because she was slipping that black satin robe down off her shoulders, and it fell to the ground like a pool of black water. And she wasn't wearing a single thing underneath, except for a mystical-looking pendant and a pair of emerald earrings.

The ones he'd given her? He glanced away from her, toward the flat stone, and saw a bit of paper lying there, with the candle flames on either side casting shadows that danced over the crude line drawing of a face. A man's face. Remarkably like his own.

He looked back at her again, a little chill dancing up his spine. "A-a-a-Aurora?"

"I needed you, Nathan," she said softly. "So I brought you to me."

He stared at her, still far too unsettled by the nude work of art standing before him to give his full attention to her words. "Brought me," he parroted.

"Manipulative magick is not something I'd normally use. But I was careful," she said, explaining herself to him as calmly as if every word she said made perfect sense—which, of course, they didn't. "I made sure the words I composed couldn't interfere with your free will," she went on. "I said, 'If he wants me, let him come to me now.'"

"I see." But he didn't. All he saw were a pair of perfect breasts, as round and firm as his fondest fantasy. And a waist he could fit his hands around. And a triangle of curls between her legs that was as shiny black as her hair.

"And you came."

He swallowed hard. Not yet he hadn't. But maybe he would before the night was over. He just hoped there wasn't going to be an earthquake or flash flood within the next hour or so. His gaze slid upward, meeting her eyes, seeing the mystery he'd always noticed there, the darkness, the night itself, glimmering back at him. Okay, then. Make that the next several hours.

She said nothing—just looked back at him, slowly turned, and from the big flat rock in the center, reached for a jeweled dagger that looked as deadly as it did beautiful. Facing him again, she pressed its hilt into his hand, with the blade pointing downward. She squeezed his fist tight around the weapon, then drew his other hand to close on it, as well.

Turning away from him again, she picked up a fat three-legged cauldron of black cast iron. And when she faced him she held it, one palm pressed to either side, arms outstretched as if she were offering it to him.

But she wasn't, because his hands were both occupied with holding the dagger. He didn't know what—

"Your ancestors performed this rite for centuries, Nathan," she whispered. "Close your eyes and open your heart. Listen to the power that still lingers in your blood. The voices of your ancestors. They're here tonight. They live . . . in you."

Something made him close his eyes. And he didn't feel like Nathan McBride, owner of a chain of pharmacies and frustrated sex maniac. He felt . . . different. Liberated. Strong. Fierce. Powerful. Male.

"As the cauldron is to the Goddess," Aurora said softly, "so the athame is to the God." Nathan blinked his eyes open, saw her holding the iron pot up to him, saw the dagger in his own hands, blade pointing down at it. Heard her whisper, "And together, they are one. . . ."

Very slowly, he lowered his arms, gently plunging the dagger into the cauldron, knowing somehow that this was what he was supposed to do. And as he did, Aurora's head tilted backward and her eyes fell closed. There was something . . . some surge of energy shooting through him, into him from where his fists clenched around the dagger's hilt, rushing up his arms and infusing his body until he felt as if he must be glowing.

He lifted the blade again, blinking his eyes open, seeing the stars and the moon above in a way he never had before. They were brighter, clearer. They seemed . . . *alive.*

Aurora gently took the blade from him and replaced the cauldron and knife on the makeshift table. Nathan couldn't take his eyes off her. It was as if he'd wanted her all his life. As if being with her were suddenly a force of nature raging inside him—something that could neither be denied nor controlled.

Aurora faced him, and he saw the same kinds of passions swirling in her eyes. "Now—"

"Now," Nathan said, gripping her shoulders, "this." He pulled her close, bent to kiss her, fed from her mouth, and hungered for more. And he knew this was right. It was right, and perfect, and he couldn't live without it. He adored her. Didn't know why or when it had happened, or what was making him realize it now. But he did. He adored her, and he didn't care if she wouldn't admit she felt the same way. She did. He knew she did.

She kissed him back as if she did.

Her hands threaded into his hair. Her body strained against his, warm and naked and wanting. He moved his hands down her back, tracing the delicate curve of her spine, then filling his palms with the swell of her buttocks and squeezing and lifting.

Her mouth tasted of honey. Her tongue was moist silk, stroking his, tasting him, driving him mad. And then her hands were there between them, working his clothes free, tearing his shirt in her eagerness to rid him of it, yanking with fierce and frightening determination at the button and zipper of his jeans. And before he knew it, he was stepping out of them, kicking his shorts aside, feeling his shirt fall at his feet. Her hands explored now, and he relished every touch, every gentle pinch and tender raking of those nails.

She turned him, and he went. She pushed him and he fell, sitting now, sucking in a quick surprised gasp when his backside came to rest upon the chill of the granite boulder. But her mouth still fed, and her hands still worked, and he couldn't notice the discomfort of the cold on his flesh for more than a moment. He felt her hands again, pressing his chest, and he lay back, and the chill sent shivers up his back as her lips did likewise to his front.

Her hungry little mouth devoured his chest, bit by bit, small white teeth nipping, plump lips working, pointy tongue torment-ing. She moved over him, straddled him, leaned down so that her breasts dangled just above his face, and he leaped at them, captur-ing one with his teeth and torturing her the way she'd done to him. Her hands were in his hair, holding him, soft pleading sounds com-ing from her throat. He gentled his mouth, sucking at her breast, feeling her relax, and then nipping her again, pinching her nipple gently between his teeth and hearing her moan in anguished plea-sure. His hand moved into the warm wetness between her legs, to explore her there as his mouth applied the exquisite torture to her breast. His fingers parted, probed, hunted, and found. Invaded and stroked. And her hips arched to ask for more.

So he gave her more. Taking his hand away, he nestled his hips against hers, and slid himself inside her, as slowly and as reverently as he had lowered the athame into the cauldron. And as he did, she tipped her head back again, closed her eyes, and the sigh that es-caped her was one of pure ecstasy as she tilted her hips to slide lower over him. And he wrapped his arms and legs around her, and rolled them both over, pinning her beneath him. Her hands closed on his backside, drawing him closer, pulling him deeper inside her. And he knew he'd never felt anything as intense as this. And likely never would.

He wanted, with everything in him, to take her hard and fast. But he denied those desires, because he wanted to see her face when she came. He wanted to feel her muscles convulse around him in pleasure. So he took his time, moving slowly, withdrawing to the very tip of him before pushing deeper, loving her with long, slow thrusts so exquisitely unbearable that his entire body quaked and shuddered.

Her breaths came faster; her hands slid upward, nails dragging over his back and then suddenly sinking into his shoulders. Her hips snapped up to meet his, faster and more demanding each time, and she breathed his name, again and again.

At her signals he moved faster, ending the tight hold he'd placed on himself, freeing his body to obey its own urges and sending his conscious mind scurrying into oblivion. There was only sensation now. Her body beneath him, her heated flesh surrounding him, holding him, her mouth, her hands, her hair, the sounds she made, the way she smelled.

And then even those things vanished in a haze of pure feeling because his body was tightening and clenching as he neared the climax he'd been longing for all his life. The one he would share with her. With this woman.

He opened his eyes, determined to know it would be as incredible for her, desperate to see and feel her own release as well as his. And he did. Her eyes met his, and he saw the feelings swirling in the onyx depths. Her jaw worked as she held his gaze and moved with him, and she seemed to know what he wanted. To see when it happened for her. And her gaze never wavered, even when she cried his name in a voice choked with pleasure. Even when her eyes widened, and her hands gripped and her nails sank deeper. Even when he thrust himself harder and faster into the depths of her beautiful body, and exploded inside her, feeling his world shatter around him. Their eyes still held. Even when he whispered, "I love you, Aurora. Dammit, I love you."

She stiffened suddenly, pushing him upward, her palms flat to his chest, and staring up at him in what looked like shock. "You . . . ?"

"Never mind," he told her. "Come here," and he drew her to him again, stroked her hair. "It's after midnight," he whispered. "Happy birthday, Aurora."

# Chapter 7

*Aurora* tried not to think about what he'd said, and focused instead on what he did. On what *they* did. On how he made her feel in a way she'd never felt before, and how no one else could bring her to this point of what felt very much like a melding of two souls. Far more than just sex.

At some point she got up, focused her energies, sat very still with her palms cupped, and willed the magick that formed her circle to shrink and concentrate itself, until it was once again that glowing orb in her hands. A swirling ball of light and energy.

As she stared down at it, she heard Nathan gasp, and glanced up to see him gazing, wide-eyed, into her palms.

"I can't believe this," he muttered.

She frowned. "Do you mean . . . you can see it?"

And it was his turn to frown. "Shouldn't I? I mean . . . you see it, don't you?"

"I see it because I'm a Witch."

But his attention was on the energy sphere again. Tentatively, he reached out with a forefinger and touched the glowing ball she held.

"Hold out your hands, Nathan," she told him. And looking at her a little uncertainly . . . he did.

Gently, Aurora transferred the energy into Nathan's hands. And he gazed down at it in wonder. "What is it?" he whispered.

"It's magick," she said simply. "The magick you don't believe in. And if you can see it, Nathan, that proves you're just a big fraud."

He shook his head. "I don't understand."

"They say seeing is believing, Nathan, but they have it backward. You have to believe in something first, *before* you can see it." He started to look up at her, but she shook her head. "Concentrate or you'll lose it."

He focused again on the glow in his hands. "W-what do I do with it?"

"I usually give leftover magick back to Mother Earth, for healing."

"How?"

She smiled. He was so wary of the power he didn't even know he had. He was a Witch, too. He just hadn't realized it yet. "Kneel down. Press your palms flat to the ground, and in your mind, see the light sinking into the earth and spreading there, spilling its healing, loving glow all through the planet."

Nathan did as she told him. When he rose again, he was looking at his hands as if he'd never seen them before. "That was incredible." He moved closer to her. "*You* are incredible."

"I'm selfish," she told him. And she meant it. She hated what she'd done to him tonight. Loved it. But hated it. She'd used him. And only when he'd blurted that he loved her had she realized just how deeply all of this might hurt him.

She didn't want to hurt Nathan.

She should tell him the truth. Now, before . . .

Nathan swept her into his arms and kissed her again, scooping her up and carrying her around the house and then inside, straight up the stairs to her bedroom—his lips never leaving hers on the way, his hands never leaving their job of caressing her body to look for a light switch. He was entirely focused, it seemed, on driving her out of her mind with wanting him again, even though she knew it was wrong. She'd done what needed doing. She'd done it in time. She wouldn't lose her powers now.

And yet she wanted him all the same. So when he tumbled with her into her bed, she didn't object. And they were still there when her aunts returned home in the morning.

Nathan saw the panicked expression on her face when the door slammed downstairs and the voices of her aunts came floating up to them. "Oh, no!" She sat up, clutching the sheet, head swinging this way and that frantically as she looked for clothes.

Footsteps pattered up the stairs. Someone called her name. She gripped his shoulder, pointed toward the bathroom door, and hissed, "Hurry!"

"Okay, okay!" Nathan jumped out of the bed, taking the sheet with him, and made it into the bathroom just as he heard a perfunctory tap on her bedroom door, followed by the creak of its hinges.

"Didn't you hear us calling, Aurora? We're home! And oh, so excited over what we found when we arrived!"

"What you—"

"These!" one of the aunts—Merriwether, Nathan thought—announced. And he wondered what prize she was showing off.

He crouched low to peer through the keyhole, first spying Aurora's pale face and stunned expression, then locating her tall, imposing Aunt Merri, arms outstretched and holding a bundle of clothes.

*His* clothes.

Oh, boy.

"Am I wrong in assuming these belong to Nathan?" the woman asked, while the other two, including Flora, who seemed in perfect health again, stood looking on.

"No, Aunt Merri. But—"

"Then you did it!" She clapped her hands together. "You did it and now you're—"

"Your powers are safe," Aurora's Aunt Fauna interrupted. He glanced toward the bed and saw Aurora frantically waving a hand as if to shut her aunt up. Just as he'd sensed Fauna had jumped in to shut her sister up. Very strange. What wasn't being said here was almost as interesting as what was. But Fauna rushed on. "You slept with a virgin before your twenty-seventh birthday, just as we told you you must. You won't lose your powers after all. And that's all you need to know, for now."

As she spoke, Aurora, clinging to a blanket for cover, lunged from the bed to silence her aunt, but Fauna had finished her little speech before she ever reached her. And Nathan felt as if he'd been hit between the eyes with a mallet.

Aurora went still, halfway between her aunt and the bed. Her head bowed slowly.

Nathan rose, wrapped the sheet around him, knotting it at his hip, and opened the door, more humiliated and angry and . . . and he didn't know what else . . . than he'd ever been in his life.

The three aunts gasped, but Aurora only stood there. She couldn't even look at him.

"Well, at least now I know why."

"Oh, dear," Fauna said in distress. "No, you don't, dear boy, not really. I was only—"

"Please leave," Aurora said, turning to her aunts. And nodding quickly, they did, backing out of the room and muttering apologies all the way. Aurora turned to him and opened her mouth.

"Don't bother," he told her coldly. "Hell, Aurora, I've seen what you can do. I suppose you'd have slept with the devil himself to keep that . . . that whatever it is."

"I don't believe in the devil. And it wasn't why I—"

"Don't lie, okay? At least give me that much." He shook his head, and reached for the clothes Merriwether had dropped on Aurora's bedroom floor. "Man, I made a real fool of myself last night, didn't I? How many times did I tell you I loved you, Aurora? A dozen, at least. What an idiot. All the time I was just part of . . . of one of your *spells*."

"That's not true. I—"

He shook his head, jeans in place, shirt draped over one arm. "Save it. I suppose that was the reason for the damn curse, as well, wasn't it? You . . . or those nutty aunts of yours, or all of you together—you made sure you'd have your virgin lover intact when the time came."

"You're right," she admitted. "But their intentions were good, Nathan. They didn't mean to hurt anyone."

He shook his head in disgust. "So am I right in assuming their damned hex has been lifted now that you have what you wanted from me?"

Lowering her eyes, she nodded.

"I don't know how you people sleep at night."

He yanked the door open and slammed out of the room, taking the stairs almost blindly, ignoring the sorry looks the other women threw him as he strode out the front door to walk home, struggling into his shirt on the way.

$A$urora was miserable. And she didn't know why. She should be happy. She'd done what was required. She would keep her powers. And yes, she'd hurt Nathan's feelings in the process, but how many times had he hurt her feelings in the past? Their whole lives he'd been hurting her.

"Why do you think that is?" a soft voice asked.

Aurora sat up in her bed, where she'd been spending most of her time. Oh, she went in to the hospital and worked her shifts, but then she came home and returned to this room, and more often than not, she shed a few tears as she tried to make sense of her misery.

Flora stood in the doorway, looking at her sadly.

"Why do I suppose what is?" she asked her aunt.

"Why do you suppose Nathan McBride has hurt you in the past?"

"Because he's a jerk, that's why."

Flora smiled gently and came in to perch on the edge of the bed. "A lot of people are jerks. But they don't hurt you. Because you don't care. No one is capable of hurting you, Aurora darling, not unless you care very deeply about them."

Aurora blinked and sat up straighter. She sniffed twice, swiped her eyes dry, and nodded. "You're right. I know it. I've known it for a while now. I do care for the idiot." She closed her eyes. "I care a lot."

"You hurt him," Aunt Flora said softly. "And if you're capable of hurting him, then . . ." She lifted a hand, palm up.

"Then he cares, too," Aurora said. "But I knew that, too. It's past tense, though. He did care. For a while. But not anymore. Not now that he thinks I only used him."

"He's still hurting, sweetheart. So he must still care."

Aurora lifted her eyes to her aunt's and felt a tiny flutter of hope try to come to life in her chest. "I love him, Aunt Flora."

"I know, dear. So tell him. No matter what happens, just tell him. And when you do, he's going to say, 'I love you, too, Aurora Sortilege.'"

\* \* \*

"I hate you, Aurora Sortilege. Detest you and despise you. I do not love you. I do not, not, *not* love you. Never have, never will. And that's final."

Nathan paced the floor of his living room whispering these reassurances to himself over and over again. Because he had a pretty little thing named Bobbie Lou or Sally Jo or something like that, waiting for him to perform, and his body was utterly unwilling. She'd shown up on his doorstep an hour ago. A stewardess he'd taken out once before. She said she remembered how strangely that night had ended and thought she'd give it another shot, as long as she was in town. And did he want to take her to dinner. And he did.

*No, I don't. I don't want to take her anywhere. I want Aurora.*

Bull. He most definitely wanted the bimbette with the copper-colored curls.

Or were they brown?

She was in his bathroom now. Freshening up, as she put it. And as he paced, she called, "If you don't feel like going out, Nate, honey, we can order in. It would be cozy, don't you think?"

Why the hell didn't she squelch that ear-splittingly irritating whiny voice so he could think?

"Nate? Sweetie?"

"Don't call me Nate," he snapped.

Her head popped out of the bathroom and she glanced at him questioningly. Copper. The curls were copper. Practically metallic.

"Sorry," he said. She smiled and stepped out farther. And there she was, wearing a skimpy black teddy and looking like a centerfold.

Nathan looked at her. Then he looked down at himself. Nothing was happening. He was having no physical reaction whatsoever. He shook his head. "Sorry, Betty Ray," he said. "But this isn't going to work. Why don't you get dressed and go home?"

Her lower lip thrust out. "It's Becky Lynn. Jerk." She slammed the bathroom door, presumably to dress.

As the door shut, there was a tap at the door behind him, the one that led outside, and he turned just as it opened. And then his heart flipped over. Because Aurora stood there. He felt a thousand pounds float away from his shoulders. He felt as if he could fly. He was stupid. He should be mad as hell.

"You told me the curse was gone now," he muttered. "But you're still messing with my head, you and those nutty aunts of yours. Aren't you, Aurora?"

She pursed her lips. "I didn't come here to fight with you. Or to listen to you rant. I came here to tell you something, and I'd appreciate it if you'd shut up and let me get it said."

He lifted both hands, palms up, and raised his brows, giving her the floor with the gesture.

"Okay," she said. She paced a few steps, pushed a hand through her glorious hair, and faced him again. "Okay. This is it. What happened between us wasn't just because of what you overheard at my house. I mean . . . it started out that way, but then . . ." She closed her eyes and straightened her spine. "Hell, you said it to me, and I can damn well say it to you." Eyes opening wide, she strode right up to him, stared right into his eyes and said, "I am in love with you, Nathan McBride, and I imagine I probably have been for most of my life." She drew a deep breath and blew it out. "There. I said it."

Nathan gaped. He searched her face and tried to stop his heart from palpitating. She meant it. She actually meant it. He lifted his hands to frame her face. "Aurora, I—"

"Here," Becky Lynn shouted, and flung something at his head. "Keep that as a souvenir, creep!" And she stormed out the door.

Aurora backed away suddenly, and as he peeled the thing away from his head, he saw her eyes filling with tears. "Oh, hell. Aurora, wait. This isn't what you think."

But she was shaking her head, backing away. "You . . . and she . . . you . . . after what we . . ."

He reached out for her, belatedly realizing he held a black teddy in his hand. He tossed it to the floor. "Dammit, Aurora, nothing happened with her. I couldn't—"

"But you wanted to. You were going to. You . . . that's why you said what you did, about the curse, and—" The tears spilled over and Nathan's heart cracked. "How could you, Nathan?" And she turned and ran the same way Becky Lynn had. With one major difference.

When Aurora left, he cared.

# Chapter 8

Oh, no. Oh, for crying out loud, he blew it! He had her, right there, knowing damn well that he loved her beyond belief. And she'd stared up at him with those big ebony eyes of hers and told him that she loved him, too.

And he'd blown it all to hell. Why had he even let Becky Lynn in the front door? Why hadn't he borrowed a page from that old antidrug campaign and just said no? He should have realized it wouldn't work, anyway. It never had.

Not until Aurora. And frankly, after that experience, he really didn't think he cared to do any comparison shopping. Nothing could be the way she was. The way they were. And she loved him. And now she was crying because he was an idiot.

Well, he had to find her. He had to fix this. There must be a way.

Okay, he'd grovel. He'd beg if he had to. He'd buy her pretty things and write sonnets and turn handsprings if that's what it took, but he wasn't going to let this incredible woman slip through his fingers. No way in hell.

He had to find her. Yes, and when he did, he'd give her something that would leave her with no doubt in her mind as to just how much she meant to him. Okay. So first, the jewelry store . . . and maybe the bank. And then he'd track her down.

*Aurora* knew he was looking for her. He called so often there was no doubt, but she wouldn't talk to him. He came by, but she refused to see him. He'd even shown up at the hospital a few times this week, whenever his schedule and hers allowed it. But she'd managed to duck him.

She stopped counting how many days and then weeks it had been since that magickal night in the circle where they'd made love. But she never stopped thinking about it. Remembering. Wishing. Even aching for him.

And then her world fell apart, the afternoon her aunts, the three of them, came to her in her room and stood around her looking sheepish and guilty.

"What?" she asked them, her spine tingling with warnings. They were up to something.

"The girls say I'm the one who has to do the talking, Aurora," Merriwether said strongly. "So I'll just come right out with it. We lied to you."

Aurora blinked. "You lied to me?" The three nodded. "About what?"

"About the reason you had to . . . er . . . that is, you and Nathan . . ."

"The reason I had to have sex with a virgin?" She felt her eyes widen. Again, the three nodded. And Merriwether said, "You see, it couldn't have been just any virgin. It had to be Nathan McBride."

"Yes," Fauna piped in, "and you wouldn't have lost your powers if you hadn't done it."

Aurora gaped and felt her legs buckle. She sank onto the bed. "I don't under . . . I can't believe . . ."

"You're going to be upset at first, dear," Flora said softly, patting Aurora's hand. "But all of this was foretold, after all. Now I'm sure you'll want to confirm it with a doctor, but you can take my word for it. You're almost certainly pregnant with Nathan's child."

"Pregnant? *Pregnant?*" Aurora's head swam. And then she did something she'd never done before in her life. She fainted.

Nathan was immersed in the stacks of books and photographs and journals he'd hauled out of his father's attic. Aside from this new obsession he'd developed for Aurora, he seemed to have discovered another powerful interest.

His family history.

And it was a rich one. It had been Aurora's words about his ancestors, that night in that magick bubble of light that had made him wonder, and now he understood.

Nathan McBride came from a long, long line of Celtic Witches. And now that he knew it, he felt oddly drawn to his heritage. He wanted to know what it meant . . . to him. He wanted to learn about and study the beliefs of his forebears.

So when he wasn't constantly trying to get a moment alone with Aurora, he was delving into the old diaries and books, and finding a wealth of information he'd been clueless about before. And it was as he was intently reading one such diary that his telephone rang, and an elderly female voice said, "If you hope to run into Aurora, try the drugstore. Not yours, your competitor's. On Main Street." That was it. The caller hung up.

Nathan frowned. Aurora hated him so much that she was shopping at the competition? Or maybe she just wanted to avoid any chance of running into him. But she knew he ran the stores from a corporate office downtown. She knew that, right?

So what was she doing in his rival's store? Hell, who cared what she was doing there? This was his chance to finally make her understand.

He got to his feet, pulled on a jacket, double-checked the pocket for the tiny box he'd been carrying with him everywhere he went, and headed out. Pouring rain. Great. He turned up the collar on the coat and ducked his head.

*A*urora hoped no one would recognize her. She was a doctor, for crying out loud. But this wasn't something she dared to do at the hospital. It was too private. Too personal. Too unbelievably stupid.

She was a doctor. A doctor knew better than to get pregnant. What the hell had happened to her that night? Why had she totally neglected to even consider . . .

Oh, hell, if her aunts were telling the truth—and Aurora was fairly certain they were—then she *knew* why. If this was meant to happen, the way they said it was, then all the protection in the world wouldn't have worked, anyway. So why kick herself?

Her eyes felt gritty and hot. She knew they were red and puffy. And she knew her hair was more mussed than combed, and that she probably looked like a drowned rat incognito, skulking through the drugstore aisles in her rain-spotted trench coat with the Druid-like hood pulled up and a pair of great big sunglasses on her nose, despite the gray skies.

She'd cased the aisle three times, and knew exactly where the stupid little home pregnancy test kits were located. She could swoop by and snatch one without anyone knowing the difference. Paying for it was going to be another matter, but she'd just have to do it. Stealing went against her belief system. So she'd muddle through and figure it served her right.

She looked around, saw no one in the aisle, lowered her head, pushed her sunglasses up on her nose, and hurried forward. Her hand flashed out and scooped up the box and she never missed a beat. She kept her quick pace up right to the end of the aisle . . .

. . . where she collided with a broad, strong chest and a familiar scent. A pair of hands she'd missed desperately came up to her shoulders to steady her.

She looked up and shoved the box she'd just grabbed into the deep pocket of her raincoat.

Nathan frowned at her. "Shoplifting, Aurora?"

"Of course not."

His brows rose. "So what is it you're buying that you don't want me to see?"

She licked her lips, took a step backward, and lowered her eyes, no longer able to look into his.

Then she noticed the tiny box that he held in his own hand. Oh, Goddess! It looked like—

He saw her looking at it, and swept it behind his back. Then his free hand came out as he hooked a finger under her chin and tipped her head back so he could stare into her eyes. He grimaced and plucked off the glasses. Then his frown creases deepened. "Aurora, honey, you look terrible."

"Thanks bunches."

"What's the matter?"

"Nothing."

"You've been crying." She turned away. But he caught her and turned her around, very gently. "So maybe it's not too late after all . . . if you still care enough to cry over me."

She swiped self-consciously at her sore eyes. "Don't be so sure it's you I've been crying over."

She meant it as a barb, but worry clouded his eyes so fast it pricked her conscience. "Is something else wrong? Is Aunt Flora—?"

"No, Nathan. Aunt Flora's fine. Really." She realized her voice had softened toward him. But his genuine concern for her aunt touched her—that he could still feel that way after what those three had pulled on him . . . well, that touched her even more.

He sighed in relief, but just as quickly scanned her face with worry in his eyes. "You sure you're okay?" When he said it he touched her face with his palm, and she closed her eyes because it felt so good to feel him again.

She wasn't okay, hadn't been okay since the last time he'd held her in his arms, but she nodded anyway.

"Aurora, let's go somewhere and talk." His voice had softened to a raspy whisper.

She almost nodded, then remembered the pregnancy test kit in her pocket. She couldn't tell him about that, not yet. And she couldn't even think straight until she knew the results. "I can't, Nathan."

He lowered his head. "You're still angry with me . . . about what you thought you saw at my apartment."

That reminder pricked a sore spot, and Aurora bristled. "What I *thought* I saw?"

Nathan nodded. "Yeah. But all you really saw was a perfectly gorgeous woman failing to interest me in the least, no matter how she tried."

Aurora narrowed her eyes and peered up at him.

"I didn't want her. That's why nothing happened, Aurora. I never wanted any of them, not really."

"You didn't?"

He smiled gently and stroked her hair. "No. I'm just beginning to catch on. All this time . . . it wasn't about spells or curses or your three crazy aunts. It was about you, Aurora. I've never been able to settle for any other woman . . . because the only woman I ever wanted is you."

His words took her breath away. Her heart hammered in her chest, and her knees turned to water. She sagged a little, but his strong hands came around her waist, and she clung to his shoulders and managed to remain upright. But there was still too much space between them.

"You told me you loved me, 'Rora. I'm hoping that's still true."

She searched his face, hesitating, and finally, bit her lip and nodded. "I've loved you since second grade," she whispered. "Maybe longer than that."

He smiled, but it was shaky, uncertain. "Then . . ." He let go of her long enough to retrieve the small box from a back pocket, and then he opened the lid. "Then marry me, Aurora."

Aurora caught her breath. The ring was a flawless diamond surrounded by emeralds glittering up at her. Its facets sparkled and shot fire even through the tears that suddenly filled her eyes.

"It will match those earrings I gave you for your sixteenth birthday," he said. "The ones you've kept all this time."

"I . . . I didn't think you remembered."

"I remember everything about you, 'Rora. Everything about the two of us, and how every time we got close I did something to screw it up. Something to hurt you."

"It wasn't only you," she argued, but he silenced her with a gentle forefinger to her lips.

"I'm never going to hurt you again, Aurora."

She wanted to speak, but she couldn't. And he lifted a thumb to wipe the tear from her cheek.

"So what do you say, 'Rora? Will you be my wife?"

She wrapped her arms around his neck, and his closed around her waist, but when he pulled her close, the box in her pocket pressed insistently between them, and Aurora remembered that he still didn't know the whole truth.

Stepping slightly away, she sniffed, reached up and stroked his hair. "It depends."

His eyes looked almost panicked. "On what?"

"How you react to what I have in my pocket."

He frowned at her, and tilted his head to one side. Then he reached down, dipping his hand into her pocket, closing it around the box. She willed herself not to close her eyes so she could watch his face as he pulled the box out and scanned the label.

Then he stared at her, wide-eyed. "You . . ." He looked at the box. Looked at her face again. "You think . . . ?"

"I'm almost sure," she said.

"We're having a baby," he whispered, shaking his head in disbelief. And then he smiled and said it again, louder this time. "We're having a baby!" His arms wound around her waist and he lifted her off her feet, holding her tight to him and spinning her around. And then he lowered her down, and bent to kiss her more tenderly than any man had ever kissed any woman. And without breaking that kiss, he took the ring from the box in his hand and slipped it onto her finger.

A smattering of applause made them draw apart suddenly, only to see that every patron in the drugstore had crowded together at the end of the aisle to watch them. Aurora wiped the tears from her face, too happy to be embarassed. He still wanted to marry her. She stared down at the glittering ring in wonder, then up into Nathan's shining eyes.

He closed his hand around hers. "Come on." As he drew her past the registers, he pulled a twenty from a pocket, tossed it on the counter and said, "Keep the change," and then they ran together out into the pouring rain toward his car.

But before they got to it, he stopped and turned to face her. Rain dripping off his nose, he said, "You didn't say yes."

He seemed so vulnerable right now, all his joy on hold, awaiting her answer, the look in his eyes telling her that his very life depended on it.

She swept one hand through his wet hair and stood on tiptoe to press her lips to his, right there on the sidewalk in the pouring rain. And then she whispered, "Yes."

# Epilogue

Nathan paced the living room of his small apartment, and wondered how the hell Aurora could be sitting so calmly on his sofa. He glanced at his watch, then at the clock on the wall, and then at the oven timer clicking madly on the coffee table.

"Is it time yet?" he asked her, for good measure.

She looked up at him, smiled gently, shook her head, and bent again to her perusal of the old books and diaries Nathan had left sitting out. "So are you going to tell me what all this is about?" she asked him.

He frowned at his watch.

"We have time."

He nodded, went to her, sat beside her. "I was curious. About my ancestors and . . . and about Witches in general, I guess."

She smiled. "You are one, you know."

Nathan's brows rose. "No. I couldn't cast a magick circle the way you did that night—wouldn't know where to begin conjuring elemental forces or any of that."

"You *have* been reading, haven't you?"

He gave her a sheepish smile, nodding once.

"But those things aren't what make you a Witch, Nathan. They can be learned. I can teach you. It's the magick that makes you what you are." She reached up to stroke his cheek. "And that's something you're born with. It's inside you. I felt it that night."

"You think so?"

She nodded, and he wondered if she could be right. He'd felt something, too. "That orb of energy would have been invisible to someone void of magick."

Her eyes danced over his face, their touch palpable. And he knew he'd always believe every word she said to him, even if she said the sun would rise at midnight.

"I hope I'm not going to have to sleep with a virgin to keep it," he said with a grin. Her gaze fell, so he leaned forward to kiss her nose. "Hey, that was a joke."

"It was a lie, Nathan. My aunts made it up. I was never really in danger of losing my magick."

"Then why—"

"This baby. They claim it was foretold. They say that you and I are supposed to give birth to—"

"To the most powerful Witch ever," he finished for her. "A little girl."

"How did you know that?"

Nathan gave his head a shake to clear it. This was all a bit too much to believe. But believe it he did. He riffled pages from one book and another until he found the passage he'd read in one of them. "My great-great-grandmother wrote it down, right here. She said that one day a McBride would father the child who would grow to be . . ." He stopped and shrugged, and instead of telling her, pushed the book into her hands so she could read it for herself. He remembered the passage. It had struck him as more moving, more memorable than anything else he'd read. It went on, about the healing gift the girl was to be born with, and how the cures for many of humanity's most dire illnesses would be discovered because of her work and her magick.

The timer pinged. Aurora closed the book, and her eyes met Nathan's. They were dark and wide and half afraid. "It'll be all right," he told her. And he glanced at the testing kit visible in the bathroom from here. "Do you want to look? Or should I?"

"I already know what it's going to say," she whispered.

He went into the bathroom, lifted the stick, and examined the shape clearly defined there. "Aurora?"

She rose and looked at him. Nathan smiled at her, and she ran into his arms. He kissed her mouth, held her close, relished the very fact that she was here with him, like this, and finally, lifted his head. "I hope she looks just like you," he told her tenderly.

# Musketeer by Moonlight

# Chapter 1

It was Halloween, and she was a prisoner in her own office. Hell, what made her think she could get the goods on an organized crime boss, anyway? She was getting a swollen head. Believing her own press. M.C. Hammer, big-city private eye. Right. The truth was that she couldn't remember a time when she'd felt more like plain old Mary Catherine Hammersmith, small-town girl.

She paced the office, pausing to glance through the smeared window at the street below. No colors down there. It was as if Newark had gone black-and-white and shades of gray—as dismal as the sky above it. The wind blew bits of paper and clouds of dirt over the pavement. The dark sedan was still parked out there. If M.C. tried to leave, its driver would follow. If she went to the safe-deposit box where she'd stashed the tape, he'd get her when she came out. If she went home . . . she shivered. The thought of that dark stairway up to her lonely apartment was not appealing. They could grab her there just as easily. She wasn't even sure it was safe to get into her car. One twist of the key might make a hell of a

noise and litter the streets with bits of a certain lady detective she'd
grown kind of fond of.

Hell.

The phone rang. She snatched it up. "M. C. Hammer Investigations."

"Ms. Hammer?"

"This is her secretary." She said it automatically. Made her
sound bigger than she was. Besides, the woman on the other end
could be anyone. One of the bad guys, maybe.

"I need to speak to Ms. Hammer," the woman said. "I'm in
trouble; I need help."

"Join the club."

"Excuse me?"

She calmed her voice. "Sorry. Ms. Hammer's out of town indef-
initely. Look, try Ace Investigations over on Fourth and Main.
They're good—they'll help you out."

The caller rung off without saying good-bye. M.C. felt bad.
They always called, and they always needed help. Up to now, she'd
been pretty good at providing it. She'd earned a reputation in the
city. They called her a tough cookie, the working woman's hero,
that sort of thing.

Right about now, she thought she could use a hero of her own.
But she'd been too busy playing hero to bother looking for one.
She'd never expected to face a situation she couldn't handle. She
was facing one now, one she'd stumbled into unintentionally. She
was only supposed to get the goods on Guido de Rocci's illicit af-
fairs, so his wife could get a decent divorce settlement out of him.
Instead she'd wound up with a tape of a phone call ordering a gang-
land hit, one that left no doubt who was in charge. Guido himself.
And stupidly, she'd told the wife. Sylvia de Rocci went soft, and
ratted her out to Guido. Seemed she got all mushy inside to learn
her hubby wasn't cheating on her after all. No, he was just running
the mob and killing people. What a sweetheart. So now Syl and

Guido were a pair of happy lovebirds, and Mary Catherine was a sitting duck with a half dozen hit men standing between her and the tape.

She could call the cops—but her phone was probably bugged, and she'd be dead before they ever got here. Besides, everyone knew the mob had a few cops in its pocket. How could she be sure the cops who showed up wouldn't be on de Rocci's payroll?

She wandered to the window again. A bus pulled up at the stop, right in front of the entrance to Sal's Bar downstairs. People got off. People got on. An idea took form.

The slug in the sedan was watching *her* front entrance, and her car. But no one could see what she did inside the office. She could take the stairs down to her own front door, but instead of going out, slip through that side door that led from the entry hall into Sal's place. Maybe slide out the bar's entrance instead of her own private one, and onto the next bus before anyone was the wiser.

"Sounds like a plan to me," she muttered. She did a quick scan of the closet. It often came in handy to have a change of clothes or two at the office. Quickly, she shed the skirt and heels she'd worn this morning and replaced them with jeans and sneakers. A leather jacket instead of the tailored blazer. A baseball cap to hide the tell-tale riot of dark curls she fondly referred to as a black rat's nest. A pair of John Lennonish sunglasses.

Glancing in the mirror, she thought she could pass for a guy. A scrawny guy, but a guy. The purse would give her away though. She emptied it, filling her pockets with the essentials, including her .38 special. Great. This was it then. There would be another bus shortly. They were in and out at this stop all day. Usually drove her nuts. Not today, though.

She took her time, moved slowly into the hall, saw no one, took the inside stairs down to the landing, and tapped on the door that led into the bar. No one ever used it, and it was locked as usual. But Sal opened it in a second, and she sauntered in like she belonged there as he gaped at her. When Sal gaped his double chin turned triple.

"Is that you, Mary Ca—"

She stomped on his foot and he shut up. "I'm not here," she told him. "You never saw me. I mean it, Sal."

Sal's silver eyebrows bunched up and he wiped his hands on his bulging white apron. "You in trouble, kid?"

"You could call it that."

"What can I do?"

"Gimme a stiff drink, and pretend you don't know me from Adam."

He shook his head, but nodded toward a vacant stool and reached for a shot glass. As he poured, he muttered, "One good man is all you need."

"So you keep telling me." She took the stool and then the drink, sipped it as she eyed the patrons in search of goons.

"If you had yourself a husband you wouldn't be in this mess."

"How do you figure that?" No goons in sight. She turned back to Sal, downed the whiskey, and set the glass on the hardwood.

"You'd be home takin' care of him, instead of out playing cop-for-hire."

"Woman's place is in the kitchen, right, Sal?"

"Worked for a hundred years, kid."

"Well, not for me. I've never needed a man around cluttering things up, and I don't plan to start now. Never met one worth the trouble anyway." She heard the squeal of air brakes and twisted her head. "That's my bus. Gotta go."

"Where to?"

She worked up a grin for him, though her heart was in her throat. "I could tell you, Sal, but then I'd have to kill you. Later." And she hopped off the stool and hurried to the bar's front entrance. The bus blocked her from the view of the goon across the street, and she joined a handful of others waiting to climb aboard. But she didn't breathe again until she was in her seat, and headed out of town.

The bus was headed to Hoboken, but since she didn't know a soul there, she got off at the terminal and caught one heading in the other direction. There was really only one place for her to go now. Her parents' place in Princeton was out of the question. First place those thugs would check. Nope, there was little choice. She had to go to Aunt Kate's house of horrors. That's what she'd called it as a kid. A gothic mausoleum way out in the sticks. They'd never track her there. Aunt Kate was an outcast, black sheep of the family. Mostly because she refused to go Christian, and kept up the traditions of the best-forgotten branch of the Hammersmith clan. Witchcraft, to put a name to it. She had an old spell book that had been in the family for more generations than anyone could count. Mary Catherine had seen it once. Dusty and faded, with a padded cloth cover that was threadbare with age.

Briefly she wondered if one of Aunt Kate's spells could help her out of this mess. But then she chased the silly thought away. All that she needed was time and clear thinking. A way to get to that tape, and get it safely to the cops without getting her head blown off. She wouldn't be safe until she did. Even if she turned it over to Guido, he'd figure she knew too much to risk letting her live. She knew the way thugs like him thought.

Aunt Kate's then. She shivered at the thought. It was All Hallows' Eve, and she'd be spending it in that spookhouse sideshow. She shook away the chill that danced up her nape, and tried to relax on the long bus ride to Craven Falls in upstate New York.

\*    \*    \*

"Hello, Aunt Kate."

Kate Hammersmith stood inside the arched, stained glass door and blinked slowly. She wore a long black dress with shiny moons and stars all over it. Homemade. Probably sewn together with spiderwebs, Mary Catherine thought glumly. Her hair was long and still dark, cut to frame her face. It made her look far younger than she was. She wore a necklace with a hunk of quartz on the end that must have weighed five pounds, minimum. "You could poke your eye out with that thing," Mary Catherine observed, just for something to say.

"You sound like your mother. What are you doing here, M.C.?"

"Aren't you even going to invite me in?"

Kate lifted one brow, then stepped aside and let Mary Catherine in. The place hadn't changed much. Muted lighting, nothing glaring or bright. Antique furniture. M.C. was no expert on guessing what period this stuff was from, but everything seemed to have clawed feet and satin. The place reeked of incense and the hot waxy aroma of recently snuffed candles.

"Well?" Kate asked, leaning back and crossing her arms over her chest.

M.C. licked her lips. "Well. I need a place to stay for a few days."

Kate's eyes narrowed and she suddenly looked way less irritated at the unannounced visit. "Are you in some kind of danger?"

"Nothing I can't handle. I just need to hang out until things cool down."

"Left in a hurry, did you?" Kate eyed her when she lifted her brows. "No luggage," she explained.

M.C. shrugged. "You look like you were on your way out. I didn't mean to mess up your . . . er . . . plans." It was Halloween. Probably crazy Kate's biggest night of the year.

Kate tilted her head. "Samhain is important, dear, but not as important as your safety. I'll stay—"

"No way, Aunt Kate. I'm fine. Honest. Not a soul in the world knows I'm here. You go on. I'll curl up on the couch and watch some TV. Maybe thumb through that old book of yours and look for spells to turn bad guys into toads. You, uh . . . still have it, don't you?" As she said it her gaze strayed to the table in the corner where the dusty tome lay open.

Kate touched her shoulder, drawing her gaze back again. "The grimoire is not a toy, Mary Catherine. The spells are powerful, particularly tonight. An amateur could cause a complete disaster by making some simple mistake—particularly if she were a neophyte with as much Pagan blood in her as you have."

A little tingle danced up Mary Catherine's spine, but she only smiled at her aunt. "I was just kidding. Don't have a cow, okay?"

Kate studied her, her eyes probing, then shook her head, making her dangling earrings—all six pairs—jangle like bells. "If you want a spell of protection, darling, just ask. I'll take care of it for you."

"You know I don't believe in that stuff," M.C. said, her gaze straying to the book again.

Aunt Kate sighed. "You're sure you'll be okay alone?"

"Sure. You go on. I'll be fine. Really."

Looking worried, Aunt Kate nodded and turned toward the door.

"Hey," M.C. called. "Aren't you forgetting your broom?"

Kate glared, but when M.C. sent her a wink, she smiled instead, waved good night, and left her alone.

M.C. wandered the living room, flicked on the TV, searched the channels. An old black-and-white version of *The Three Musketeers* was playing, and she watched that for a while, but her gaze kept straying back to the dusty book on the table. Surely it wouldn't hurt to just peek?

No. She'd promised Aunt Kate.

Glancing back at the screen, she shook her head in disgust. How could any man hope to hold his own in a fight with those silly ruffles hanging from his sleeves? And those hats! For crying out loud, were they supposed to look heroic with puffy plumes jutting out of their hats? She decided the Musketeers must have all been gay, and further judged she'd far rather have her .38 in hand during a crisis than one of those fragile-looking swords that seemed like they'd break in a strong wind.

Despite the ridiculousness of the film, though, she felt her heart twist a little when D'Artagnan leapt between his lady fair and the evil villain, vowing to protect her with his life.

Too bad heroes like that weren't around these days. She wouldn't even mind the stupid hat.

The book called to her again, and this time Mary Catherine got up and wandered over to it. She reached out to touch it, drew her hand away, then reached out again and gently flipped some pages. And she paused when she read, "Spell of Protection." The thing looked pretty simple. You were supposed to be in a spot where the light of the moon fell on you, during its first quarter. Light a white candle. Envision the protection in whatever way worked for you—a bubble of white light or a strong stone wall around your body were given as examples. Then, keeping that thought in mind, you just repeated the invocation written on the page.

Hmm.

Mary Catherine glanced sideways at the tall window, and saw a thin beam of moonlight peeking between the heavy velvet curtains. Hmm. She meandered over there and opened the curtains, and sure enough the moonlight flooded the room. It wasn't a quarter moon. But wouldn't a full moon be even better?

*If* you believed in any of this nonsense to begin with, which she did not.

She casually walked back to the table, where the moonlight spilled brightly over her and the book. Two candles sat there, one on either side of her aunt's precious old grimoire. One was pink and one was red. No white ones in sight. But a candle was a candle, right? And a long wooden match was laid there just begging to be lit. What the hell.

She struck the match and lit it, touching its flame to both candles because, hey, two candles were better than one.

She grinned. This was kind of a fun way to spend Halloween.

Okay, next steps: envision protection, and say the chant. She tried to imagine a bubble of white light surrounding her, and then tried picturing a bulletproof wall. But her mind kept straying back to that scene in the movie, where the Musketeer had vowed to protect his lady with his life. Cornball bunch of crap.

She read the words on the page, and heard the clock singing backup to her chant by striking midnight.

Without warning, something exploded and a ball of smoke enveloped her. Coughing, she waved it away, and suddenly she had the distinct feeling that she wasn't alone in the room anymore.

# Chapter 2

Alexandre sat up and rubbed his head, eyes closed tightly. He wasn't certain what had happened. He'd been in the midst of a minor skirmish, setting to rights an insult to the king of France, when he'd heard a lady calling to him from afar. Fair damsels in need of aid were nothing new to Alexandre. He was sworn to protect the king, of course, but there were plenty of Musketeers available to the king at all times. Alexandre often got sidetracked protecting ladies in distress. He didn't mind the task at all, especially considering the delicious ways the fair maids often expressed their gratitude. He must have been clubbed on the head while distracted by the odd cadence of this particular lady's voice.

At any rate, he heard nothing of his enemies now, and imagined they'd fled, as his opponents often did before he'd finished with them. Clutching his rapier in one hand and righting his chapeau with the other, he got to his feet and peered through the odd smoke that surrounded him.

And then he went still and blinked in shock. He was no longer

in the Provençal village where he'd faced off against the three ruffi-
ans only moments ago. He was inside a château, and staring into
the very wide and frightened eyes of a beautiful—if oddly
dressed—young woman.

He gave his head a shake and looked again. She was still there.
Frightened as if she were looking at a ghost. Her eyes gleamed like
dark sapphires in the moonlight, and her hair was a delightful mass
of raven curls he imagined would feel like silk twined round his fingers. Never mind the odd clothing, or the odd feeling in his head. A
beautiful woman like this one certainly took precedence over such
trivial worries.

"*Bonjour, mademoiselle,*" he whispered, quickly removing his
chapeau with a flourish and bowing deeply. Sheathing his sword, he
gripped her small hand and drew it to his lips. Ah, warm salty skin,
and a telltale tremble. She liked him already.

The hand in his jerked away fast. "Who the hell are you?" the
fair lady demanded. "Wha-what are you doing here?"

He straightened, smoothed the luxurious plume, and then replaced his hat. "So it is English you prefer," he said. " 'Tis well I
speak it fluently. I am Alexandre, one of the king's finest Musketeers, my lady."

"Get real," she said. "You are not."

"But I am." He took a step closer. She backed up, and it surprised him. "Do not fear me, pretty one. I am . . . a bit disoriented,
but believe me, I have only come to help you."

"He-help me?"

"*Oui, ma petite.* I heard you calling out for help—a protector, a
hero I believe you cried for." He rubbed his perfectly pointed beard
with his fingers. "It is a bit of a blur, but I do recall that much."

She shook her head back and forth slowly, taking another step
away from him. "This is crazy. This is nuts. You can't be here; this
can't be happening."

He shrugged, smiling to himself, quite familiar with the power of his presence on females. "Many a lady has been overwhelmed by my charm, little one. Do not be concerned. It is not a dream, *ma belle*. I truly am here. At your disposal." He let his gaze stray lower, to her lips, which looked full and tempting, and added, "Anything you need, pretty one, I assure you, I can provide." As he said it he moved closer.

The lady whipped a tiny weapon, which vaguely resembled a black powder pistol, from somewhere beneath the clothing she wore, and pointed it at him. "Don't you come one step closer, mister."

Amused, he reached out to snatch the toy from her hands. "What is this silly thing?" He gazed down the barrel, fingers grazing the trigger. The lady lunged forward, knocking the rounded end upward, away from his nose, just as the small device exploded in his hands. He felt his chapeau sail from his head and heard the looking glass behind him shatter. Alexandre dropped the weapon to the floor. *"Mon Dieu!"*

"You nearly shot yourself, you idiot!" she shouted. "Or did you?" Gripping his shoulders, she scanned his face, hands running up and down his arms in a most familiar fashion.

His fear faded quickly, and his notorious smile returned. "Ah, do not fear for me, lady. I am unharmed. But . . . eh . . . you may examine me further, if it would reassure you." He took advantage of her closeness to clasp her waist and pull her tight to him.

She drew back and punched him in the jaw so hard that Alexandre staggered backward and wound up landing on his derriere. But he never stopped smiling at her. "So," he said, rubbing his jaw, "you are shy, *non*?" He retrieved his hat from the floor, frowning at the neat round hole in the front of it.

"I'm the farthest thing from shy, Al. Touch me again, and you'll wish I were."

He was quite confused by her reluctance. Never had any lady sought to withhold her favors from him. They tended to swoon at a mere glance. But he'd already noticed this one's strangeness. Perhaps her mind was unbalanced. Pity. She was truly magnificent. He shook his head, sighing in disappointment but resigned to defeat. His first. Perhaps she'd come around yet, but for the moment he sensed it might be best to stop trying. "Very well, *ma chérie*. I will not touch you again. Until you request it, at least." He got suavely to his feet, smoothing one hand over the long, wavy locks he wore and brushing at his breeches.

"Don't hold your breath."

"Nonetheless, never let it be said that Alexandre failed to come to the aid of a lady in need."

"What I need is to know who does your hair. Captain Hook?"

"Why were you calling for help?" he asked, ignoring her puzzling question.

She looked at the floor, shook her head. "This is unreal."

"I can see you are greatly distressed. Has some rogue insulted your honor, then? Shall I call him out, teach him a lesson he will not soon forget?"

She closed her eyes and he noticed how thick and dark her lashes were, resting upon her fair cheeks. "You're the one who's gonna be distressed. I think I—I think I messed up."

"It is understandable, *chérie*. You are only a woman, after all."

Her head came up, eyes narrow. "Watch it, Al."

"I am only saying that whatever is wrong, I can make it right. So, tell me now, what has befallen you?"

"It's what's befallen you we have to worry about," she said.

He frowned at her. "I do not understand."

"Do they have Witches where you come from, Al?"

He lifted his brows. "*Oui*, but they are not a problem. If they get out of hand, we simply hang them." Then he frowned. "You are not a Witch, are you, lady?"

"No. Not . . . exactly. But . . . well, maybe you'd better sit down."

"If you wish it." He tucked his damaged hat under his arm and walked to the settee, but he didn't sit until she did. "Now," he said, "tell Alexandre what troubles you . . . but first, *ma chérie*, tell me your name."

She blinked. "Oh. It's Mary Catherine Hammersmith. But I go by M. C. Hammer. It's . . . sort of a joke."

"My lady Hammer," he repeated, lowering his head respectfully. "Now, why are you so troubled, eh?"

She looked decidedly sheepish. "I got into trouble. I needed help. And I found this . . . old book . . . with a . . . an incantation. . . ."

"A Witch's spell?"

She nodded. "Right . . . a spell for protection. And I said the words out loud . . . and I must have messed it up, because the next thing I knew, you were here."

He smiled slowly, and lifted a hand to gently pat her head. "Poor Lady Hammer . . . you truly believe that you have brought me here by witchery?"

"Oh, I'm pretty sure of it."

"What makes you so sure, little one? Perhaps I simply heard your lovely voice asking for protection, and followed the sound to find you here."

"Well, that wouldn't have been possible, Al. See, you . . . you sort of . . . traveled . . . through time."

He studied her face. Poor, disturbed beauty. Surely he could find a way to pull her from her delusions! He must. She was entirely too beautiful to be a lunatic.

"You don't believe me, do you? This is the future, Al. The year is 1998."

"Oh, sweet Lady Hammer. Sssh." He ran his hand through her hair. "You will be all right. I will find help for you, I vow it."

She closed her eyes, poor little thing. "I can prove it," she said.

"Oh?" He so wanted to help her get well. He wasn't certain, but he didn't think it would be quite chivalrous to seduce a lunatic. So until he cured her . . .

"See that little box over there?" she asked, pointing.

He followed her gaze and nodded. She picked up a smaller item, thumbed a button, and the box came to life all on its own. *"Sacre bleu!"* he shouted, leaping to his feet as tiny Musketeers, his own comrades, battled their enemies, all the while held captive inside the box! He drew his sword and lashed out at the thing, but its face was impenetrable.

The poor S.O.B. was still swinging his sword at the television set when the front door burst open and Aunt Kate appeared. Mary Catherine sank a little deeper into the sofa cushions at the glare her aunt sent her. She just stood there, looking from Al to M.C. and back again. Then, hands going to her hips, she shouted, "Mary Catherine Hammersmith, *what* did you *do?*"

# Chapter 3

*P*oor Al. He'd just sat there looking stunned as Aunt Kate explained what happened to him. He hadn't believed it at first, of course. But by the time they'd shown him the electric lights, the microwave, and Aunt Kate's smoke-belching Buick, he'd pretty much accepted the truth.

Now, Kate paced while Mary Catherine sat beside Al on the settee. She felt like a kid called into the principal's office. "You should have listened to me," Kate muttered. She went to the book, glancing down at it. "Is this the spell you used?"

Getting up, Mary Catherine went closer and peered over her aunt's shoulder at the book. "Yeah, that's it."

"This spell specifically calls for the moon's first quarter. I can't believe you'd use it during a full moon! And on All Hallows' Eve, of all nights!"

M.C. shrugged. "I didn't exactly expect it to work."

"Work? You quadrupled its potency!" She glared. M.C. looked at the floor. "And what about the white candle? I don't see one here." Kate looked at the candles on the table. "Red and pink? You used these, didn't you?"

M.C. nodded. "Is that bad?"

Kate eyed Al, then M.C. again. "Red is for passion. Pink brings true love. Honestly, Mary Catherine, what were you thinking?"

Again M.C. shrugged. "Mostly about *The Three Musketeers*," she muttered. "It was on TV."

Kate frowned. "Well, that explains it. You wanted protection. You got yourself a protector—in exactly the form you were envisioning." She rolled her eyes, shook her head. "Goddess preserve us from neophyte Witches."

"I am not a Witch," M.C. said flatly.

"I think Alexandre would disagree with you there."

Al looked up at the mention of his name. He'd been sitting, pretty much ignoring them. But now he seemed to straighten his spine as he got to his feet and came forward. "Can this . . . this spell be reversed?"

Aunt Kate looked at the book again, drumming her painted fingernails on the page. "I think so. It will take some research, but . . ."

"Well, that's just great," M.C. muttered. "Meanwhile, I'm right back where I started, with the biggest criminal in seven states out to do me in."

Kate blinked. Al gaped at her. M.C. realized she hadn't told either of them just how much trouble she was in. Nor had she intended to. She wasn't a whiner, and she certainly didn't want to drag either of them into this mess. "Forget I said that. It's nothing I can't handle. Go on, Aunt Kate. Figure a way to send Al back where he belongs."

Kate tilted her head. "I can't do that, M.C. The only one who can reverse your spell is you. I can help, but—"

"*Non!*"

At his declaration, Kate and M.C. both turned toward Al in surprise. "Whaddya mean, no? You have to go back," M.C. said.

He stared straight into her eyes, and his were very dark, very deep. If it weren't for the long, crimp-curled hair, pointy beard, and stupid hat, she thought, the guy might actually be attractive.

"I am a Musketeer," he said, still holding her with his penetrating stare. "You brought me here to help you, Lady Hammer, and help you I shall."

Lowering her eyes, she shook her head. "It's not like there's much you could do, Al."

When she looked up again, he wore a knowing smile. "You know very little about what I can do, pretty one. Besides, no Musketeer would leave a lady in this situation. This criminal . . . he means to murder you, *non*?" She shrugged, and Al shook his head. "I will stay," he said firmly. "And when I've dispatched the villain, only then will I allow you to send me back . . . if you can."

Sighing heavily, M.C. lifted her chin. "What do you plan to do, Al? Challenge him to a sword fight? Look, I know you think you're some kind of superman, and maybe you are, in your own time. But you wouldn't stand a chance against this guy. He has weapons you haven't even imagined. Machine guns, and a dozen goons to do his bidding. You couldn't begin to—"

"Enough!" Al spun around, putting his back to her, arms crossed at his chest.

"Now you've gone and insulted him," Aunt Kate scolded. "I swear, M.C., didn't your mother teach you a thing about tact?"

M.C. threw her hands in the air. "I'm just trying to keep him alive, for crying out loud!" He didn't face her. He tapped his foot on the floor, waiting, she figured. She cleared her throat, moved closer, put her hand on his shoulder. "I apologize, Al. I didn't mean to insult you or question your . . . abilities. I just . . . well, hell, I dragged you here by mistake, and I feel bad enough about that already. If you go and get killed, I'll never be able to live with myself."

"And if I return, leaving you behind, never to know whether this . . . this goon person succeeds in taking your life . . . I would not be able to live with myself, *chérie*."

She nodded. "I guess I can understand that."

Slowly he turned to face her again. "It is a question of honor, lady. I cannot leave you to face a killer alone. It is that simple."

M.C. tore her gaze from his and sought assistance in Aunt Kate. Kate sighed, shaking her head. "You won't be very successful in sending him back if he doesn't want to go. Besides, there are consequences to working magick on people against their will, Mary Catherine. It just isn't done."

Lowering her head in defeat, M.C. surrendered. "Okay. You can stay. But"—she looked him over again, head to toe—"but we're going to have to give you a makeover. I mean, the boots are cool, but the rest of this getup . . ." Kate elbowed her, and she realized she was on the verge of insulting him yet again. She cleared her throat. "It would be better if we dressed you in clothing more typical of what people wear in this day and age."

He rubbed his pointed beard thoughtfully. "I see. Yes, it is obvious people dress . . . quite differently today." This with a disapproving glance at her jeans and T-shirt.

M.C. looked at him with raised eyebrows. Then she reached up and removed his hat, eyeing the elegant, wavy locks underneath. "We'll have to start by chopping off this hair."

His smile was slow and almost . . . sexy. "No need." He reached up and removed the offending hair. "Frankly, my lady, I find the wig as offensive as you obviously do. I wear it only when I must."

"Sort of like me with panty hose," she said, grinning. Underneath, his own hair was dark, pulled behind his head and tied there with a thong. She wondered how long it was, and impulsively reached around his head to tug the thong away. Then, without thinking, ran her fingers through his hair to shake it loose. But her hands froze in mid-motion as his eyes, darkening, met hers.

"Maybe we should still cut it," Aunt Kate suggested.

Unable to look away, M.C. shook her head. "No. No, I think it's . . . it's fine." Why was her voice all hoarse?

"At last, something about me you like," he said softly.

Remembering herself, she drew her hands away from his hair. "You . . . um . . . you should shave."

His dark brows drew closer. "Men of this time do not wear beards?"

She averted her eyes. "Some do."

She didn't look up, but she could hear the smile in his voice. "But you would prefer to see me without mine?"

"I really don't care one way or the other. It was just a suggestion." She peered up to see him studying her. He was entirely too convinced of his own appeal.

"Come, Alexandre," Aunt Kate said. "I'll show you to the bathroom and explain how everything works. M.C., while we're up there, you run next door and ask Mrs. Johnson to loan us something for our guest to wear. He looks to be about Mr. Johnson's size."

Al started up the stairs. M.C. headed for the door. But before she left, she saw her aunt gazing worriedly at the red and pink candles on the table, a perplexed frown between her brows. She shook herself, though, and hurried up the stairs.

M.C. got the clothes, along with a curious glance from Mrs. Johnson, delivered them to her aunt, and then waited. She spent her time checking the cable listings, thinking she might be able to give Al a few lessons on life in the nineties by letting him watch television tonight and explaining things as they went along. She figured she'd best get him a gun, too, and teach him to use it. She really didn't see how the man was going to be any help to her at all. In fact, worse than that, he was an added burden. Now she had to worry about keeping him alive as well as protecting her own skin. Hell, things had gone from bad to worse, and they showed no signs of improving soon.

Aunt Kate cleared her throat, and M.C. turned, then jumped off the couch as if someone had goosed her.

Al stood at the foot of the stairs. The faded jeans fit him like a surgical glove, and the T-shirt strained to contain him. The guy was built like Stallone. Broad chest. Big shoulders. Biceps to die for.

Even when she could finally drag her eyes away from his body, she still couldn't catch her breath. His hair gleamed, neatly pulled back again. The beard was gone, and underneath it he looked like . . . like . . . he belonged on the big screen. A leading man to make the actresses' pulse rates go up.

He smiled then, and M.C.'s stomach convulsed. The man was absolutely, drop dead gorgeous.

"Oh, dear," Aunt Kate murmured.

He sent her a puzzled glance, but focused on M.C. again, moving forward. "Will I blend in now, do you think?"

"Not in this lifetime," she muttered, suddenly conscious of the fact that she hadn't run a comb through her tangles in hours. He looked worried. She bit her lip. "You look great, Al. You really do." He looked better than great. He looked like a Grade A hunk with a French accent. He looked like a *Playgirl* cover in search of a home. Her throat went dry.

His smile got bigger. "Good. It feels strange . . . but comfortable. Far more so than the dress of my day. Although I see nowhere to fasten my sword."

She looked across the room to where he'd left his weapon standing upright in a corner. The ornate handguard glittered and she wondered if it was real gold. "Men don't carry swords these days. I thought I'd teach you to use a gun."

He frowned. "If you're referring to that volatile toy you pointed at me earlier, I think not. A sword and my own wit are all I need."

"But the men we're up against will have guns, Al. And—"

"You can carry all the . . . *guns* . . . you need, my lady Hammer. For me, my rapier will be sufficient."

She clenched her jaw. "You're very stubborn, you know that?"

He only smiled.

"It's autumn," Aunt Kate commented. "We'll get him a

longish coat to wear, and no one will notice the sword at all. It's not a big deal."

"It will be a big deal if he gets a forty-four-caliber hole blown through that magnificent chest of hi—" She cut herself off, bit her lip.

Al moved forward until they were standing very close to each other, nose to . . . magnificent chest. "Something else about me that meets with your approval, *non*?"

"I'm only saying I would like to keep you in one piece, you arrogant, feather-hatted, Don Juan wanna-be."

"Ah. All the same, I am glad you find my . . . chest to be . . . *magnifique*, Lady Hammer. And I promise . . . I will remain in one piece, for you."

She swallowed hard, and told herself she was not the sort of woman who would respond to such outrageous, ego-based flirting. So why were her knees so weak?

"You can't keep calling me Lady Hammer, either," she said.

"What shall I call you then?" He touched her chin with a forefinger, lifting her head slightly so he could search her eyes. "Sorceress? Enchantress? *La Belle Femme?*"

"M.C. will be fine," she rasped.

"It does not suit you. I will call you Mary Catherine, as your aunt does. A lady as beautiful as you are deserves a name equally so."

Her throat was dry.

"Did the women of your time really fall for these lines, Al? I know perfectly well that I look like hell."

His fingertips brushed a curl from her cheek. "If this is what hell looks like, my lady, then I shall resolve to sin far more often."

Her cheeks heated. She couldn't believe it. She was blushing!

Beyond him, Aunt Kate sighed heavily, snatched up the pink and red candles, and tossed them into the garbage pail.

# Chapter 4

M.C. settled onto the settee beside Al—not too close, of course—and thumbed the remote. The set came to life, and Al shot it one startled glance before regaining his calm and eyeing her instead.

"So, now you will tell me the secret of the little box with the tiny Musketeers trapped inside, *non*?"

She closed her eyes and prayed for patience. "There are no tiny people inside it, Al. It's just pretend." He cocked one eyebrow at her. "Make-believe," she said. He still frowned. "It's just moving pictures of people in costumes. Like a play."

The frown vanished. Wonder replaced it, and he stared again at the set. "But the players . . . they are so small."

"That's only a picture of the players. They aren't really there. See . . ." She sought an explanation he could understand, but found none. Then she glanced up when her aunt came in from another room, carrying her Polaroid with her.

She handed it to M.C. "Maybe this will help."

"Perfect. Sit still, Al." She pointed the camera at him and pressed the button. He jumped to his feet when the flash went off, then rubbed his eyes. "Sorry about that," she said. She took the photo the camera spit into her hand and watched it, waiting. In a few moments the image came clear. Al, looking like some lonely woman's fantasy come to life. Every inch the modern-day hunk. He didn't look a thing like a Musketeer now in his jeans and T-shirt. He could fool anyone—until he opened his mouth.

But what an attractive mouth it was.

*Stop that!*

She lifted her gaze from the photo, only to encounter the real thing, staring at her curiously. "Here," she said. "See? This is called a camera, and it takes pictures of people. Look."

He took the photo from her hand, then blinked down at it. "This . . . this amazes me."

"It's a photograph," she told him. "A similar kind of machine takes moving pictures of actors, and then the pictures are sent into the television set for our entertainment. Understand?"

Again he looked at the screen. Finally, he nodded, still staring. "And what sort of play is this?" he asked, pointing.

M.C. took the photo from him, tucked it into her back pocket, and then glanced toward the TV. "Oh, that's just a game. Two teams competing to see which wins. It's called football. Waste of time, really." The camera cut to a group of cheerleaders. Al gaped and nearly fell on the floor. M.C. snatched up the remote and changed the station. "Here's a movie. A story, you see? If we watch together, I can explain things to you as we go along, and maybe you'll understand the modern world better."

"What . . . what sort of . . . story?" he asked, his gaze riveted to the screen as the opening credits of *Casablanca* scrolled past.

M.C. sighed as she always did when Bogie was nearby. "A love story. Sit down, Al. Relax. This is a terrific movie."

"A terrific *old* movie," Aunt Kate said, shaking her head. "Surely you don't expect him to learn about the modern world by watching this?"

"Sssh! It's starting." M.C. sat down again, thumbing the volume up a few notches.

Kate rolled her eyes. "He should be getting some rest. It's late and—"

"Aunt Kate, go on up to bed. Al and I will be fine."

Kate eyed her. "*Star Trek* is showing on channel 12." She said it without much hope in her voice. M.C. ignored her. "*Indiana Jones* is on 26 . . . or maybe the late news would be—"

M.C. sent her aunt a quelling glare.

"I found the . . . er . . . ball of foot game to be interesting," Al suggested.

M.C. looked at him with raised brows, then turned to her aunt. "He's becoming a nineties guy already." She got to her feet, pointing at Al with a decisive forefinger. "You are going to sit here and watch *Casablanca*. And you," she said, turning to Aunt Kate, "are going up to bed before you fall asleep on your feet."

Kate put her hands on her hips. "And what are you going to do, young lady?"

M.C. smiled. "Make popcorn. What else?"

She sauntered into the kitchen to do just that, and when she returned, Al was alone, riveted to the TV screen, Aunt Kate having finally surrendered and gone to bed.

Al dug into the popcorn with delight, and M.C. explained the film as it went along. The cars, the guns, the airplanes, the war. But when it ended, Al turned to her in confusion.

"He let her go," he said, shaking his head.

M.C. sniffed and rubbed at her eyes. "I know. It's a beautiful story, isn't it?"

"Beautiful?" He searched her face. "But you are crying! I thought you said this was not real! Make-believe, *non*?"

"Of course it's make-believe." She averted her face, rubbing the tears from her lashes briskly.

"Then . . . why do you cry?"

"Because it's so sad!"

"And yet you love it all the same? Though it makes you cry to see it?"

She nodded. Al frowned. "You are a foolish woman, Mary Catherine. And that . . . that story is foolish as well. He should not have let her go."

M.C. tilted her head and studied Al's face. "Well, I'll be . . . You were as moved by the film as I was, weren't you?"

"*Non!*" he said. "I told you, it was foolish. He loved her. He should have taken her away with him and let the war be damned."

He said it with such passion that she found herself staring at him in surprise. "You feel pretty strongly about it, hmm?"

Al nodded hard, then met her eyes. "Nothing is more important than love, lady. Not war, nor peace, nor marriage. Nothing."

Lowering her gaze, she said, "You sound as if you've been in love yourself."

Al shook his head slowly, but his gaze remained riveted to her face. "I have known many women, *ma belle*, but I have not loved. Some of them . . . claimed to love me, but it was my position, my sword, not me. The romantic image of the Musketeer. One day, I will find a woman who will love the man, rather than the colors he wears and the rapier he wields."

"I'll bet you will," she said softly.

He nodded, more gently this time. "And when I do, *chérie,* I will not let her go the way your foolish Rick of the magic box did. I will fight for her. I will die for her. I will even . . . even surrender my sword for her."

She blinked, amazed at the way her heart tripped at his words.

"You think I am foolish," he said, lowering his eyes.

"I think," she said, "that this woman . . . will thank her lucky stars."

He smiled, and handed her the television guide her aunt had been perusing earlier. "Another play," he said.

"Aren't you tired?"

Staring deeply into her eyes, he said, "I am more awake than I have ever been, *ma petite*."

She felt her cheeks heating, so she averted her face, burying her nose in the magazine, flipping pages. She didn't think she'd ever met a more hopeless romantic in her life. Who'd have guessed the French flirt was really such a softy? "Oh, here's one. This time you'll get to see what I do for a living as well as learn about life in the nineties." He frowned as she set the book down and turned to channel 8, where *V. I. Warshawski* was about to begin.

*Alexandre* was amazed at the strength and independence of the woman on the screen, and slowly realized that Mary Catherine was like her. He had no idea how to deal with such a woman. And yet, as the film progressed he understood better the kind of danger she must be facing.

When it ended, he turned to M.C. "Like the woman, you feel you have no need of a man to protect you, *non?*"

"Right," she said. And she said it firmly.

"Yet, you must have been afraid. For you sought help from the book of magic."

She shrugged her small shoulders. "I . . . was only playing around. I didn't expect it to really work . . . certainly didn't expect a Musketeer to show up."

She smiled, and as it had before, her smile touched him on some very deep level. Made his stomach clench tight like a fist.

"I think you were afraid. Are you still, Mary Catherine?"

She lowered her lids to hide her eyes, and he knew she was. But thought herself too strong to admit it.

"Tell me about this trouble you are in," he said.

Nodding again, she began. And when she had told him all of it, he found himself amazed at her cleverness in having eluded her pursuers for as long as she had. At disguising herself and escaping even as they watched her every move. She was truly an unusual woman. Unlike any he'd known.

"You do not have to go back," he suggested. "You could go far away, leave this . . . this evidence behind."

"I can't do that," she said. "Guido de Rocci is a killer, Al. If I don't put him away, he's just going to hurt someone else. I can't let that happen."

He stared at her for a very long moment. "Finally, something about you I understand," he said softly.

"Do you?"

He nodded. "It is . . . a matter of honor, is it not?"

She stared at him thoughtfully for a long moment. "Yeah," she said. "I guess it is."

"Then I shall help you to retrieve this evidence."

She blinked as if surprised. "But how? I told you, they're watching the bank. Oh, they might let me get in and grab the tape, but there's no way I'll get out of there once I have it."

"*Oui*, they are watching. But they are watching for you, Lady Hammer. Not me."

Her brows bunched together, creasing her forehead. "Not . . . you?"

"I shall go into this . . . this bank, and retrieve the tape for you. It is simple, *non*?"

Her frown eased. "It *sounds* simple." Then she caught her lower lip in her teeth, shaking her head slowly. "So why do I have the feeling it won't be?"

"You worry for nothing, *ma chérie*. I am a Musketeer. This is only a small task, and barely worthy of my skills."

She thought for a long moment, even got to her feet and paced the floor. But finally she turned to him and nodded. "All right, we'll try it. But you have to understand, Al, it's going to be dangerous."

"I am not unfamiliar with danger, Mary Catherine."

She searched his face. But he got the feeling she didn't quite believe him. "You'd better get some sleep. Tomorrow's going to be a big day, and you'll need to be on your toes."

He frowned at the unusual turn of phrase. "A wise suggestion," he finally said.

"Come on, I'll take you to the bedroom." She reached for his hand, quite without thought, he was certain. But when his closed around hers, he felt the shudder that worked through her. And more. The warmth of that small hand nestled within his larger one. The pull of a longing that seemed to well from somewhere deep inside him. The tingle of an attraction more powerful than any he'd known. And he realized then what she wanted.

"There is one thing I must tell you, lady, before I rest."

She tugged her hand gently, but he only drew it to his lips and kissed its silken flesh before finally releasing her. "Go . . . go ahead," she said, but her voice trembled just as her hand had when his lips had caressed it.

He sighed. "I am a Musketeer, and as of this moment, my mission is to protect you, and to see to it that your pursuers are dealt with. This is my task, Mary Catherine, and until it is done, it is where all my attention must lie."

She tilted her head to one side. "I'm not sure what you're getting at."

He nodded. "I am being unclear. What I am saying is that as long as I am your protector, I cannot make love to you."

She blinked twice, and then her eyes opened wide. "Wh-what?"

"I am sorry, *ma chérie*. It is a part of my personal code of conduct, you see. I cannot be distracted, even for a moment. Not until you are safe, and my task complete."

She gaped for a moment. Then snapped her jaw shut. "Of all the nerve! I swear, Al, I've never met a more conceited, cocksure, arrogant—"

He surged to his feet, and in one smooth motion swept her into his arms, dipped her backward, and bent over her to kiss her mouth, because he knew how badly she wanted him to. She went stiff in his arms, but as he worked her lips with his, her body melted, and her mouth relaxed, and he made love to her with his tongue until she trembled all over.

Then he straightened, careful not to release her until he was sure she wouldn't fall. Her eyes were wide and glassy, her breaths quick and short. "Do not be angry with me, pretty one. I, too, find it difficult to wait. But for now, you must go to your chamber alone, and I will rest here . . . and dream of the time when my job is done and I can give you what we both desire."

Her faced flushed, still panting, she clenched her fists and glared at him. "The only thing I *desire*, Al, is to get this tape to the police, Guido de Rocci behind bars, and you back in your own time and out of my life for good. Understand?"

He smiled very gently. "*Oui, ma petite*. I understand, *perfectly*."

She made a growling sound like that of a lion about to spring, then whirled and stomped away from him and up the stairs to her room. Alone, and angry at him for denying her. He lowered his head, shaking it slowly. Poor *petite*. It frustrated him as well. And for the first time, Alexandre was tempted to forgo honor, deny his own code, and give in to the rapture he would find in her arms.

But no. He was a Musketeer.

He laid his rapier beside the settee within easy reach, and curled onto the cushions for a night he was certain would provide little rest.

# Chapter 5

She didn't sleep well. Her rest consisted of punching her pillow, and wishing it were Al's gorgeous face—that and wondering why the hell she'd reacted to his kiss the way she had.

He was arrogant, all too sure of himself, lecherous, and infuriating.

But he kissed like he'd been born to it.

And she reacted like a woman too long without a man. That was all there was to it, she decided. It wasn't him, it was her own unplanned celibacy that had her hormones raging when he touched her. She'd never been good at choosing men. Every time she got involved, the guy turned out to be a loser, and so she'd decided to avoid the opposite sex entirely. That had been over a year ago. She guessed her body had its own opinion on the subject.

So maybe she should try again. But not with Al. Absolutely not with Al.

Why not?

Hell. He was too sure of himself, too old-fashioned, probably to the point of being chauvinistic, and he was going back where he came from just as soon as all of this was over.

And that, she realized, was the heart of the matter. He was going back, and there was no sense in her forming some sick attachment to him in the meantime. No sense at all.

All morning M.C. and Aunt Kate helped Al practice the role he was about to play. They talked him through it over and over again. Waiting for his turn in line, what he'd say to the teller at the window, how they'd take him into another room where he'd insert his key into the box and the banker would insert hers. He'd memorized everything from the box number to the fact that he must address the teller as Mr. or Ms. rather than "my lady," or *"ma chérie."*

M.C. believed she'd thought of everything.

Before noon, he seemed ready. Aunt Kate had run into town to buy him a dark-colored trench coat that reached to mid-shin, since he was so damned insistent on wearing his sword. She'd also had a copy of the safe-deposit box key made. M.C. thought it best, just in case, and she put the extra key in her jeans pocket where she could get at it in a hurry if she needed to. Despite Al's protests, they'd managed to talk him into wearing the Kevlar vest that M.C. had practically lived in for the past few days. And in spite of his objections, Mary Catherine was going to be waiting right outside the bank to back him up if all hell broke loose.

Her stomach was churning when all was finally ready and she got into Aunt Kate's car to drive back to Newark. She was forgetting something. She was sure of it.

Al, on the other hand, was far less concerned about the job at hand than he was about their mode of transportation. He eyed the car warily before getting in, then took his passenger seat looking a bit pale.

"It's perfectly safe, Al," M.C. assured him. "Put your seat belt on." When he frowned at her, she demonstrated by fastening her own. Lips tight, he pulled the belt around him, and snapped it.

"Good," she said, and then turned the key.

The motor came to life, and M.C. shifted into gear and pulled onto the street. Al's hand gripped her knee, and for once, she was certain it *wasn't* a come-on. His knuckles were white, and the pressure pretty intense. She closed her hand over his. "Easy, Al. There's nothing to this, I promise."

He met her eyes and seemed unsure. "We are traveling very quickly, are we not?"

She glanced at the speedometer. "I'm going thirty. We're practically crawling."

Another car approached, and Al looked up fast, eyes widening. "Watch out, lady!"

His shout startled her so much that she jammed the brakes and came to an abrupt stop in the middle of the quiet street. The other car passed, its driver sending her an odd look. M.C. shook her head, glancing in the mirror and thanking her stars that no one was behind her. She'd have been rear-ended for sure.

Sighing, she turned to Al. "Look, Al, I've been driving for over a decade now. Will you relax? Please?"

He closed his eyes slowly. "Forgive me," he said. "You must think me very cowardly."

She shook her head slowly. "I think you're only about half as nervous as I'd be in your shoes. Listen, Al, this is going to get worse. Once we hit the highway we'll be going a lot faster, and there are going to be lots of other cars on the road with us. Are you going to be okay with this?"

He licked his lips, nodding slowly. "It is just so new and strange to me."

"I know. You'll get used to it, I promise. Look, do you trust me?"

He stared into her eyes for a long moment. "Oddly enough,

Mary Catherine, I do. It is good, *non*? Since I am placing my life in your hands?"

She smiled. "I'm an excellent driver."

The blast of a horn made Al jump out of his skin and whirl around. M.C. glanced back to see a car behind them. She let off the brake, pressed on the accelerator, and got moving.

By early afternoon, they were back in Newark, and she thought it was a good thing Al had been given several hours to get used to traveling by car before facing the city traffic. What a mess. At any rate, he'd calmed down a lot. Enough so that he was now asking questions about how the car worked, and whether he could try driving it himself. The very thought had her almost as nervous as he'd been when he'd first got into the thing.

She parked a block away from the bank. Her hat and sunglasses were firmly back in place now, and she wore her leather jacket like a shield. "That's the bank, over there," she said. "You won't have to cross any streets. That's a lesson in itself around here. I'll stay here, where I can keep an eye on you in case anything goes wrong. Okay?"

"Yes, fine. I know what to do." He glanced around, his nervousness gone, every bit the protector now. "Do you see any of your enemies about?"

She dragged her eyes from Al and looked around. Then she nodded. "That dark sedan with the tinted glass, right across from the bank. That's one of Guido's goons inside it."

Al spotted the car and nodded. "Perhaps you should await me elsewhere," he suggested. "You'll be alone, unprotected while I retrieve the tape."

"Not quite unprotected," she said, and she took out her gun, then gave the cylinder a spin. "He comes near me, he'll wish he hadn't."

"I still don't like leaving your side, Mary Catherine, with one of them so close."

"He doesn't know this car, and he can't possibly recognize me from there. Go on, Al. Get the tape. It's the only way to end this thing."

Sighing heavily, he nodded. "I will be as fast as possible, my lady." He fiddled with the door handle for a minute, finally made it work, and started to get out without undoing the seat belt. It tugged him back down, and M.C. reached over to release it for him. Impulsively, she touched his shoulder. "Be careful, Al."

"Do not worry," he said, then he smiled at her and got out, striding purposefully toward the bank in his long dark coat, looking this way and that all the way there. Inconspicuous, he definitely was not. At least his sword didn't show.

His sword. It was at that precise moment that M.C. realized what it was she'd forgotten. This bank had been robbed six times in the past two years. As a result it had been equipped with metal detectors at the entrances and airportlike X-ray machines. "Oh, hell!" She had to stop him. But she'd never get inside with her gun. Quickly she pulled it from her jeans and jammed it under the front seat.

She jumped out of the car and ran toward the bank to stop Al, but he was already heading through the entrance. By the time she got to the door, a security guard was guiding Al to the X-ray machine and asking him to walk through it. She shoved the door open, lunged inside, saw the X-ray guy's eyes bug out as he looked at the screen, and then saw three security guards pull their weapons and head for Al, even as he reached for his sword.

"Al, no!" she shouted. Too late. In a flash the weapon was in his hand, whipping to and fro like lightning. The guards' guns sailed from their hands as if they'd sprouted wings. The bank's alarm shrieked like a banshee, and Al smiled, his eyes gleaming as he held the guards at bay. He was *enjoying this*, she realized in disbelief.

He backed past her toward the door, glanced her way briefly, and inclined his head. Then he was gone, out the door with the guards in hot pursuit. Already she could hear approaching sirens.

She looked outside to see the dark sedan pulling slowly away from the bank. No doubt Guido's goon had a record and didn't want to be caught within a mile of a bank robbery. She looked up and down the street for Al, and caught sight of him as he leapt nimbly from the sidewalk to the hood of a parked car, swung his sword in an elegant arc to fend off his pursuers, and then leapt off the other side. She should go after him, she thought; she should help him.

But he'd all but told her to go after the tape. And she could always bail him out of jail—or the loony bin, where he'd more likely end up—later.

Poor Al. She hoped the cops didn't shoot first and ask questions later. She knew she'd better hurry. He'd never survive without her.

Quickly she went up to a frightened teller. "I know this is a bad time," she said, "but this is truly an emergency. My life is in danger unless I get into my safe-deposit box right this minute."

"I'm sorry," the woman said. "But in the middle of all this, I can't possibly—"

"Please. I'm not kidding you, I could be killed if you don't help me."

The woman searched M.C.'s face, frowning. Then nodded. "All right. But . . . be discreet. I could lose my job for this."

"Thank you."

Within a few minutes, M.C. had the tape. Getting out of the bank with the cops there questioning people proved to be another challenge. But she found herself pausing to eavesdrop as she overheard the guards who had returned from the chase, telling their story to the police.

"The man was insane," one said. "Some kind of acrobat or something."

"Look what he did to my uniform!" said another, fingering the neat slash across the front of his shirt. "He coulda killed me."

"No way," a third commented. "He was too good. If he'd wanted to kill you, you'd be dead."

"Man, I never saw anything like it. He ducked into an alley, and we thought we had him cornered. But then he jumped onto a Dumpster and did a backflip right over the fence. And he wasn't even winded!"

Poor Al. Out there, being pursued like a fox by hounds, in an unfamiliar city. But she shook her head in wonder at the way he'd handled himself. She almost wished she could have seen it.

She tucked the tape into her pocket and sidled over toward the group of customers who'd already been interviewed. Briefly she thought about handing the tape to one of the cops on the scene, but it was too risky. If he were honest, he'd insist on taking her with him to the station, and that would leave Al alone on the run. If he were less than honest . . . She knew full well that there were several cops on Guido de Rocci's payroll, and it would be just her luck to pick one of them.

No, she wasn't handing this evidence over to anyone other than the top guy. The D.A. himself. But first, she had to find and rescue her self-appointed bodyguard before he got himself killed.

A cop gave the group of customers the okay to leave, and she slipped out with them. Then she ducked her head and pulled her cap lower as the dark sedan passed slowly by. Circling the block like a damned hungry shark. She couldn't walk around searching for Al. Not yet. She had to get to the car. She'd drive around looking for him. It would be safer that way. At least she could make a run for it if they recognized her.

The guy in the sedan passed her, and did a double take. Oh, hell. He was picking up a car phone now. She walked faster. She was nearly to her aunt's beat-up Buick when a second dark car pulled to a stop at the corner just beyond it. A man got out. Suit, sunglasses. Damn.

She ran for the car as the thug came toward her on the sidewalk, his hand reaching inside his tailored Italian jacket. She thought of her own gun, tucked under the front seat of the car. Hell. Almost there. She grabbed the door handle.

A hand gripped her arm, spun her around, and she stood face-to-face with Guido de Rocci himself. The barrel of a handgun jammed into her belly, and she held her breath.

"The tape," he rasped. "Hand it over, or die."

"I gave it to the cops already, de Rocci. And I hope they fry your ass."

"You're a liar," he said. "Hand it over."

She met his shaded eyes and simply shook her head. "Shoot me and those cops will be all over you like ugly on an ape, pal. From the feel of it, I'd say there's no silencer on that piece of yours."

"Oh, I'm not going to shoot you, Miss Hammer. Not here, at least." He tugged her away from the Buick, just as the other car came to a halt in the street beside it. And she knew if they got her into that vehicle it would be all over. She closed her eyes and prayed for a miracle.

# Chapter 6

The miracle she was praying for appeared. Guido de Rocci stood on the sidewalk, facing the street, holding her pressed up against her aunt's Buick, his gun jabbing into her belly. His goons in their dark sedan had pulled to a stop in the street beside the Buick.

When de Rocci suddenly stiffened, she didn't know why. Until she looked downward. Al crouched comfortably on the sidewalk behind the man, and the tip of his sword nestled at the base of Guido's spine.

"Unhand the lady," Al said softly. And his eyes glittered.

He was smart, her Musketeer. The guys in the car couldn't even see him down there. The oversized Buick blocked him from their view.

Guido didn't move.

"Release her, man, or I'll run you through!" Al put a little more pressure on the sword, and Guido flinched.

"Okay, okay." He let his grip on M.C. go, but still kept the gun in her belly.

"Now tell your men to drive away." Again Al shoved the sword.

Guido grunted, and his jaw went tight. But he nodded to his goons. "Take one more turn around the block."

The dark sedan moved slowly away. But M.C. still didn't relax. Tough to relax with the barrel of a .44 in your gut.

"Very good, sir," Al said, and he got to his feet as soon as the other car was out of sight. "Now, put your gun down, and perhaps I shall let you live."

"You're some kind of lunatic. I can blow the broad away with no more than a twitch of my finger, pal, so put your blade down or she's history."

"If you shoot her, the soldiers from the bank will come running," Al said.

"Soldiers? What the hell are you, nuts?"

At that precise moment, one of the cops leaving the bank stepped out, glanced their way, and pointed right at Al. Several others followed as he came running, shouting that he'd spotted the suspect. The commotion took Al's attention away from Guido for the briefest instant, and Guido whirled on him, gun raised.

With barely a sideways glance, Al flicked his sword, almost carelessly, and the gun flew from de Rocci's hand and skittered across the sidewalk. Then Al backhanded the mob boss, and sent Guido sprawling.

The creep reached for his gun, even as M.C. was yanking the car door open and snatching up her own. She aimed it at his head. "Lie still, you slug. Al, get in. Quick!"

The cops ran closer, reaching for their weapons now. Al dove into the car, clambered into the passenger seat, and pulled M.C. in behind him. She slammed the door, turned the key, and laid rubber, cutting into traffic and drawing a half dozen horn blasts and hand gestures on the way.

Moments later, she heard the sirens. Hell, she was being chased by half the cops in Newark, and probably half the mob hit men as well. Traffic was bad. Almost at a standstill up ahead. She glanced at Al. He stared back, looking worried. And then she smiled and jerked the wheel. She laid just the horn as the car bumped over the curb and onto the sidewalk. People scattered like autumn leaves in front of a strong wind. She took out a few parking meters, but figured it was them or the pedestrians. She swung left, the wrong way down a one-way street, but the fastest route away from the city. By the time she emerged on a side road, she'd lost them. Lost them!

"Hot damn, I'm good," she said, and slowed the car down to keep from attracting notice, turning onto less and less traveled streets until she was completely away from the city.

Al didn't answer. She looked his way, and saw how pale he was. Looked as if he might lose his lunch, too. "You okay, Al?"

He swallowed hard, and nodded. "Of course," he said. "The question is, are you?" The dazed expression left his eyes, and they filled instead with concern as he scanned her face. "Did that brute harm you, Mary Catherine?"

"No. But he would have." She drew a deep breath and prepared to eat crow. "You were . . . pretty incredible back there, Al. I didn't think you'd stand a chance against de Rocci and his gun-toting goons. I mean, with nothing but that sword. But you . . ." She shook her head and sighed. "You saved my butt, Al. I owe you one."

He looked away, almost as if he were embarrassed by her praise. "It is what I came here to do," he said. "And what I have spent most of my life doing. You should not be so surprised."

She nodded. "My mistake. I suppose a guy who fights for a living learns a few things along the way."

"You suppose correctly."

She reached over to touch his shoulder. "I'm sorry I doubted you."

He said nothing. Insulted at her surprise, she figured.

"Look, Al, I've never known a man like you, okay? I mean, most guys . . . hell, they aren't tough like you. They haven't needed to be. The world's too modern. They don't need to hunt for food or cut wood for fires or learn to fight. They've got grocery stores and fuel oil and sophisticated weapons. Just aim and shoot your way out of trouble. Simple. Barely any skill to it. A trained monkey could do it."

He finally looked at her. And he was smiling when he did, which relieved her a little bit. He'd saved her life, after all. Insulting him was the last thing she'd meant to do.

"It works to my advantage, their softness."

"Does it?"

He nodded. "That man seemed to think that because he had his pistol in hand, he had nothing to fear. He did not expect me to resist."

"I guess you taught him a thing or two," she said, and she couldn't help smiling back. "I wish I could have seen his face when you flicked that sword of yours and sent his gun sailing. I'll bet he looked like an air-starved trout."

Al frowned and tilted his head. "His mouth was open. And his eyes did seem to bulge a bit."

Mary Catherine laughed out loud, tipping her head back. "You're something, Al. You really are."

Al nodded, but his expression turned serious. "It will not be so easy next time," he said.

M.C. felt her smile die. "You're right. He's not going to underestimate you again." But then she brightened and patted her pocket. "But we're halfway home, Al. I got the tape."

Al sent her an approving glance. "I knew you would. What must we do next, to bring this de Rocci to justice?"

Mary Catherine licked her lips in thought. "We have to get the tape to the district attorney. I don't trust anyone else. I want to personally put it into his hands. But it won't be easy."

"Nothing worthwhile ever is."

"You got that right." She took another turn, picking up speed. "We're going to have to ditch the car, Al. De Rocci's seen it, and by now the cops have the plate number. Then we'll find a place to lay low, call the D.A. and set up a meeting."

Al nodded. "A wise course of action," he said.

"By the time we get settled in, D.A. Hennesey will be out of his office for the night. I doubt his home phone is listed." He looked at her curiously, and she clarified. "We probably won't be able to reach him until tomorrow."

"Then our immediate concern is for a safe place to spend the night," he said, cutting right to the heart of the matter.

"Right. We'll head into the next town, leave the car at a diner, and call a cab to take us to a motel."

"A cab?"

"A . . . car for hire," she explained.

Al frowned, rubbing his chin. "Would the . . . er . . . police not be able to question the driver of this . . . cab, to find out where we'd gone?"

M.C. clapped a hand to her forehead. "You're right. Hell, how are we going to get anywhere without a car?"

Al looked at her as if she were sprouting a second head. "You were right before, Mary Catherine. The modern world has made things far too easy."

*Al* kept it to himself, but he'd been as amazed by Mary Catherine's strength as she had been by his ability. Any other woman he'd known would have been in tears, become paralyzed with fear, or simply fainted away, had she found herself in a similar situation. A lowlife manhandling her, a weapon pressed to her tender belly. But Mary Catherine had defied the dog, insulted him, refused to cower.

She was, quite simply, amazing.

He suggested she drive far from the city, into as rural an area as the modern world had to offer. And instead of "ditching" her aunt's contraption, whatever that meant, he'd persuaded her to trust its care to a farmer. Indeed, he'd managed to talk the kind man into letting them rent a pair of horses for the night, leaving the car as a sort of collateral to ensure their return.

The man's eyes had widened when Al had offered him a handful of gold coins in exchange for the use of his horses. He'd examined them carefully, while M.C. had elbowed Alexandre in the rib cage.

When he looked her way, she whispered, "Those coins are probably worth a fortune, Al!"

"Nonsense. 'Tis a pittance."

"Not in this day and age. If you have any more, hold on to them, for heaven's sake."

He shrugged, quite befuddled. But the man pocketed the coins, grinning hugely, and was only too happy to comply when Alexandre asked him to keep the car in his barn overnight. To protect it from the elements, he said, though his true motive was to keep it from prying eyes.

He thought he'd done quite well, until the farmer led two graying, swaybacked mares from his barn, decked out in worn saddles and bridles whose straps were split with age.

"Are these the only two you have?" Alexandre asked, running a hand along one horse's neck and feeling the matted coat in dire need of grooming.

" 'Fraid so," the man said. "Take 'em or leave 'em."

"Er . . . Al?"

Alexandre shook his head at M.C., then addressed the man. "Perhaps I shall give you more coin upon our return. So that you can purchase some oats for these animals, and perhaps a brush."

The man frowned, unsure about whether he'd just been insulted, but unwilling to let the possibility of more gold slip by him. Finally he nodded. "That'd be real kind of you, mister."

Alexandre nodded. "Then I shall, provided you keep all of this to yourself. The lady and I do not wish to be disturbed tonight."

The farmer smiled widely, and winked. "Mum's the word."

"Al," M.C. said, and she tugged on his long coat this time. He turned to her. "We'll only be needing one horse," she told him. "Unless you want to see me fall on my butt."

Alexandre frowned. "You do not ride?"

"Never have. And won't start now if we have a choice."

"A choice, my lady, is one thing we do not have. I shall teach you. Fear not."

She tugged him aside, her voice low. "Al, I mean it. I don't want a horse all to myself. Can't I just ride with you?"

His heart tripped over itself. So it was his closeness she craved, even still, after all she'd been through today. He stroked her hair and fought the desire rising like a tide within him. "I'd like nothing better than to hold you close to me in the saddle, sweet one. But I've already explained why that cannot be. Not yet," he added, lest she think he did not return her ardor.

Her jaw dropped. She closed it. "Get over yourself, Al. I'm scared to ride one of these smelly beasts all by myself, and that's all there is to it!"

He smiled slightly and nodded. "Of course you are. You, a woman who stands face-to-face with an armed blackguard, and looks him in the eye without a trace of fear. Of course you're afraid of an old, plodding horse."

"But it's the truth! I am!"

He closed his eyes briefly, the exquisite agony of self-denial like a firestorm in his gut. "Soon," he whispered, leaning closer and looking into her eyes. "It will be soon, Mary Catherine. And worth every second of waiting. I promise."

He held her gaze with his, and saw a gleam of passion flit into her eyes. But she blinked, hiding it quickly, looking away. "You're an arrogant jackass."

He laughed softly. "Nonetheless, neither of these mares looks strong enough to carry us both. Much as the thought of holding you nestled between my thighs with your back pressed to my chest, and my arms tight around your waist, might tempt me. I am afraid we have no choice."

She pressed a hand to her belly, biting her lip, a little breathless, he thought.

He turned back to the man, nodded his thanks, and scooped Mary Catherine off her feet and into his arms. He deposited her gently into the saddle, held her waist until she seemed to get her balance. It surprised him when she changed position, moving one leg to the other side so she sat astride, rather than sidesaddle, but he made no comment as he then bent to adjust the stirrups for her. A second later, he swung easily onto his own mount.

Then he turned to her. "Hold to the pommel, lady, and hand the reins to me."

She gripped the pommel until her knuckles were white as Alexandre set his horse into motion at a slow, easy pace.

"Great," she muttered. "So I suppose I'm stuck here on this animal's back until we get to the nearest motel, right?"

"Quite wrong, dear lady. We will be far less likely to be discovered if we make camp in yonder woods. Very deep in them, I should think."

"But . . . but, Al, I'm hungry. We haven't eaten. And we don't have blankets or . . . or *anything*."

"We have all we need, Mary Catherine." He looked back at her, wondering how a woman could be so capable and yet so utterly helpless at the same time. "Have no fear. I am your Musketeer, Lady Hammer. I will feed you and keep you warm. On my sword, I will."

He saw her pale, and then her throat moved as if she were trying to swallow and couldn't.

# Chapter 7

She had no idea what he was looking for as they plodded deeper and deeper into the state forest that bordered the farmer's property. But he was definitely looking for something. Scanning the trees, eyeing everything around them, until finally, he nodded and drew his horse to a halt.

"This will do nicely."

M.C. looked around. "What will do nicely?"

"This spot. To make camp." He dismounted and walked to her horse, clasped her waist in his big hands, and lifted her down. As soon as she put weight on her legs, she felt the burn and pull of muscles she didn't know she had. Her rear end hurt. Al saw her wince, and smiled. "No doubt it will be worse in the morn. If I could have spared you the riding, I would have."

She shook her head and limped toward a soft patch of ground to sit. Al led the horses away from her, to a stream she hadn't even noticed before, and let them drink. Then he took an ancient-looking length of rope from one of the saddles, slicing it neatly in half with a dagger he'd pulled from his boot. "I'll picket them nearby, where there's grass," he said, and led the horses farther along the stream's bank.

M.C. leaned back on her hands and wondered what she'd got herself into this time. She was stuck here, alone with Al in the middle of the forest, for the night. Al, who'd somehow wound up with the idea that she was burning up with lust for him. Not that he wasn't attractive. He was. Very. Okay, so he wasn't the kind of man she'd toss out of bed for eating crackers, but he wasn't her type, either.

She frowned, realizing how little sense that thought made. Her types—the types she'd usually ended up dating, way back when she'd still been dating at all—were losers. Oh, they always seemed okay at first. But then they'd reveal themselves. There was Mike, who'd kept hitting her up for money. Kevin, who'd been busted for dealing drugs after their second date. And Tom, who'd been married. The slug.

And there was Al. A guy who put honor above everything else, who could handle a sword like some kind of master, and who was so polite it was sickening. A guy who'd refused to leave her until he knew she was safe.

Definitely not her type. Al was no loser.

Problem was, he had to leave. But why was that so important, anyway? It wasn't like she was going to go and fall in love with him or anything. Why not enjoy the guy while he was here?

He appeared then from the trees, his arms loaded down with limbs and deadfall. Dropping the pile to the ground, he shrugged out of his coat and crouched beside it. His jeans pulled tight to his backside when he crouched like that. And the black T-shirt he wore clung. He had great arms. Hard. Nice.

M.C. got up, deciding to keep her thoughts in line by keeping busy with other things. "I'll help gather wood," she said.

"Nonsense, lady. Gathering wood for the fire is a man's job."

Aha. There it was. She'd known there had to be something

wrong with him. No man could be as perfect as he was beginning to seem to her. He was a chauvinist.

"This is the twentieth century, Al. There are no men's jobs or women's work anymore. Women in this day and age can be police officers or firefighters or world leaders if they want to. And men cook and clean and change diapers."

He went still, his back to her, still crouching over the fire he'd begun to lay on a bare spot of ground. "I have offended you," he said softly. "I am sorry, Lady Hammer. Chivalry . . . is a part of being a man, in my time. It is difficult to understand how it can have become an insult in only a few centuries."

"Chivalry." She repeated the word.

Sighing deeply, Al resumed piling dried leaves and twigs, adding larger pieces of wood on top of them. "Yes. The men of my generation are not fools, Mary Catherine. It has never been a matter of believing a woman *incapable* of doing heavy work. Only a matter of believing she should not have to do it."

"I see."

He straightened, turning to come close to her, and then dropping to one knee in front of her. "I do not think you do. In my time, Mary Catherine, we cherished our women. Treated them as the precious, beloved creatures they are. The only hope for the continuation of our race, the mothers of our children." He took her hand in his, tracing its contours with the tip of a forefinger. "Look at this hand. Beautiful, delicate . . . capable, yes, but small and fragile." Then he turned their clasped hands over, so his was on top. "Mine, however, is large, hard, and calloused. Rough work, unpleasant tasks . . . are beneath a creature as magical as a woman. She . . . you . . . should be adored, treasured—respected as the beautiful being you are. The mother of mankind. Not asked to bruise this lovely hand on something as far beneath you as gathering wood."

She couldn't breathe. His voice had gone soft and deep, and it touched nerve endings somewhere inside her that came to life all at once. Then he brought her hand to his lips, and kissed it gently. "A woman like you should be given anything she desires."

"A-and . . . what if what she desires is to help gather firewood?"

He lifted his head away from her hand, but it tingled where his mouth had touched. Holding her gaze pinned to his, he smiled slightly. "Then she should gather firewood."

"You . . . don't think I'm too weak for the job?"

"Weak?" His brows rose. "I've never known a woman with your strength, Mary Catherine. But even the most fragile female has the ability in her to capture a man's heart—to bear his children. Surely the latter task takes far more strength than to gather branches from the forest floor. More strength, perhaps, than that of any man."

"I imagine so."

"I'll start the fire," he told her. "If you wish to gather more wood, then do so. But if you'd rather rest from the ride, consider me your humble servant." He bowed his head.

For just a moment she had the craziest feeling that she was some kind of queen, and the grass underneath her a throne. Whoa, what a sensation! She had to concede he wasn't exactly a chauvinist. There was, she decided, a difference between chauvinism and chivalry.

Al rose and returned to his pile of kindling, pulling a flintstone from his pocket and crouching again.

Mary Catherine got up and went to crouch beside him, reaching into her own pocket. "You can put the stone away, Al. I have something better."

He eyed the lighter in her hand. "Another wonder of your modern world?"

"You're gonna love this," she said, and she flicked the lighter. He smiled when a flame appeared. She touched it to the dried leaves at the base of the pile and watched the flames lick up at them, catch, and begin to spread to the kindling.

"Wonderful," he said.

M.C. sat back on her heels as the fire took hold, and she began to think that maybe being up here with him all night wasn't such a terrible thing.

"So, did you mean all that stuff you said about women, Al, or is that a line you use to charm them out of their pantaloons?"

He laughed softly, shaking his head. "I meant it."

"You really believe a woman can do just about anything a man can?"

"Some women," he said. "You, for example."

"That's good, because I want to ask you to do something for me. And it might not be the kind of request you're used to getting from women."

He met her eyes, a reflection of the growing fire dancing deep in his own. "Ask me anything, Mary Catherine."

She smiled at him. "Teach me how to use that sword of yours."

His eyes opened wide, but then his lips curved, and he shook his head slowly. "Why should that request surprise me coming from you? If you wish to learn, Mary Catherine, I will teach you."

This night was looking better and better.

"But first," he said, "I will find us something to eat." He added larger pieces of wood to the fire, then rose, glancing around the woods. "I saw signs of deer nearby. Also possum, and quail."

"Um, I'd rather go hungry than eat a possum, Al."

He bowed slightly. "Then I shall not bring one for your dinner."

He didn't bring her a possum. He brought a wild turkey big enough to feed a dozen people. M.C. had busied herself gathering more firewood and making a neat stack of it. She'd checked on the horses twice, and was beginning to get bored and more than slightly worried about Al, though she knew she probably should have known better. Then he showed up with the turkey. He'd quite chivalrously taken care of the nastier parts of preparing wild game far away from camp, lest her delicate female stomach protest.

She was glad of it, too.

This bird he brought was ready for the oven. Or the campfire, in this case. It didn't look anything like what she was used to seeing in the grocery stores or on Thanksgiving tables. It was skinnier, longer, and not as smooth and shiny.

She was surprised when he began cutting it up with his dagger. It was stupid of her to have expected him to roast it whole, she mused; it would have taken half the night. Then he skewered hunks of meat, and using forked branches to hold them up, set them to cook over the fire.

Before long the tantalizing aroma had her stomach growling out loud. He pretended not to notice, but she knew he had to hear it. Then she wondered why she cared.

He turned the meat until it was done, then handed her a sizzling, perfectly browned breast portion. One bite and she was in heaven. "God, this is good," she mumbled, and ate some more.

Al seemed equally enamored of his own helping of turkey. But as M.C.'s stomach got full, her mind turned to other matters. "Al, how did you get this bird without a gun?"

He reached down to his boot and withdrew the dagger. Then replaced it, as if he had answered her question.

"But . . . you couldn't just sneak up on the bird and—"

He shook his head. "The dagger is perfectly balanced. An excellent throwing blade."

M.C. blinked. "You *threw* your knife at the turkey? And you hit him?"

Al tilted his head. "It would hardly be worthwhile to throw the dagger and miss him, Mary Catherine."

"Oh. Well, how practical." She finished her meat, licked her fingers, and got to her feet. "So will you show me how to use the sword now?"

"Of course." He got up as well, his rapier dangling from a belt at his waist. He wasn't wearing the coat now, so the sword was in plain sight. M.C. stepped forward and reached for it. Al dodged her, shaking his head. "*Non.* You must learn *before* I entrust you with the actual weapon."

M.C. frowned at him. "How am I supposed to learn without a sword?"

"I brought you a . . . a practice sword," he said, and nodded toward the large tree behind her. She saw a long, narrow stick—a branch with all its twigs and leaves stripped off—leaning against the massive trunk.

"You want me to use *that*?"

"For now," he told her. "Trust me, Mary Catherine. I have no desire to lose a hand or to see you lose an eye when you make a misstep. This will be safer."

"You sound like my mother. 'You could put an eye out, Mary Catherine.'"

"A wise woman, your mother. It would be a shame for harm to come to such beautiful eyes."

She averted her *"beautiful"* eyes now, turning to pick up her stick instead of letting him see her blush yet again.

"They're like rich brown velvet, you know," he went on.

"Or mud," she replied.

Al chuckled, and it did something wild to her insides. He had a sexy laugh—she'd give him that much. She gripped her stick and turned to face him. "So what do I do with it?"

Al lifted his sword, holding his opposite hand up in the air behind him. "*En garde,* my lady."

# Chapter 8

Wielding a sword was nowhere near as easy as Al made it look. M.C. discovered that while trying to mimic his graceful moves with her stick. To her credit, she only whacked him upside the head twice, but he had a bright red welt to show for it. Still, he'd kept his patience, and she thought she'd mastered a move or two by they time they finished.

"Now," Al said, gently closing his hand on the hilt of her branch and taking it from her. "Try it with a real sword."

She was breathless, and she had no doubt her face was bright red from exertion—while he stood there as relaxed as if he'd just been napping. No doubt about it, the guy was in great shape. She, on the other hand, definitely needed to do more aerobics. Or something.

He dropped the stick to the ground and pressed his gleaming sword into her hand. "Like this," he said, guiding her fingers around the grip, then covering them with his own. "Ready?"

She nodded. Al stepped away from her . . . a good three feet away, and that made her grin. "How can I fight without an opponent?"

He smiled back at her, and it made her heart skip. "For now, your opponent is going to have to be make believe, *ma belle*. Imagine Monsieur de Rocci standing before you."

M.C. narrowed her eyes. "That should help immensely. Can I castrate him?"

Al frowned. "You are more bloodthirsty than I realized."

"Only for de Rocci," she said, and she lifted the sword as he'd shown her. "It's heavier than the stick," she said, then she brought it down in a sweeping arc.

"*Bon.* Now thrust! Parry! Dodge! Block!" As he shouted commands, she obeyed, and she couldn't deny she felt incredibly powerful wielding the weapon—though not exactly graceful, nearly tripping over her feet once. Still, when she finished, he nodded in approval. "You are an excellent student, Mary Catherine. You learn quickly."

She nodded, smiling, breathless. "I only wish you were going to be around longer." Then she bit her lip. She hadn't thought about his leaving lately, but now the idea made her inexplicably sad. And not just because he wouldn't be around to give her lessons.

She actually *liked* the guy. Amazing.

"I wish it, too," he said softly.

"What was your life like before I stole you away from it, Al?" Her voice was softer than usual, she realized.

"Ah, my life before." Did he sound wistful? "It was a grand adventure, Mary Catherine. To be a Musketeer is every Frenchman's dream . . . or it is in my time. I am respected and admired, even envied, by everyone I meet."

A man of stature, she mused. Successful and in love with his work. "Did you have any family?"

He lowered his eyes. "I was my parents' only child. They died of a fever when I was still young, so I was reared by my uncle, who had served with the Musketeers before he finally married and settled down. He is gone now, too. I have no family. But then, a Musketeer is better off without one. My life is my work, you see."

"And love?"

Shrugging his broad shoulders, Alexandre smiled. "When love comes, *it* will become my life. For true love alone, would I lay down my sword. Until that day comes I am happy to fight for right and the honor of the king. Each day brings a new challenge, a new adventure."

"A new woman . . . ?"

His smile changed to one filled with mischief. "Sometimes. A warrior never knows which day will be his last, so he tends to make the most of his nights. But sex is not love, my Lady Hammer. Those moonlight trysts meant nothing, neither to me nor to the ladies involved. And I think you are wise enough to know this."

She wondered if it would mean anything if *she* were "the lady involved." Then told herself it didn't matter. He stepped closer, brushing a damp tendril of hair from her face. "You are tired now, and it has grown late. We should rest."

Her throat went dry. "All right."

Al stoked the fire, then laid the saddles on the ground to use as pillows. He put them very close together, she noticed. Then he picked up his long coat. Stretching out on the ground, he pulled the coat over him, then held one side up and looked at her. "Come, Mary Catherine. You know you've nothing to fear."

"I know," she said, maybe a tad defensively. "I'm not afraid." Or if she was, it wasn't for the reasons he was thinking. Lying so close to him all night long—and not touching him—was going to be a challenge. It wasn't Al she was worried about, it was herself. Did women come on to men in his time? What would he think of her if she—

What was she thinking? He was the one obsessed with sex, not her. And since he'd vowed not to touch her until his role as protector was fulfilled, she didn't have a thing to worry about.

Did she?

"Mary Catherine?"

His brows were arched as he lay there waiting for her, looking like a centerfold—except that he had his clothes on. M.C. sighed and went to him, slid underneath the coat, and laid her head on the saddle.

"Good night, my lady. Sleep well."

" 'Night, Al," she said, but she didn't think she was going to sleep.

She did. Must have, because when she woke up, her head was no longer pillowed by the saddle, but by something far warmer, soft and firm at the same time, and with a much nicer smell.

She opened her eyes to the brilliance of dawn, and realized what it was. Al's chest. And his arms were wrapped around her, one hand buried in her hair. One of her legs had decided to rest atop both of his, and her arms were twined around his waist.

He smelled good. God, he did, and he was so warm and hard underneath her. She lifted her head, wondering if she could slip away before he woke. But when she looked at his eyes, she found them open, staring into hers, a fire burning in their depths.

"*Mon Dieu*," he whispered. "You are . . . so beautiful."

His lips were only inches from hers, and pulling her closer, like magnets. Drawing her. She didn't fight it. She let her mouth be tugged to his until their lips touched. And then Al's arms tightened around her, and he kissed her. His mouth pushed at hers until she opened to him, then his tongue slid inside to lick and caress. She'd never known her mouth could be such an erogenous zone. She'd never been kissed like this. Tenderness and passion at once. She wanted him. It hit her like a bullet between the eyes. She wanted to make love to this man. Here. Now.

She was practically on top of him now, and as he continued kissing her, she moved the rest of the way. Her legs straddled his, and she felt his arousal pressing hard between them. But then his hands came to her shoulders, and gently, he lifted her away.

"Never," he whispered, "has temptation been so difficult to resist."

"For me, either." She leaned forward to kiss him again, but he held her away.

"Yet resist I must." He closed his eyes, as if in pain. "But if desire can kill a man, I'll not live much longer."

"Al, don't . . ."

"We mustn't. It was my vow, long ago—the code by which I've lived. I am your protector until you are safe. And only that."

M.C. went stiff, staring down at him in disbelief. "You're kidding, aren't you?"

"If I make love to you now, Mary Catherine, my thoughts will be of nothing else for days to come. I will be distracted, even weakened by a desire this fierce, the memory of a pleasure sweeter than any I've known. *No* . . . I cannot."

M.C. rolled off him and got to her feet. "Fine. That's just fine with me, Al. I didn't want to anyway!"

"I have hurt you." He rose and came to stand behind her, his hands massaging her shoulders. "Make no mistake, *ma chérie*, were it not for my vow, for honor's sake, I—"

"Oh, to hell with you and your damned honor."

She pulled away, busied herself dousing the dwindling fire, scooping dirt over the coals.

"You do not mean that."

"Let's just get out of here, okay? Let's just find a phone, call the D.A., and set up the appointment."

He stood where he was. "This is as difficult for me as for you, Mary Catherine."

She ignored him, embarrassed, downright stung by his rejection. "We'll have to find a car. Can't use Aunt Kate's even if no one's found it by now. The cops have probably called her by now—they'd have traced the plate number and—"

Mary Catherine stopped talking and bit her lip. "Oh my God."

Al was beside her in a second, his hands gripping her shoulders again. "What is it?"

"The license plate. Oh, God, why didn't I think of this last night? Al, Guido saw that plate. He can probably track down the car's owner as easily as the police can!"

"Your aunt?" he asked, looking worried.

"She could be in danger. We have to call her, Al, tell her to get out of the house and lay low for a while." She looked into his eyes, shook her head as a ball of dread formed in the pit of her stomach. "And we'd better do it fast."

The woman was a bundle of contradictions. First she denied wanting him, a habit that had begun to make him doubt himself for the first time in recent memory. Then she'd made it all too clear that she *did* want him. And then she'd become angry, unable, or perhaps—as stubborn as she was—un*willing* to understand his reasons. But all of that had fallen by the wayside when she'd realized she might have inadvertently put her aunt in danger.

As they rode side by side, he watched her. The way her eyes took on such intensity when she was worried. The way the wind tossed her dark hair and the morning sun made it gleam.

He'd wanted many women, had most of them. But never had he felt anything like what he was feeling now. It wasn't just stronger, it was different. An entirely new brand of desire he'd never felt before. And it left him with the odd sense that everything he'd experienced before had been only a faint foreshadowing of this . . . this new and powerful feeling.

Would it fade once they'd given in to its demand and made love together? That was the way it usually worked for Alexandre. But he had a feeling it wouldn't be the same this time. Nothing seemed the same this time.

When they finally arrived back at the farm, the farmer greeted them with a smile and a wave from his front porch. Mary Catherine was off her mount almost before it came to a stop, and heading up the steps. "Please," she said breathlessly, "I need to use your phone. I'll pay you for the call, but—"

"Sure, sure. Come on inside. So how was your ride? The horses look none the worse for wear."

Mary Catherine didn't answer, just hurried past him and into the house. Alexandre watched as the farmer leaned through the door and pointed, then turned to face him again, grinning expectantly.

Alexandre dismounted and took another gold coin from his pocket, handing it to the man.

"Thank you kindly," the older man said, smiling.

Al nodded and turned to remove the saddles.

"Oh, now, don't you bother with that."

"The animals are hot," Al said. "They need to be rubbed down."

"And Tony will take care of it," the farmer insisted. Then he cupped his hands and yelled, and a young man emerged from the barn. As he hurried across the lawn toward the house, the farmer said, "See, I took them coins you gave me yesterday into town this morning and had 'em appraised. When I found out what they were worth, I figured I could afford to hire me a hand around here."

Alexandre frowned. Perhaps Mary Catherine had been right about the coins' value.

Tony arrived, looked at the horses, then at the farmer. "These are the ones? When's the last time they were groomed, anyway?"

"Been a while," the farmer said, chuckling. "Tony here is real experienced with horses. He'll have 'em in tip-top shape in no time."

Alexandre saw the way the boy's hands were already moving over the animals' coats. It was obvious he not only knew about horses, but cared about them. At least one good thing had come of his visit here.

Then the bang of the door drew his gaze, and he saw Mary Catherine standing there, looking pale and wide-eyed.

"What is it, *chérie*? Did you reach your aunt with the telephone device?"

She nodded, closed her eyes. "Guido de Rocci answered the phone."

Alexandre shook his head, not certain he understood.

"He's there, at her house, Al," she went on. "He has her, and he won't let her go unless we give him the tape."

# Chapter 9

There was no time to find another car. M.C. backed Aunt Kate's car out of the farmer's dim, dusty barn without a thought about how many cops might spot it on the road. If she saw flashing lights behind her on the way, she would keep right on going.

"It will be all right," Al said softly, touching her shoulder, drawing her gaze.

She glanced his way as she drove, saw the concern in his eyes. But not for Aunt Kate. His worry was for her, and for what she might be feeling right now. "How can you be so sure of that?" M.C. asked. "For all we know Aunt Kate could already be—"

"No." Al said it firmly. "De Rocci isn't stupid. He wants to trade your aunt for this tape. He cannot do that unless he keeps her alive."

M.C. tried to keep her eyes on the road, tried to keep her speed to within ten miles an hour above the speed limit, though every instinct was to press the pedal to the floor. If she showed up with cops in tow, the whole thing could turn into a standoff, with her odd, eccentric aunt playing hostage. Aunt Kate would be in far less danger this way.

"What do you want to do when we get there?" Al asked softly.

She glanced at him again, surprised that he would ask. He was the expert in fighting here. But she was the expert on nineties goons like de Rocci. "I don't think we have a choice, Al. I'll have to give him the tape."

Al's lips pursed.

"What?" she asked. "You think it's the wrong decision, don't you?"

"I think . . . you're wrong about one thing. We *do* have a choice. And we have to make it carefully. Mary Catherine, do you really think de Rocci will let you or your aunt leave that house alive once he has the tape?"

M.C. sighed, grating her teeth. Al was right. He was so right. "No, he won't. He can't. We'd have him dead to rights on unlawful imprisonment, breaking and entering, maybe assault. And he has to know I can testify as to what I heard on that tape, even if the tape itself is long gone."

"Then we cannot turn it over."

"But Al, what else can we do? He's there, and you can bet he's not alone. He knows we're coming, and he'll be watching for us. How can we . . . ?"

"There's always a way, Mary Catherine. Trust me."

She looked into Al's eyes, and realized that she did trust him. She'd trust him with her life. When the hell had she decided to believe in him this much? But no matter, she had. And she nodded to tell him so.

"Good," he said. "And let us not forget, your aunt Kate is not *entirely* without resources of her own."

\*   \*   \*

They left the car nearly a mile from the house, hidden behind a neighbor's hedges on a side road. Then they walked. And not on the narrow lanes of the suburban-leaning-toward-rural town of Craven Falls, either. They crossed back lawns and vacant lots, skirting the edges of trees and bushes and woodlots where they could. And soon the gothic white elephant was in sight. Flat roof, widow's walk in need of another coat of white paint, curlicues of wood trim everywhere. Tall, narrow windows, their curtains drawn tight like closed eyes, as if the house were sound asleep.

A parked car with two men inside sat opposite Aunt Kate's driveway. A shadowy form lurked just beyond the back door. From their position behind some trees in the back lawn, they could glimpse him when he moved.

"They'll have a man at the front door as well," Al said. "What we need is another way inside. But first"—he glanced toward the car out front—"we should eliminate some of the contenders."

"Even up the odds," M.C. said. "Gotcha. I can take care of the ones in the car, Al. All I need is a roll of duct tape, a length of garden hose, and a pair of shears." She glanced around. "I imagine I can find all of that in the toolshed."

Taking her arm, he started toward the shed, but she shook her head at him. "No. Look, try to get a look inside, make sure Aunt Kate's okay. I can handle this part alone."

He frowned. "I think we should stay together, lady. It would be safer."

"I'm a big girl, Al. And I'm worried about my aunt. Please, I'll feel so much better knowing you're close by, keeping an eye on her."

Closing his eyes, he nodded once. "All right. I know you're more than capable." Then he closed his hand on her outer arms and drew her close to him. "Be careful, *ma chérie*." And he kissed her, hard and fast.

She blinked, tried to catch her breath, gave her head a shake. "Don't let them hurt her, Al. I'm counting on you."

"You have my word as a Musketeer, Mary Catherine. No harm will come to your aunt."

As soon as he said it, she knew it was true. Amazing how much faith she'd come to have in him. She looked at his face, dark eyes blazing into hers, one last time, then crouched low and made a dash to the toolshed. She didn't pause, but yanked the door open and ducked inside. Then she peered back toward the house to see how Al was doing, and caught her breath.

He gave a hop, reaching overhead to catch hold of a tree limb. Then he swung back and forth, faster and faster, his body sailing higher into the air each time, and finally, on the biggest upswing yet, he just let go.

His momentum carried him higher, and he flipped in midair before catching hold of the edge of the flat, tar-coated roof. Carefully, he pulled himself up and crept toward the widow's walk at the center.

M.C. couldn't believe it. He could have broken his neck. Shivering, she glanced through the shed's dusty window toward the guys in the car, but they hadn't moved. Didn't seem as if they'd noticed a thing amiss.

She flicked the lighter to see in the darkness and foraged for the tools she needed. It didn't take long to find them. She let the lighter go out, pocketed the shears and the tape, and carried the length of hose in one hand. As an afterthought she pulled out her gun with the other. Just in case. Then she crept out of the shed and across the lawn, keeping low, using the hedges for cover. When she ran out of hedges, she dropped to the ground and crawled right up to the car, which the fools had left running. Hadn't anyone ever told them how dangerous that could be? She ripped off some tape with her teeth, stuck the hose into the exhaust pipe, and wrapped it up tight. Then she took the other end of the hose with her as she wriggled on her back underneath the car. Right under the driver's seat, she found the air vent, and she stuck the hose right there.

Then she shimmied out again and made her way to the back-yard, all without once being seen.

She smiled to herself. She was good.

But Al was better.

When she looked up she saw a length of rope dangling from a hidden corner of the roof. He'd left her a way inside.

What a guy.

When she crept down the attic stairs, praying none would creak and give her away, she wished to heaven she knew where everyone was. She got to the second-floor hall and started down it on tiptoe, passing each closed bedroom door with her ears straining and her heart in her throat.

Then one opened just as she moved past, and she was pulled in-side. A big hand covered her mouth, and the room was utterly dark. She struggled . . . but briefly. That wide chest behind her; that scent. She stilled, waiting. The hand left her mouth, and she whis-pered, "Al?"

"*Oui, ma chérie.* Who else?"

"Did you find them? Is my aunt all right?"

"She is fine. In the next bedroom. De Rocci is with her. As far as I can tell there are two others in the house, one at the front door, one at the back. It would be best if we could eliminate them at the same time."

"That way neither has time to warn the other."

"Or to warn de Rocci," Al said. "The men in the car?"

"They'll be sleeping by the time we get downstairs." She couldn't see his frown, but knew it was there, all the same. "I'll ex-plain later. Trust me, Al, they're not going to be a problem."

"I do trust you," he said. "It is odd, being in battle with a woman at my side. But even more strange to feel so certain she is equal to the task. You are . . . you are a special woman, Mary Catherine."

"Glad you realize it," she said. "Now let's get this show on the road."

"I'll take the back door," he told her. And she had no doubt he'd already checked the two men out, and decided the guy by the back door was bigger, or meaner, or more dangerous. Not that she minded.

"Let's make it quick and quiet, okay?" She didn't wait for an answer. "Meet you at the bottom of the stairs." Then she ducked out the door and headed down.

Al came behind her, and he squeezed her hand at the base of the stairs before they turned in opposite directions. M.C. drew her gun and crept into the living room. It was dim, but not all that dark, despite the fact that the lights were all out and the curtains drawn tight. She could see the guy fairly well. He was looking outside, expecting visitors from there, not from within. She crept closer, lifting her gun. She was almost right behind him when she heard a dull thud, a low grunt from the back of the house, followed by what had to be a body slumping to the floor. The goon heard it, too, and spun. But she clocked him with the pistol butt before he came to a stop, and he sank to the floor like a limp noodle. M.C. pocketed the gun, yanked out the duct tape, and used it to tie him up. A little more over the mouth. Perfect.

She headed back to the stairway and met Al at the bottom. "Done?" he asked.

"*Fini,*" she replied. He grinned at her and they took the stairs together. "Now what?"

"Now, I go back to the roof, and you to the door of your aunt's room."

"Ah, we enter from two directions."

Al nodded. "But take care. Do not stand directly in front of the door, Mary Catherine. I've no desire to lose you now."

She caught her breath. Silly thing for him to say. He'd be going back when this was over. Losing her was inevitable. She gave her head a shake to rid herself of that thought. "Don't worry. I've done this sort of thing once or twice."

He nodded, and headed up the attic stairs. She gave him a minute to get into position, then strode up to her aunt's bedroom door and, standing to one side of it, reached out and knocked.

"What is it?" de Rocci growled.

"Mr. de Rocci? It's M. C. Hammer. I brought that tape like you said."

She heard footsteps coming nearer, a voice cussing. "What the hell—how did you—?" The door was flung open. De Rocci stood there, gun in hand, looking up and down the hall. "Where are my men?"

"They sent me up," she said. She hoped she sounded convincing.

De Rocci eyed her, glancing beyond her nervously, and finally gripped her arm, pulled her into the bedroom, and closed the door behind her. She had a brief moment to notice her aunt, tied to a chair in one corner, a gag over her mouth. The poor thing was wide-eyed with fear. But then all hell broke loose. De Rocci pointed his gun at M.C., yanked her weapon from her waistband, and demanded, "Give me the tape!" Before she could react, the window behind him shattered as Al swung through it like some kind of superhero.

Al landed in a ready crouch, his sword appearing in his hand so suddenly that she never saw him draw it. De Rocci whirled and fired. Aunt Kate sent a fierce look at his gun and muttered something from behind her gag. It was all over in a heartbeat. The bullet slammed into Al like a sledgehammer, knocking him to the floor. His sword skidded across the hardwood, bumping M.C.'s feet and stopping there, and before de Rocci could turn around, she had that baby in her hand. But she hesitated, trying to remember what the hell to do with it. De Rocci's weapon was aiming at her as her fist clenched on the cool hilt.

And Al yelled, as if through grated teeth, "Parry! Dodge! Thrust!"

She sliced de Rocci's gun hand, and he dropped the weapon, cursing furiously. He lunged forward to retrieve it, but she lashed his rear end with the flat side of the blade, and he went sprawling on his face.

Al grabbed the fallen gun and held it on de Rocci. "Enough," Al managed. "It is over."

"Al!" M.C. dropped to her knees where he was. He'd pulled himself into a sitting position. His shirt was soaked in blood. She reached for him.

"Not yet, *chérie*. Untie your aunt, and use the ropes to bind de Rocci tight. Do it now. Hurry."

She nodded, understanding his urgency. He was going to lose consciousness soon, and he wanted to know she was safe before he did. She rapidly untied her aunt's hands and feet. "Are you all right, Aunt Kate? Did he hurt you?"

Kate nodded yes, then shook her head no, then reached up to undo the gag while M.C. rushed across the room to truss Guido de Rocci up like a Christmas goose. When he started cussing at her, she pulled the duct tape and smacked a strip across his mouth. "You're going down, de Rocci," she told him. "For a long, long time!"

There was a thud behind her and she turned, her heart aching as she saw Al lying on the floor, limp and unconscious. She ran to him, fell to her knees again, and yanked the T-shirt up and the Kevlar vest open so she could see the damage.

"Don't panic, Mary Catherine. The bullet didn't hit his heart," her aunt said softly. "It was headed that way, but I managed to give it a nudge."

M.C. frowned when she saw Al's wounds but didn't avert her eyes. She tried to wipe the blood away to see the injury better. "What are you talking about? What nudge?"

"Don't forget who I am, Mary Catherine," Aunt Kate said. "I

pushed the bullet upward. So it would only hit his shoulder, the fleshy part, if my aim was any good."

"Al doesn't have any 'fleshy parts.' " Dabbing more blood away, M.C. caught her breath. Her aunt was absolutely right. The bullet had gone into his shoulder. She pushed a cloth tight to the wound to stop the bleeding. "I can't believe it," she muttered.

"How can you still doubt? M.C., you managed to conjure yourself a Musketeer, and you still don't believe in magic?"

M.C. stroked Al's face with one hand, pressing a cloth to the wound with the other. "If there were really such a thing as magic . . . ," she whispered.

"What, Mary Catherine? Tell me."

She closed her eyes. "He'd stay."

But he wouldn't stay. It was over now, and she was safe. And it would soon be time for Al to return to his own time. His own duties. His own life. M.C.'s eyes burned inexplicably, and her stomach churned, and her heart felt as if it was breaking just a little bit.

"Call the police, will you, Aunt Kate? And the D.A. And an ambulance for Al."

Aunt Kate nodded, reaching for the phone. "We won't need the ambulance though. A scratch like that we can tend right here." M.C. opened her mouth, but her aunt shook a finger. "Don't you go doubting me again, young lady."

Lowering her head, M.C. sighed. "I won't."

# Chapter 10

Between the two of them, Aunt Kate and M.C. managed to get Al into the bed. He came around while they were doing it, argued a bit, but finally resigned himself to submitting. He was outnumbered anyway. Sirens were screaming closer by the second, so at least de Rocci and his goon squad wouldn't be sitting around the house much longer.

M.C. rolled her eyes and shook her head a lot when Aunt Kate used one of her concoctions on Al's wound, but the stuff seemed to stop the bleeding almost immediately.

Frowning, she leaned over the jar and sniffed. "What's in that stuff, anyway?"

"Some healing herbs, disinfectant, and cobwebs, dear. Now run into the bathroom and bring me some gauze and tape."

"Cobwebs?" M.C. asked with a gasp.

Al, who'd been lying back on the pillows, sat up a little, eyes widening with alarm. "Cobwebs?" he echoed.

Aunt Kate sighed heavily. "Fine, I'll get the bandages myself." And with a huff she headed off to the bathroom.

M.C. sat down on the edge of the bed, and instinctively stroked Al's dark hair away from his forehead. "Are you really okay?"

His mischievous grin appeared to reassure her, though she could still see the pain reflected in his eyes. "I have been far more grievously wounded than this, and survived, Mary Catherine. But if you wish to sit there and worry for me, I won't object." With his uninjured arm, he reached up, ran his hand slowly over her cheek. "You are beautiful when you are worried."

She lowered her eyes. "You never give up, do you, Al?"

"Never. And now, *chérie,* you are no longer under my protection."

She met his gaze, let him see for once that she felt the same way he did. "Unfortunately, you're lying in bed with a hole in your shoulder at the moment."

"It is of little importance. I will not be using my *shoulder, ma petite.*" His fingertips danced over her temple, and she shivered.

Licking her lips, she noted, "We have an audience."

Then there were footsteps thundering up the stairs, and the bedroom door burst open. Uniformed officers lunged inside, weapons drawn.

"And more arriving all the time, *non?*"

"Afraid so," M.C. said. Then she turned to face the cops. "You can put those down. The bad guys are gift-wrapped and waiting for delivery." And she nodded toward de Rocci even as she was reaching into her pocket for the tape. "That one's the baddest of the bunch, and this tape will prove it."

Holstering his gun, the first officer stepped forward. Another came behind him. "You'd best run outside and check on the two in the car. I don't think the carbon monoxide has killed them yet, but . . ."

The second cop was gone before she could finish. The first one reached for the tape, but M.C. pulled it back. "I'd just as soon put this in the D.A.'s hands myself, if it's all the same to you."

$\mathcal{T}$he two in the car were hauled away by ambulance, while the others were taken in the backs of police cars. D.A. Hennesey insisted M.C. come with him, but she shook her head.

"I'm not going anywhere until I make sure Al's okay."

The D.A., a short, balding man with wire rims that made him look more like an accountant than a crime fighter, nodded. "I understand that, Ms. Hammer, but this is necessary."

"No it isn't. You have the tape."

"And de Rocci has other men in his employ, if all you've told me is true. Once we get your statement on the record, he'll have no reason to send them after you."

"No reason but revenge, you mean."

The D.A.'s brows went up. "Well, yes, there is that."

"I'm not afraid of him." She glanced at Al, sitting up in the bed now and sipping some brew Aunt Kate had whipped up, while Kate sat in a chair beside him to make sure he took every drop.

"Go with Monsieur Hennesey, Mary Catherine," Al urged. "I want you safe."

She frowned.

"I will be fine," he promised.

"And I'll see to it he is," Aunt Kate said. "Go on, honey, get this over with. We have things to do, you know." This with a meaningful glance at Al.

Things to do. Right. They had to send Al back. Holding his gaze for a long moment, M.C. said, "Don't do anything without me, okay? I want to have a chance to say . . ." She couldn't say the last word. Good-bye. It was too final. Too sudden. She didn't want to say it now. Maybe . . . maybe not ever.

Al's eyes darkened as they held hers—almost as if he were reading her thoughts. "I will be here waiting when you return, little one. I promise you."

Nodding hard, blinking at the burning behind her eyes, M.C. turned to the D.A. "All right, let's get this over with."


$\mathcal{I}$t took forever, or at least it seemed like it did. By the time M.C. got out of the local police department where the D.A. took her statement, it was well after dark. Big, black clouds had rolled in so that not a single star was visible in the sky. Matched her mood, she thought. She figured by the time she got back, Aunt Kate would have everything ready for Al's return trip. She'd have found the right spell in that big book of hers, and she'd have gathered up whatever obscure herbs or glittery crystals or eye of newt they might need.

Pausing at the front door, M.C. took out the photo she'd snapped of Al that first night. She'd been carrying it with her ever since. She stared down at his face, traced his shape with her finger, and wasn't surprised when a teardrop fell from her cheek to land upon his image.

Sniffling, she tucked the photo away, and opened the front door.

The first thing she saw when she walked inside were the candles. Two rows of tall, elegant taper candles formed a path across the floor. They alternated in color, pink and red. She'd never seen so many candles all lighted at once.

She figured it must be part of whatever ritual Aunt Kate had devised.

Then the scent wafted up to tickle her nostrils, and she glanced downward. Rose petals littered the floor like confetti between the two rows of candles.

Frowning, M.C. took off her shoes, shrugged out of her jacket, and stepped onto the silky-soft path. "Aunt Kate?" she called.

No answer. But the candle-and-rose-petal path led up the stairs. And as she followed it, she heard soft music.

Lord, but this must be one complicated spell! At the top of the stairs, the path continued down the hall, and turned, going right through the open door of the guest room. "Where is everybody?" M.C. asked. Still no answer.

She moved on, into the guest room.

Candles glowed from every surface. The entire bedroom floor and the bed itself were cushioned with the tender petals. And a vase stood beside the bed with a dozen deep red buds nodding from their long, slender stalks.

And then Al came out of the shadows and crossed the room toward her. He stopped right in front of her, drew his sword, dropped to one knee, and held the weapon balanced on his upturned palms. Head bowed, he lifted it. "My gift to you, my lady," he murmured. Then he laid it at her feet. Taking her hand in both of his, he pressed his lips to her palm. His kiss was warm, and wet, and it left her skin tingling.

And suddenly she understood. This was it, the grand seduction. The one she'd been waiting for, dreaming of, wanting, since she'd first met him. But the pleasure of her surprise was dampened by the knowledge that this was also his way of saying good-bye.

She shook that thought away as he rose, still clinging to her hand. They'd have this. They'd have this one night, to remember.

"Aunt Kate?" she asked softly.

"Out for the evening," he replied, his voice low, tender, almost a caress in itself.

"And all of this?" She waved a hand to encompass the room.

He cupped her face between his palms. "For you," he told her. "All this . . . and more, were it mine to give."

"You certainly do know how to treat a lady." It was meant to sound flippant, light. But her voice trembled instead.

"No, *ma chérie*. I have never wished to treat any lady the way I wish to treat you. I swear it on my sword."

She blinked, her eyes burning again.

"Mary Catherine . . . ," he began.

"No," she said quickly. "Don't say any more. I hate crying, Al, and you're putting me damned close to it."

"But why?"

Why? Because she didn't want to let him go, dammit! He was the first man who'd ever made her feel this way, and she knew she'd never feel it for any other. Why, when the unthinkable had finally happened to her, did it have to be with a man who couldn't stay? How could she vow never to fall in love and then do just that, when she knew it was impossible?

*Fall in love.*

Oh, God, that was exactly what she'd done!

"Mary Catherine?" His eyes searched her face.

She blinked away her shock, shook her head, and slid her arms around his waist. "Shut up and kiss me already."

He smiled. Devilish, that smile of his. Then he pulled her close, and kissed her thoroughly. His mouth worked hers, his tongue probed and explored, and locked together, they stumbled toward the bed, and fell onto its nest of rose petals.

Al never stopped kissing her as he tugged and pulled at her clothes, removing them one by one. His mouth traveled. Over her jaw, down to her throat, and lower. He muttered in French as he mouthed her breasts, and then her belly, and then her thighs. Sweet, erotic endearments, nearly as arousing as his touch.

She struggled with his clothes, too, until he pulled her into his arms without a stitch between them, and proceeded to make love to her more sweetly than she'd ever imagined possible.

And when her climax mingled with his, and she whispered his name, she knew she loved him even more now than she had before.

What, oh what, was she ever going to do without him?

They lay twined together for a long time as the candles burned low, Al stroking her hair, her back, holding her close and tenderly in his arms. But finally, he sat up a bit, looked down at her almost adoringly, and whispered, "It is time, *chérie*."

"I know," she whispered, and she couldn't keep her feelings in check any longer. M. C. Hammer, tough-as-nails lady detective, began to cry.

"Mary Catherine! What is wrong?"

She sniffled, tried to stop the tears, but failed. The touch of his gentle fingers on her damp cheeks only made her cry even harder. "I—I'm sorry, Al. I just . . . I just wish you didn't have to go."

"Go? Go? But my love, I thought you understood!"

She blinked, staring up at him. "Understood . . . what?"

"I gave you my sword. Sweet Mary Catherine, with it goes my heart. I told you once that I would only give up my sword for the woman who would be my true love, did I not?"

Shaking her head slowly, she stared at him.

"I love you, Lady Hammer. And love is more important than anything else. More important than life or death . . . or time itself. I will die before I will leave you, my love . . . if . . ." He searched her face, then turned his gaze away.

"If?" she prompted.

"If you feel the same," he told her softly, not looking at her, almost as if he were afraid to look at her.

Her heart swelled until she thought it would burst, and she ran one hand through his satin hair. "Oh, I do," she whispered. "Al, I really, really do. I love you."

He turned to meet her eyes, his wide and brimming. "Ah, *ma chérie,* do you mean it?"

She nodded hard. "But Al, can you really stay? Are you sure you want to?"

"I would live upon the moon itself, if it meant I could be at your side, my love." He kissed her, long and lingeringly. Then holding her nestled against his chest, he continued. "I have no ties to the past that would require my return. Your Aunt Kate said the decision to stay or to go was mine. And you yourself told me my gold coins are worth a fortune, Mary Catherine, so I can make my way."

"Oh, I have a few ideas about how you can earn a living, Al. You're not without certain job skills, you know."

"No?"

She nibbled his chin. "You sure you won't mind having a Witch in the family?" she asked him.

"If you can tolerate a Musketeer as a husband, then I can withstand a Witch as an aunt," he whispered.

M.C. blinked. "H—husband?"

"*Oui*. If you will have me."

Her smile was slow, but straight from the heart. "You'd better believe I will. And Al, there's another partnership I have in mind for us. Besides marriage, I mean."

"Oh, is there?"

She nodded. "Umm-hmm. But . . . um . . . we can talk about that in the morning." She pressed closer to him, curled her arms around his strong shoulders, and pulled him to her for another kiss.

"Very late in the morning," he whispered, and he held her even tighter.

# Epilogue

Alexandre held his wife close to his side as they stood outside the door of her office in Newark. She'd told him her wedding gift to him was waiting here, though to his way of thinking, she'd already given him the gift of a lifetime just by agreeing to be his.

He was slowly getting used to this modern world. Everything moved quickly, too quickly at times, but with Mary Catherine at his side, he could adapt to anything.

He loved her. Adored her, and knew he would never regret his decision to remain at her side. He'd searched for a woman like her all his life. One who would love him for the man he was, rather than the colors he wore or the sword he carried. He'd had to travel through time to find her, but find her he had. And he would never, never let her go.

She squeezed his waist and smiled up at him. "Here it is," she said, and there was laughter in her voice.

"Where?" Alexandre asked her, looking up and down the hallway in which they stood. He saw nothing but the office door.

"There," she said, pointing.

He looked to where she pointed, seeing only a strip of white across the glass panel of the door.

"Go on, peel the tape away."

Frowning, Al leaned forward, got hold of one edge of the sticky white paper—"tape"; he vowed to remember all these new words—and peeled it slowly away.

Underneath the stuff, he read the words newly painted upon the glass, and smiled, his heart filling until he thought it would burst.

TWO MUSKETEERS INVESTIGATIONS
ONE FOR ALL, AND ALL FOR ONE!

# The Con
## and the Crusader

# Prologue

*Jack* McCain pulled the last weed in his grandma's vegetable patch and wiped the dirt off his hands on the seat of his pants.

"Good job, young man," Grandma said from her perch on the front porch. "Now you can have that ice cream I promised you."

Jack sighed. "I don't see why I couldn't have had it before."

"Because you hadn't earned it before. Now you have. It's what I keep telling you, boy. Hard work pays off. A lazy man will never get ahead in life."

"Ahh, phooey." Jack climbed up the front steps. His back ached and he thought he might wind up with blisters on his fingers by morning. "I'm never gonna do hard work when I grow up. I'm gonna use my brains, and make a fortune, and never pull a weed again."

Grandma got to her feet with an effort, and held the screen door open. Jack went inside and headed to the kitchen to wash his hands while Grandma dished up the ice cream.

"You'll find," she said as she set two dishes on the table, "that hard work can be its own reward. Why, when you see those vegetables growing, don't you feel awfully good about yourself? Knowing you had a hand in them? When we pick a fresh tomato off the vine, don't you feel—"

"All I feel is that it would've been a heck of a lot easier to buy a tomato at the A&P." Jack dried his hands on a towel and sat down at the table, almost too tired to enjoy the ice cream now, he thought glumly.

"Oh, you have so much to learn, boy," Grandma said. "Just how do you plan to get ahead in life if you aren't willing to work for it? Hmm?"

Jack shrugged, shoveled a spoonful of ice cream into his mouth, and decided he wasn't too tired to enjoy it after all. "I don't know. If I could find that wishin' well you're always talkin' about, I'd wish myself a million dollars and then I'd pay someone to do the weeding."

His grandma clicked her tongue and shook her head. "That well only appears to people when they truly need its magic . . . people who are deserving. So the legend goes, anyway."

"Well, I need it," Jack moaned. "Look at my hands!" He held one palm up for his grandma's inspection, while scooping up another bite with his free hand.

"But even so," Grandma went on, "the wishes aren't free. You have to earn them just like anything else in life. There's a stone beside that well. My grandmother saw it once, and she memorized the words that were engraved there, and told them to me, and I've told them to you."

"Yeah, yeah," Jack said, rolling his eyes and knowing Grandma was about to recite the old poem yet again. She never got sick of telling her crazy wishing-well stories.

And sure enough, she did. In her singsong voice that was reserved only for reading bedtime stories or poems.

"Make a wish upon this well, but wishes don't come free.
Make a promise here, as well, and your wish you will see.
A voyage will you take then, your promise to fulfill.
And when you've kept your vow, I shall appear here on this
   hill.
With one more wish to grant you, one more gift to bestow.
Any wish you care to make; to stay, perhaps, or go."


Grandma got a sappy look in her eye as she recited the verse.
Jack just finished his ice cream and shook his head. He didn't even
think that well was real. He'd looked for it time and time again, but
he'd never found it. Well, it didn't matter. He was smart. He had the
gift of gab, his grandma said. He could talk anyone into doing just
about anything. Why, just last week he'd conned Mary Ellen Mc-
Madden into doing his math homework for him.

Nope, Jack McCain wasn't going to spend his life pulling weeds
or getting dirty. He vowed it. Wishing well or no wishing well, he'd
make his fortune, and he'd make it without working his tail off for
it, too!

# Chapter 1

$\mathcal{I}$t wouldn't have been all that uncomfortable without the hand-cuffs. Jack had no doubt whatsoever they were little more than a prop being used for effect. To drive home a point.

"So really, guys, who put you up to this?" he said, smiling his most winning smile at the backs of their crew cuts. The two cops in the front seat didn't seem to notice. "I mean, it's obviously a joke, right?"

"Sam, did you tell this clown he had the right to remain silent?" one crew cut said to the other.

"Sure did."

"Hmph. Wouldn't know it, would you?"

"Nope."

"Aw, come on, guys, gimme a break." His spotless Armani suit was picking up lint from the seat, and he shuddered to think where that lint might have come from.

"You've had all the breaks you're getting, pal. You've run your last con."

"That's bull! For cryin' out loud, guys, I gave up conning the upstanding citizens of Hillcrest a long time ago. I've gone straight, and you know it."

"Right." One of the cops turned in his seat. "Now you only con drug lords."

"Yeah," said the other. "And organized crime bosses, right?"

He shrugged and tried not to look too sheepish. It was true, he'd turned the confidence game into an art form, and he'd swindled some major bucks out of some big-time criminals. But it wasn't like they couldn't afford it.

"Beats digging ditches for a living," he said, admitting nothing.

"You never were one to want to get your hands dirty."

The cops exchanged a glance, a nod, and all of a sudden the cruiser slowed and pulled off to the shoulder. The two cops turned in the seat to look back at him. And he would have loosened his collar if his hands hadn't been cuffed behind his back. It was getting damned warm in this car. And they were basically in the middle of nowhere. Not a house for a mile in either direction, and he knew that, because he'd grown up in one of them. His grandmother's run-down farm house, abandoned now. He hadn't been back there since she'd died and the government had taken it for back taxes. Dear old Grandma. She used to say there was a wishing well around here somewhere. One that really granted wishes.

A fairy tale to give a lonely kid hope, that's all her stories were. You didn't get what you wanted by wishing for it, or by working your fingers to the bone for it the way she had, either. You got it by using your brains, and going out, and taking it from those who had it in spades.

"What's this," he asked, and he tried not to sound nervous. "You gonna rough me up now? Should I be hoping for a passerby with a camcorder?"

The cop named Sam smiled, shaking his head. "We have you

cold, Jack. You know that, right? That swampland you sold to Arturo, the phony stock sales, all of it. We can make this bust stick."

Jack only shrugged. "I can't imagine a judge and jury feeling too vindictive against me for picking on poor, defenseless kingpins like Arturo," he said. "Not that I'm saying I did."

"Like I said, we can make it stick. But we don't have to."

Jack's attention was caught and he looked up slowly.

"We can help each other out," the cop went on. "You give us a hand with our little problem, and uh, we'll see what we can do about yours."

"You want to make a deal with me," he said slowly, finally understanding what this little bust was all about. "But what do I have that you could possibly want—"

"Oh, come on Jack. You know damn well what you have. We've been trying to bust Arturo for months, but he's slicker than Satan. Slicker than *you*, even."

"You can give us names," said the other cop. "Dates, places, times. Where he's been, who he's been talking to."

"Yeah," Jack said. "Right. And get my head blown off an hour later. No thanks, guys. I think I'll take my chances with whatever trumped-up charges you can think up to try to pin on me."

Sam shrugged, shaking his head slowly. "Thing is, Jackie, my boy, that's liable to happen either way."

"Huh?"

"Well . . . we got leaks. I mean, we do what we can, but it happens, you know? So chances are, Arturo already knows you've been picked up. And my guess is he knows why."

Jack was silent for a long moment. Then he said simply, "Shit."

"You cooperate with us, we'll keep you in protective custody until he's safely behind bars, my friend. You don't . . . well, we'll take you downtown, spend a couple of hours questioning you, and then turn you loose."

"In full view of anyone who cares to be watching." Jack could fill it all in pretty easily. "Anyone being Arturo, who'll figure I spilled everything I knew, and pop me at the first opportunity."

"Gee, do you really think he'd do that?"

"Sarcasm doesn't become you, Sam."

"So? You gonna tell us what you know?"

Jack sighed, shook his head, and glanced behind him for about the fifth time. "I don't think I'm going to get the chance to, fellas." He said it calmly. He was noted for keeping a cool demeanor under any circumstances—wise-cracking his way through life-and-death struggles, interrogations, death threats. He was also known for making a lot of money without lifting a finger. It had been his goal for as long as he could remember to get rich without working for it. Grandma always told him he'd have to pay the piper some day. Looked like that day had arrived.

The dark sedan that had been a discreet distance behind them sped up, closing the gap.

"Shit," Sam said. "We've got a tail."

"Gee, do you think?" Jack asked, just as another car suddenly pulled across the road in front of them. The two cops drew their guns, and Sam grabbed the mike with his free hand and started yelling for backup. Four goons in very nice suits and very dark glasses got out of their vehicles with automatic weapons.

"Jesus, forget the damn radio and gimme the keys to these cuffs!" For once, Jack's coolness deserted him. Sam tossed a set of keys into the backseat. By the time Jack turned ass backwards to snag them in his cuffed hands, the bullets had started flying, and he ducked low. He heard glass shatter, a dull grunt, constant blasting, but none coming from within the car. He lifted his head just long enough to see what he wished he hadn't. The two cops in the front were full of more holes than Swiss cheese, and the bad guys were approaching from the driver's side of the car. He ducked again. There was no time to unlock himself. Just to stuff the keys into a back pocket, wrench open the passenger-side door at his back, and roll through it into the ditch at the roadside.

He hit the ground, got up, and dug in. Running for all he was worth, hoping the maniacs didn't see him, he ducked into the nearby woods.

Shouts, gunshots, and running footsteps followed.

Shit. They'd seen him, all right. And they were thundering after him, even now.

His grandma had been right. Crime didn't pay, and dammit, this was a fine time for him to realize it. These guys meant *business*. Deadly business.

They were gaining on him. Tough to run very fast with your hands trussed up behind your back, and roots leaping up to trip you every few feet. A bullet whirred past his ear, and he spotted what looked like a curving stone wall just ahead, mostly overgrown with vines and brambles. Cover. It wasn't much, but if he dove beyond it, it might block a few bullets. Buy him another second or two of life.

He ran full tilt, reached the little wall, and dove headfirst over it.

Only, it wasn't a wall. He figured that out when he didn't hit the ground on the other side. It was a well. And he was plummeting down into inky darkness, and no bottom in sight.

If the landing didn't kill him, the bad guys would. No way out. "God, don't let me end up like this. If I had one more chance, I'd work for a living. I swear I would. Get me out of this one and I'll prove it. I'll work harder than I ever have in my life! Honest, I will!"

His only answer was a powerful thud when he hit the bottom.

# Chapter 2

Emily Hawkins wiped the sweat from her brow, and eyed the unplowed ground that stretched out in front of her. She'd been driving the damn mule all morning, and had little more to show for it than an aching back and a few crooked furrows.

So far, her experiment was failing. But failure was not something she could tolerate easily. Nor would she. If it killed her she would raise a crop, sell the grain, and make the final mortgage payment on time. She would. Oh, no one else believed it. Everyone in this town had urged her to sell the farm before her husband was even buried. And when she'd told them all that she intended to keep it, to run it herself, and make that payment rather than sell it for the criminally low offers her neighbors and local banker had made on the place, they'd laughed at her.

*Laughed!* At *her*!

"Well, we'll just see who's laughing when I've finished!" she huffed, and yelled again at the mule. "Come on, Molly! We've work to do!"

"Aunt Emily?"

She stopped what she was doing and turned to see her precious ones, Sarah Jane and Matthew, staring up at her. Beyond them, one hand on either shoulder, stood Mary Brightwater, the local schoolteacher.

"Your children are wanting their lunch, Mrs. Hawkins."

Emily bit her tongue before she could tell the schoolmarm to mind her own business. "I was just on my way."

Mary was clean and shiny, yellow hair spilling from beneath her pretty bonnet. Young, fresh. She made Emily feel like a dirt-covered crone.

"I'll be happy to help," Mary said with a youthful smile, sunlight glinting in her hair.

"I can manage just fine," Emily replied, taking a small hand in each of hers. Then, remembering her manners, "But you're welcome to join us, if you like."

"I would, thank you. I've been wanting a word with you, you know."

Emily crooked a brow, certain she was about to be on the receiving end of yet another lecture on a woman's place, and the futility of her efforts. As a foursome, they trekked across the wide-open expanse, down the slight incline to the pretty white clapboard farmhouse beyond. There was a well in front, its pump handle freshly painted. And a small barn off to the left, in need of a new coat itself. But there were only so many hours in the day. The wide front porch was swept clean and the house was in order, though. Sarah Jane and Matthew raced ahead. Emily watched Sarah's auburn braids flying behind her, and thought again that she would do anything, *anything*, to keep this place for the children. They'd lost so much already. . . .

The children played outdoors while Emily prepared lunch, and despite her insistence that she needed no help, Mary pitched in anyway.

"Mrs. Hawkins . . . Emily," Mary began as they sliced cheese and bread that wasn't quite as light as it should have been. Oh, how Emily missed the days when she'd had time enough to cook a proper meal. "May I call you that? I hope you don't mind my speaking plainly to you. I know it's not my place to advise you, but I feel I must."

Emily closed her eyes and sighed. "Say what you will. But know that I will not be swayed."

"I'll say it then. You simply cannot continue trying to run this farm and raise these children on your own."

Emily met Mary's eyes straight on. "I shall tell you what I've told everyone else. I have no choice." She went to the window and looked out at the children playing in the yard. "Look at them, Mary. They lost their mother when they were almost too young to know her."

"Your sister was a fine woman," Mary said. "Everyone thought so."

"Yes, and no one thought I could ever fill her shoes. But I have. I came here and cared for those two as if they were my own. I married my sister's husband to halt the town gossips pecking about how improper it was for us to be living together as we were. I love them. And I would do anything for them."

"You've more than proven that."

"Now that Clem is gone, I'll take his place as well. I can do this, I know I can."

"It's too much for one woman. Any woman, even you."

The words sounded almost like a compliment, but Emily thought her ears must be deceiving her.

"Look at you, Emily. You've grown thin, you have dark circles under your eyes, no doubt from lack of sleep. And your hands." As she spoke she gripped Emily's wrist and turned her palm up. "Lordy, when these blisters break you'll be unable to grip a wooden spoon, much less the reins of that mule."

Emily pulled her hand free, turning away. She could not admit defeat. She *would not*. "So what do you suggest? That I give up? That I let this place go to the bank for lack of one final payment?"

"No. I don't suggest that at all."

Emily turned around to stare at the young woman. "You don't?"

Mary shook her head. "I am aware that's what everyone else has been telling you to do, Emily, but I've seen enough of you to know you're not the type to do things the easy way. Nor to give up easily. And moreover, if there is any woman who could achieve this, you are she. In fact, I *want* to see you succeed."

"You do?" Emily was bewildered.

Mary nodded. "I've never known a woman as strong as you are, Emily. And I'd dearly love to see you prove once and for all that the men of this town are wrong. I simply have a suggestion for you. One which I think would make things a good deal easier."

"My goodness." Emily had to blink away her shock. "I . . . I'm surprised."

"Sit," Mary said. "And try to keep an open mind."

Emily sat, and Mary poured coffee into two tin cups, then brought them to the table and took a seat of her own. "Emily," she said, "what you need to enable you to bring in the crop and keep this farm, is a man."

Emily's shoulders slumped. "I had so hoped you would have a *plausible* suggestion." She sighed. "I've no time for courtship, nor flirting, nor fixing my hair in hopes of enticing some man into wedlock. I vow, Mary, I'm not the sort of woman a man would want anyway."

"You're joking, surely. Why, Emily, I can name a dozen men who would break their legs racing to the altar for you!"

Emily met her eyes. "For my land, you mean. For this farm."

Mary's eyes widened. "Is that what you truly believe?"

"It's what I know. I am a thirty-five-year-old widow with two children to raise. I've carrot-hued hair that refuses to be tamed, and since I've begun running this farm I've become hard in all the places a woman should be soft. My hands are callused, my face is sun-burned. Please, need I go on?"

Mary only shook her head as if in disbelief. Very polite of her. "And I cannot afford to hire help just now," Emily continued.

"No, of course you can't. But . . ." Mary paused, licked her lips. "What if there were a way you could get a man to do the work around here without hiring one . . . or courting?"

Frowning over her cup, Emily looked up. "Whatever do you mean?"

"Emily, there is a statute still in effect in this town. I came upon it while teaching my class about local government and how it's run. The mayor gave us a look at the town's statutes. And that's when I saw it. It dates back fifteen years, to a time when Hillcrest seems to have had a severe shortage of . . . men."

"A man shortage?"

"Um-hmm. And with the prison nearby, men were being trans-ported through here all the time. So the law was written and passed by the town council, and then signed by the governor. Any single woman or widow who owns property may choose a prisoner to marry. The man goes right back to jail if he mistreats, dis-pleases, or tries to leave his bride. He has to agree to the terms she sets beforehand."

Emily felt her eyes widen; felt hope spring to life for the first time in months. But then she sighed and lowered her head. "It . . . it would be impossible. He'd expect . . . certain . . . things . . ." She met Mary's eyes again. "With Clem, it was different. We were Anna's sister and Anna's husband, bound together for the sake of Anna's children. We were friends, and helpmates, but never . . . never husband and wife. Not . . . not *really*."

"I see."

"Of course . . . I suppose if I could find a prisoner who could never possibly be interested in . . . in such things . . ."

Mary sighed. "All men are interested in . . . such things."

"I mean with me. Suppose I were to get one older than me?"

"Men love younger women."

"A lot older, I mean."

Mary tilted her head. "You want him to be strong enough to work, don't you?"

"Mmm, that's true. Younger, then. Yes, that's it! I'll find one so young he wouldn't dream of . . . of *such things* . . . with a woman of my age."

"Oh, now we're getting there! It will positively scandalize the entire town!" Mary said this as if it were a good thing.

"And it isn't as if it would be impossible. I'm hardly attractive."

"Oh, Emily, this will drive Mr. Sheldon absolutely mad!"

Emily lowered her eyes to hide the flash of anger in them. "Sometimes I think he only holds that mortgage over my head to force me into accepting his marriage proposal. I hate to be so suspicious of him, but . . . well, he *is* a banker."

"Never mind him. Go fix yourself up, Emily! There's a whole group of prisoners due in this afternoon. I'll finish the children's lunch. Go on now. Go!"

"I hardly see why I need fix myself up at all."

Mary eyed her, then shook her head. "The prisoner has to agree to this too, you know. You mustn't scare him so badly he'd prefer serving his sentence to marrying you."

"Oh," Emily said, glancing down at her dirt-streaked dress. "All right, then. I suppose . . ." She turned to go to the well for water, and as she went, she asked herself just what she was thinking. But then, this might be the only way. "I can do this," she muttered, bolstering herself, raising her chin. "I can. I must. For the children."

\* \* \*

$\mathcal{J}ack$ shook himself, lifted his head, and realized that he was still alive. Then he realized something else, as well. He wasn't at the bottom of any well. In fact there was no well in sight. He thought he'd glimpsed it when he'd first opened his eyes, but when he looked again, there was nothing there.

And for just an instant his grandmother's wishing-well fairy tale had whispered through his mind. But that was ridiculous.

At any rate, there was no one shooting at him now. He was on a dusty road. A group of men were shuffling past him, all looking like extras from a cheap Western: unshaven and dusty, wearing faded jeans and tattered hats. Some wore leg-irons, some handcuffs, some both. At the front and rear some guys in antiquated prison guard uniforms strode along with rifles.

"What the hell . . . ?"

"Get up, fellow." A booted foot nudged him in the rib cage. "Come on, now. It ain't that long a walk."

"No, look, I'm not one of these—"

"I *said* get up." This time the fellow moved his rifle, just a little, enough to remind Jack it was there.

Jack got up. "Look, you're making a mistake. I'm not—"

"Back in line."

"But I don't belong in line. I just—"

Thud. The rifle butt drove into his belly hard enough to send the wind gusting out of him. He dragged in a breath when he could, and took his place in line, doubled over, but at least he was in line. Damn, but this was weird. Where the hell was he?

Up ahead a town came into view. Only it was more like a handful of buildings in the middle of nowhere. Little Town on the Prairie or something. The dirt track led to it, through it, and vanished. He'd freaking landed in nowhere land. "What the hell is this place?" he asked.

"Hillcrest. Prison's just up yonder."

"Hillcrest my ass." He looked, then looked again. There was nothing, no camera crew, not a vehicle in sight, but he could still swear he'd fallen into the middle of a movie set. He'd see Eastwood toting a six-shooter any minute, he was sure of it.

"Now, look'ere, Mr. Fancy-duds, I've had just about enough of your lip."

"Mr. Fancy-duds? Gee, you oughtta be on stage with witty lines like that, pal."

"I ain't yer pal." The guy spit on the ground. "But these other fellas in line will be, once you're all in prison together. Gee, you think they'll like you?"

Jack took a look at the filthy, smelly, oversized, dangerous-looking bunch of convicts around him, and wished for Arturo's gangsters again. "Listen, mister, I don't know what the hell this is, but there's been some kind of mistake. I don't belong here."

"Then how'd you git here? Fall down outta the sky?"

"I don't know." Jack felt dizzy and disoriented. He tried to go back over the last few minutes as he remembered them but they made no sense. Maybe he'd been shot after all, or hit his head when he fell into the well and this was just . . .

Wait a minute. The well. Grandma's *wishing well*?

Nah. Couldn't be. . . .

Maybe. He *had* sort of made a wish. *And* a promise. Hadn't he?

"Hold up there!" someone called.

Jack glanced ahead, saw a pair of horses galloping toward him, one pulling a . . . a buggy. With a fringe on top. Jesus H. . . . The other horse carried a rider wearing a badge.

"Look, I think I must have banged my head. *Hard.* Could you check?" he asked the ugly guard.

"You don't shaddup and *I'm* gonna bang your head." The guard looked toward the rider. "What is it, Sheriff?"

The sheriff dismounted and walked over to the now-halted

buggy, leaned inside to talk to someone Jack couldn't see, and came back out with some papers. "I uh . . ." The sheriff pushed his hat back and scratched his head. "Hillcrest has an arrangement with the prison. It uh . . . it goes back a ways, but it's still on the books and . . . well, I know this is highly irregular, but . . ." Shaking his head, he thrust a sheaf of papers into the guard's hand. The guard surprised Jack by being capable of reading them, then he looked up at the sheriff.

"You have *got* to be kiddin', Sheriff."

"It's the law," the sheriff said. "And she qualifies, and she's *insisting*."

Frowning, the guard sighed. "Well, the law's the law, I suppose. Is she *sure* about this?"

"There's no talking her out of it, I'm afraid," the sheriff replied.

The guard shook his head again. "So, uh . . . which one does she want?"

The sheriff went to the buggy, and came back again. "Ahem . . . er . . . which one is the youngest?"

The guard looked the prisoners over, rubbing his chin. "That would be Johnny over there. Twenty-one. Killed a family of seven and burned their house 'cause their wagon splashed mud on him one day."

The sheriff paled. Shaking his head, he walked to the buggy again. Then turned back. "How old's the odd-lookin' one?"

"Hey!" Jack said when they both looked at him. But they just waited. "Twenty-eight," he finally answered. "And I'm not odd-looking, and furthermore, I'd like to know just what the hell is—"

"She'll take him," the sheriff said.

"Now wait a minute! Who'll take me, and where, for Pete's sake, and—"

The guard shook out the papers. "Says here he has the right to refuse the offer."

"He'd have to be a raving fool. I mean, hell, man, look at the alternative." And with that the sheriff gazed up at a distant hillside, where the most grim-looking place on the planet loomed; gray stone, high walls, barbed wire, and armed guards in towers.

"That there is Hillcrest Prison, Mr. Fancy-duds," the ugly card said almost in Jack's ear. "And that's where yer headin' if you turn the lady down. Frankly, I hope you do. I'd like to see just how long a tenderfoot like you would last up there."

Jack shivered. "Look, guys, if you'd just tell me what the hell is going on here . . ."

"Town statute," the sheriff said. "Any land-owning female who is either single or widowed may, at her discretion, choose a prison-bound male to marry her—"

"*Marry?*"

"Yeah." The guard elbowed him in the ribs. "Trade one prison for another, eh pal?" Then he laughed so loud Jack could smell his breath.

"You can refuse, of course," the sheriff said. "But if you agree, you have to play by the rules. No beating her . . ."

"*Beating her?*"

". . . no consorting with lewd women, no drinkin', no gamblin', and you can't leave her, 'cause if you do, you go right back to prison. Got it?"

"Uh . . . yeah. Sure. But as I've been trying to tell this gentleman here, I'm not on my way to prison. I'm . . . I'm sort of lost, and I just stumbled onto this group of . . . er . . ."

"Right. In handcuffs."

Jack tugged, remembered, and felt the first stirrings of panic take hold. "But this isn't fair. Look, I really don't . . . I mean I wasn't . . ."

"I know it's an arcane law, son," the sheriff said. "Hell, it's fifteen years old, written back in seventy-five when the town was founded."

Jack pulled out of his panic long enough to note, "You can't even add, and they made you sheriff?"

"I can too add. Eighteen seventy-five plus fifteen is ninety, and that's exactly right. Eighteen ninety."

Jack blinked. Then he looked around him at all the others. "This is a joke. You guys are all in on it, and this is some kind of a—"

"Come 'ere and meet the widow Hawkins, son." The sheriff gripped his arm and tugged him over to the buggy. Then he rapped on the door. "Come on out, Miss Emily. Might as well get a good look at him and make sure about this. I mean, hell, he's not only way too young for you, he's slightly insane to boot. You sure about this?"

She was old? They wanted him to marry some old lady named Miss Emily? The widow Hawkins? Good God!

She peered out the window, but had a big bonnet on and a fan in front of her face. All he could see were a pair of eyes. Green eyes. And they didn't look like the eyes of an old lady, either. A few reddish wisps of hair had escaped the bonnet. Not gray, but a pretty color. Like a sunset.

She met his eyes, and her gaze locked with his for just a minute. She looked scared, nervous, and maybe a little embarrassed. And then she spoke in a deep, rich voice that sounded the way melting butter would sound if it could speak, he thought.

"I know this is very odd, sir. But I assure you, it's perfectly legal. And . . . and necessary. All I will expect from you is honest work," she said. "Nothing more."

And her eyes met his once again, a quick glance, filled with meaning. "Nothing more," he repeated, getting the message loud and clear. "You sure you want a husband, lady? Sounds more like you need a hired hand."

"If I could afford a hand, sir, do you think I would be opening my home to a criminal?"

"I am *not* a—"

"It's either me, or prison, sir. So are you going to get into this buggy or continue walking with your . . . companions?"

He glanced back at the guys he'd be rooming with at the prison, then at the ugly guard who seemed to have it in for him. Nobody was listening when he said this was a mistake. And he might have stood a chance of making them listen if he could explain any of this. But he couldn't. At least with the lady, he might have a chance to figure things out. From behind those prison walls, he didn't think he ever would. Drawing a deep breath, he met those green eyes again and said, "I'm getting in."

He thought she sighed very softly . . . in relief? "Good."

The sheriff opened the buggy's door. But the lady . . . Miss Emily . . . stopped him. "Take off those hand shackles, Sheriff."

The sheriff glanced down and then frowned. He gripped the cuffs, shaking his head. "Dang. I don't know who put these on you, pal, but I've never seen their like around here. I doubt my keys will—"

"That's okay. The keys are in my back pocket."

At that the sheriff frowned.

"I told you, Sheriff, I'm not a criminal. I was arrested because the cops thought I could give them some information. They intended to let me go, even gave me the keys and then all hell broke loose and I wound up here, and I still don't know how. . . ."

"Ah, hell," the sheriff said, pulling out the key and unlocking the cuffs. "Shut up, already."

"I gotta warn you, Miss Emily," the ugly guard put in, "this guy talks a blue streak. Crazy talk, too. Why, he'll talk till your ears bleed, if you let him."

Jack glanced up at the woman in the buggy and thought he detected a smile in her eyes, but she looked away before he could be sure. He rubbed his wrists where the cuffs had chafed him and finally climbed into the buggy, taking the seat across from her.

The sheriff got back aboard his horse. "Just so you don't get any ideas, mister, I'll be escortin' you back to Miss Emily's place. And the preacher will be there waiting. There won't be any chance to go running off, so forget it if that's what you're thinking. And if you want to change your mind, now's the time to do it."

He sat there, hearing the sheriff, but looking at the lady. Curiosity made him lift his hand, touch the fan she held, and gently push it aside so he could see her face. And when he did, he wondered why the hell any woman as beautiful as this one would have to resort to such an odd method of getting herself a husband. His eyes slowly traced over high cheekbones, lean features, full pink lips. And more curling strands of cinnamon hair framing the rest.

"I'm uh . . . I'm not gonna change my mind, Sheriff," he said.

She blushed a pretty shade of pink, but there was just a hint of alarm in her wide green eyes.

# Chapter 3

"It . . . doesn't look as if you've been well treated," Emily said. Anything to break the strained silence that filled the buggy. He was, she noticed, a handsome man. Though his suit was very odd. She'd never seen one like it. He must be from back East. He had dark brown hair, tousled now. A hard, strong face, though it was scratched in several places, and there was a bruise along the side of his temple.

She hadn't thought this through quite thoroughly, then, had she? She should have chosen an ugly man. Though the others she'd glimpsed would have likely frightened the children. And she certainly didn't want that.

He reached up to touch the bruise. "Oh, they didn't do this. I was . . . it uh . . . happened before."

"I see." She didn't. Not really. "I . . . um . . . I don't even know your name." She smiled uneasily.

"It's Jack," he said. "Jack McCain." He held out a hand.

Emily took it, hesitantly, but the warmth and strength that surrounded hers when she did made her even more uneasy. His grip was firm, tight. She pulled her hand away, averting her eyes. This was not going to be as easy as Mary had made it sound.

"Well, Mr. McCain—"

"I kind of think it's safe for you to call me Jack," he said, interrupting her. "If we're going to . . . you know . . . get married." He lowered his head, shook it slowly. "I can't even believe all this."

Tilting her head, Emily studied him. He looked upset. Confused. "What were you arrested for, Mr. . . . er . . . Jack?"

His head came up, eyes meeting hers. He had blue eyes. Very blue . . . and very piercing. When he looked at her it was as if he were looking more deeply than anyone ever had before. "It's a long story. And you wouldn't believe me if I told you." He frowned, searching her eyes. "It is *really* eighteen ninety?"

Blinking rapidly, she caught her breath. Lordy, but what if he *was* slightly insane, as the guard had suggested? "I . . . yes. Why does that surprise you?"

"Because I . . ." He lowered his gaze and shrugged. "Never mind. It sounds crazy even to me, and I'm the one living it. Tell me something, Emily, is there a wishing well around here?"

Again she frowned and searched his face for signs of lunacy. But he had the look of a normal man asking a perfectly normal question. "There is a story about a well, not far from where you just were, with the prisoners. It . . . well, there are tales about it. I don't know of anyone who's ever seen it." But she had seen it. She'd seen it herself one day. But it had been gone the next. "Some say it truly can grant wishes." She shrugged. "I've never been much for believing in such things myself."

His lips thinned. "You ever try it?"

"Making a wish at a well?" She hesitated. "I'm embarrassed to admit it, but . . . yes."

"What did you wish for, Emily?"

His voice was soft . . . but she felt it brushing against her nerves like a touch. He was disturbingly intense, this man. "That is personal."

"Did it come true?"

She drew a breath. Did it? She'd wished for a means to keep the farm, give the children a wonderful, happy upbringing, and perhaps . . . find some kernel of happiness for herself in the process, though that part of her wish was the least important of all. "I suppose," she finally answered, "that it is still too soon to tell. Tell me, Jack, do you like children?"

His eyes widened, and it seemed she'd succeeded in distracting him from this odd talk of wishes and wells. "Why? Do you *have* children?"

Smiling at his distress, she nodded. "Two of them. Sarah Jane and Matthew. Of course, they're actually my sister's children, but she . . . she died when they were just babies. So naturally I came here to care for them."

"Naturally." He was staring at her even harder now. "How old are they?"

"Sarah Jane is five, and Matthew is seven," she said.

"And uh . . . where is their father?"

He seemed truly interested in her situation. Of course, he would be. It was soon to become *his* situation as well. "I suppose I may as well tell you the whole of it. I married their father shortly after arriving here. Clem was a good man, and my sister loved him dearly. He was well respected in Hillcrest, but that didn't stop the townsfolk from gossiping about an unmarried woman living under the same roof with a widowed man and raising his children. So we married, and that ended the gossip."

Jack's brows bent until they touched. "How very . . . practical."

"It was best for the children."

"Uh-huh."

Emily didn't like the speculative look in his eyes, so she went on with her story. "Clem died two months ago, leaving me with the farm, and one rather large mortgage payment due in the fall. If I can't raise a crop, I will lose the children's home to the bank, and that is unacceptable. But though I've tried, I fear I cannot do it alone."

"And that's where I come in," he said slowly.

She nodded, trying to look bright and hopeful. "Yes. And Mr. McCain—"

"Jack."

"Jack. When this payment is made, and the farm is safe, I will let you out of our . . . arrangement."

His brows went up. "You can do that?"

She nodded hard. "I've checked this statute thoroughly, and while you are forbidden from leaving me, I remain free to end our . . . marriage . . . at any time. So long as the decision is mine, you'll have fulfilled your obligation, and will be considered a free man."

"So . . . I'm sort of a summer rental?"

"Don't you see how perfectly this works out? I'll get to keep the children's home, you'll get your freedom. All in exchange for a few months of hard work."

"Hard work," he repeated, and for a moment he seemed to be thinking. But then he nodded. "It is . . . a pretty fair deal," he said. "But maybe it would've been better if you'd chosen somebody else. Emily, uh, you had no way of knowing this, but I . . . I don't know the first thing about farming."

The glimmer of hope vanished. "You don't?"

"I'm sorry. Maybe you should send me back with the sheriff and wait for someone else. I don't belong here. I'm . . . I'm kind of lost and . . . hell, I don't even know how I *got* here." He shook his head. "I need to figure this out, find out how I'm supposed to get back where I belong, and what all this means, and . . ." He ended with a deep sigh.

Emily's heart contracted just a little in her chest. The maternal

side of her, she supposed. He did indeed look lost. Alone and confused, though she didn't know why.

"Perhaps . . . I can help you find those answers."

He looked up slowly.

"It is the least I can do. I'm asking a great deal from you, Jack. You
can learn farming. I can teach you that. But what I can't do is bring in
a crop on my own." She lowered her head. "I need your help, Jack.
And if you'll give it, wholeheartedly, I'll do everything I can to help
you get back to . . . to wherever it is you call home. You have my word
on that." She smiled, very slightly. "Do we have a bargain?"


$\mathcal{S}$he had him the minute she said she needed him. Jack didn't think
anyone had *ever* needed him for a damn thing. Not once. But she
seemed to be in a bind, and he seemed to be in a position to help
her out of it.

And despite all the other unbelievably odd things that were happening to him, he found he wanted to.

There was a suspicion rattling around in his brain. One almost
too absurd to even bear considering. But he was considering it anyway. Suppose that well he'd fallen into *had* been the one from his
grandma's tales. He remembered begging for another chance,
promising to work harder than he ever had in exchange for it. And
he remembered his grandma reciting that verse. Something about
the well appearing again once a person had fulfilled his end of the
bargain. Well, crazy as it sounded, he didn't know how else to explain all of this. So maybe if he worked hard enough, he'd find that
well again and he could wish himself right back to good ol' 1999.

Either that or he'd suffered a massive concussion when he'd
fallen, and this was all one big hallucination. Yeah. Maybe that was
it. It seemed more likely.

The buggy rattled to a halt, and Jack glanced out to see another
woman, a young blonde, holding the hands of two of the cutest

kids he'd ever laid eyes on. Red-haired, freckle-faced cherubs with green eyes like their aunt. Beyond them a guy in black stood with a book in his hand. The promised preacher, no doubt. And again he wondered just what would drive a woman like Emily to do something so drastic.

He eyed her, and found he really wanted to know. God, she looked nervous. "Emily, I want you to tell me one thing before we go through with this," he said, thinking back to when she'd chosen him from the crowd. "Why me? I mean, there were a lot of men there. So why did you pick me?"

She looked away, shrugging, not answering him.

"When you first arrived out there, you asked the sheriff for the youngest. And you asked my age before you chose me. That has something to do with it, doesn't it?"

To his surprise, her face turned crimson and she looked away. "I . . . I . . . thought choosing a younger man would simply help to avoid . . . complications."

"I don't think I follow."

Lifting her chin, she met his eyes. "I'll be blunt, then. I wanted a man young enough so there would be no danger of him . . . wanting to be . . . intimate with me. This is a business arrangement. Nothing more."

He absorbed that bit of information, failing to see any logic in it. "How old are you, Emily?"

She bit her lip and, lowered her head. "Thirty-five."

He nodded. "So you figured no twenty-eight-year-old man could possibly be attracted to a woman so ancient." For some reason it bothered him a great deal to have her thinking that way.

She looked up fast, a little flare in her eyes. "I'm *hardly* ancient, Mr. McCain."

"Exactly, Miss Hawkins."

Her eyes widened, and she looked away. "It's Mrs. Hawkins."

"If I'm reading you right, and I think I am, then I'd say for all intents and purposes, it's Miss."

He saw her throat move as she swallowed convulsively. "This is a business arrangement between us," she reminded him. "That's all." Then she met his eyes, but it seemed as if she had to force herself to. "I've told you my situation, set forth my terms. Do you agree or not?"

He glanced out again, saw the sheriff dismounting, gun in his holster at his side. It didn't look like he had much of a choice in the matter. For now. At least until he could figure out what the hell had happened to him, and whether or not this was all some kind of delusional episode caused by a bullet wound or a concussion.

And being married to a woman like this one for the summer didn't seem like such a terrible chore. Even if she had made it pretty clear that it was a hands-off sort of proposal. He was a professional confidence man. And he was beginning to see her as a challenge.

"I agree to your terms, Miss Hawkins. And I'll abide by them until you change your mind."

The look in those green eyes told him she knew exactly what he meant. "I won't be changing my mind," she said.

He nodded and gave her one of his winning smiles. "If you say so." Then he got out of the buggy and reached up to take her hand and help her down, just the way he'd seen gentleman cowboys do in the movies.

She took his hand, stepped down into the brilliant sunshine, and looked up at him. On the surface, she looked strong, determined, and stubborn to Jack. But he'd made a life out of reading people. And he could see beyond the surface of hers.

Miss Emily Hawkins was just a little bit attracted to him. And the feeling scared her to death.

# Chapter 4

Emily shifted nervously from one foot to the other when Reverend Waterman asked, "Are we ready to proceed, then?"

She looked at the stranger standing beside her, and for just a moment, panic fluttered in her belly as if she'd swallowed a hummingbird.

"If you have any doubts, Miss Emily, then now's the time to say so," Sheriff Stonewall said slowly. "We can take him right on up to the prison while you give this thing some more thought."

She sensed the man beside her stiffen, and almost gasped aloud when his hand curled protectively around hers. "Emily and I have made a bargain, Sheriff," he said. "She's not going to back down now."

Mary Brightwater quickly nodded. "You're doing the right thing, Emily," she said.

"Am I?" Emily bit her lip, but her doubts fled when she felt a small tug at her skirts and looked down at Sarah Jane.

Innocent green eyes stared up at her, darting every few seconds to the stranger, Jack McCain. "Is he gonna be our new uncle, Aunt Emily?"

Emily swallowed the dryness in her throat. But before she could answer, Jack was hunkered down, eye to eye with her precious niece. Little Matthew crept closer, nervous but protective of his sister in spite of that. "You must be Sarah Jane," Jack said. Then he glanced at the boy beside her. "And you're Matt, right?"

"That's right," Matthew said, straightening to his full height.

"Well, you can call me Jack. I'd tell you to call me Uncle Jack, but I figure that's a title I'm gonna have to earn. Can't just waltz in and claim it, now can I?"

The children glanced at each other, then back at Jack once more, nodding their agreement. "Now I'm gonna need an awful lot of help from you two. Your Aunt Em needs a hand running this farm, and there's a whole lot about farming I don't know. But I'll bet you can teach me most of it."

Matt's chin rose a notch. "I sure can," he said.

"Me, too," Sarah Jane put in. "*I* can even show you how to milk the cow."

Emily thought Jack's face pulled into an almost grimace, but if it did, he covered it fast. "That's great," he said. "But right now I need your help with something else." He turned to little Matthew, his face very serious. "I'd like to marry your Aunt Em, today, Matt. But you being the man of the house, I figure I can't do that until I get your permission. What do you think?"

Matt glanced up at Emily. "Do you want to marry him, Aunt Emily?"

She found she couldn't speak. For some reason her airways seemed choked off, so she simply nodded.

Matthew returned Jack's gaze. "You have to promise to be nice to her," he said. Then Sarah Jane whispered something to him, and he nodded. "And nice to us, too."

"And take us fishin'!" Sarah Jane put in. "Like Pa used to do."

"Yeah," Matthew said. "And . . . you gotta kiss her sometimes."

Emily felt her face heat. *"Matthew . . ."*

"He does, Aunt Em. Pa never did. Never once, that I saw, and all the married folks in town are always doin' it. I think you're supposed to when you're married."

She could feel Jack's eyes on her, but she couldn't look back at him to save her life.

"I'll do that," Jack said, and she knew his eyes were still on her. "But only if she wants me to."

"Okay then. I guess it's okay if you marry her."

Jack nodded and offered Matthew his hand. Matthew took it and shook in a very grown-up manner. "Now," Jack went on. "I'm gonna be needing a best man for this wedding. And your Aunt Emily needs a maid of honor. You two think you'd like the jobs?"

Emily couldn't remember the last time she'd seen those two little angels light up the way they did then. Sarah Jane smiled so hard her eyes crinkled at the corners. And Matthew just beamed.

Truly this man couldn't be so bad. No man who treated children so kindly could possibly be. But a new worry began creeping into Emily's mind. The children could easily fall in love with a man like Jack McCain. What would it do to them when he left again in the fall? Goodness knows they'd lost so much already: their mother, their father.

But not their home. She'd see to that. And she'd simply have a talk with Jack about trying not to get too close to them. This would work. It had to work. For the children.

Lifting her chin and facing the preacher, she nodded once. "I suppose we're ready to proceed, Reverend Waterman."

"Very well." He opened his Bible and began to read. The sheriff looked on in unveiled disapproval while Mary watched with a dreamy expression in her eyes. And when the ceremony ended and the preacher intoned, "You may kiss the bride," Jack turned to

Emily, and for just a second she thought he might be every bit as nervous as she was. She didn't want to be dragged into those powerful arms, kissed by this handsome man. Not now, not this way, in front of all these people. She was terrified all at once, not of him . . . but of what her own reactions to such an experience might be.

Jack stared into her eyes for one long moment, and then he reached out, took her hand very gently in his much larger one, and lifted it to his lips. She felt his breath, his heat, as he brushed a soft kiss across the back of her hand. And she tingled all the way to her toes. Oh, my! She'd never felt such a tingle before.

Trembling all over, she whispered, "Thank you," for his ears alone. For she was certain he'd seen her fear, and deliberately spared her the embarrassment of being kissed full on the mouth in public.

"No," he said softly. "Thank *you*." And then he smiled, and it took her breath away.

*What have I just done,* she wondered. *And what in the world do I do next?*


*D*amn, *I'm good.* Jack smiled to himself after the ceremony was over. For just a second there, it had looked as if Miss Emily was going to change her mind. And he knew right then that anything— even a sham marriage—was preferable to doing time in that prison on the hill beyond town. So he'd put his talents to work. You want to win a woman's trust, you be good to her kids. And conning a couple of kids was easy. Treat them like adults, show them some respect, and they'd respond every time. Kids liked that kind of crap. As for the lady, she'd be a little tougher. But he was getting the feeling that the mere suggestion of sex scared the hell out of her, and the fear in her eyes at the thought of kissing him had pretty well verified that theory. So he'd turned on the schoolboy charm, and kissed her hand.

She'd been relieved. And *grateful*. And that would go a long way toward getting things off to a good start here. Hell, he only had to convince her to put up with him until he figured out what the hell had happened to land him in this place and how to get back where he belonged. It would be the easiest con he'd ever played, and it would keep him out of prison in the meantime. Nothing to it.

Jack had pretty much determined that this was not a delusion or a dream. Or a joke. Somebody would have slipped up by now and given it away. No, it was lasting too long, and had too much detail to it, to be anything other than real. Somehow, something had happened when he'd fallen into that well. And he was pretty sure he'd truly landed in Hillcrest, Oklahoma, in the year 1890. It sounded crazy. It *was* crazy, but here he was, and there was pretty much no denying it.

So while he was here, he might as well make the best of it. And the best of it was not going to be found in any nineteenth-century prison.

So he'd just bide his time here. And sure, he'd have to do some farm work to earn his keep, but hell, how hard could it be?

He turned to his pseudo-bride, wearing his best smile. The sheriff and the minister were already walking away, shaking their heads in disapproval. What did he care if they didn't want to stay for the party? He was starving, and looking forward to a big celebratory meal, and maybe even a slice of pseudo–wedding cake.

"You'd best come on inside," Emily said to him. "You can't get any work done in those clothes."

Wait a minute. Work? Already?

"Clem's things ought to fit you fine. We might still get that north field plowed before dark if we get busy."

The man didn't seem to know anything. Lordy, but she ought to have listened to him when he'd said as much, but she couldn't quite believe any grown man could be so completely ignorant about simple farm work.

But she'd been wrong. He was worse at driving the mule than she was, for heaven's sake. And by the time she'd shown him how to do it three times over, they'd wasted a solid hour of the afternoon.

Still, any help was better than none at all, she supposed. At least she was able to return to the house and get the other chores done at a decent hour for a change. And she couldn't remember the last time she'd managed to have a suitable supper ready before the children started complaining that they were hungry.

Jack hauled himself through the front door at dark, and he looked for all the world as if he'd been dragged through the dirt by a runaway horse and beaten with a sizable club. His face bore so much dirt that his eyes seemed to be peering at her from a dark hole.

"My goodness," she said, hurrying forward and easing him into a chair. "What happened?"

The children looked at him with wide eyes. He only shrugged. "I *plowed*." Then with a sigh, he shook his head. "I didn't get the whole field done. Three-quarters of it, though."

Closing her eyes, Emily sighed. "It was half done when you started," she said.

"Yeah. And I'm having trouble swallowing that you did all that by yourself and lived to tell the tale."

Sarah Jane giggled behind her hand. Matthew looked puzzled. "My dad used to plow the north field in one afternoon, Jack," he said.

"Then your dad must have been one heck of a man," Jack replied, apparently taking no offense.

Matthew smiled. "You'll get the hang of it in no time."

Emily had her doubts. "I kept your dinner warm," she said, bending to the oven to remove the steaming plate. Jack's stomach growled noisily, and Sarah Jane giggled again.

Jack sent her a playful scowl and got to his feet with a groan, eyeing the heaping plate. "Man, that smells good."

Emily shrugged, and tried not to feel the rush of pleasure. "It's nothing special. Roast beef and vegetables, biscuits and gravy. There's blueberry pie for dessert."

His wide eyes went from the plate to Emily's face. "You *made* all that? On that thing?" He glanced at the wood stove that took up most of the space in one corner of the kitchen. And as she nodded, he leaned over, inhaling the steam and closing his eyes. Then he opened them again. "And there's pie, too?"

She couldn't help but smile as she nodded again. That he should be so impressed before he'd even tasted a bite . . . and she *had* gone to more trouble than usual, though she'd told herself again and again not to.

"I'll go wash up," he said quickly. "Where's the . . . uh . . ."

"The well is right out front. Didn't you see it there?"

"Oh. Right, the well." He shook his head and turned to limp back outside.

Emily set his plate on the table, and wiping her hands on her apron, followed him. She found him by the well, pumping water into a pail. As she approached, he plunged his hands into the cool water, tipped his head back, and sucked air through his teeth.

She walked up to him. "Let me see them."

"What?" he asked, turning quickly.

"Your hands, Jack. Let me see them." When he didn't move, she reached out and took his hands, pulling them from the water and turning his palms up. "Mercy!"

"That bad, huh?" He glanced down at his hands and made a face.

"Jack, you should have stopped. Lord, you won't even be able to hold onto the plow tomorrow. Look at you!"

"Well, this isn't exactly the kind of work I'm used to."

Emily frowned at him as she quickly untied her apron, took it off, and dipped an end into the water. "Just what sort of work *are* you used to, Jack?" As she spoke she gently washed the dirt from his red, blistered palms.

Jack had gone still. He just stood there, silent, as she dipped and washed, dipped and washed. His hands, his forearms, his neck. Running the cool cloth over his face, she stopped suddenly. "Jack?"

"What?"

"I asked what kind of work you usually do. Did you fall asleep on your feet?"

"I . . . no . . . it's just . . . I'm not used to being . . ." His eyes met hers.

Emily lowered her head. "Oh."

"You must be pretty disappointed in me so far, huh?"

Lifting her head again, she shook it. "No, Jack. You're trying your best, and that's all I can ask."

"It's not gonna be enough, though. Emily, we're gonna need some more help around here if we have any shot at getting that crop of . . . of whatever it is you plan to plant—"

"Sorghum," she interrupted.

"Right."

"But I have no money to pay for hands, Jack. I've explained that to you."

"Yeah, well, how about you just leave that part to me?"

She tilted her head. "I don't understand."

"I have an idea. Tomorrow, I'll go into town. And if I can't con . . . er, convince . . . two or three plowboys to come back with me and help get that crop in, then my name isn't Jack McCain."

She shook her head slowly. "Don't you think I've tried? It won't work, Jack. Nobody works for nothing."

"Hey. Trust me. Okay?"

She looked up at him. Shook her head. "We'll lose a day's work if you spend it in town."

"Then we'll gain a week's work when I get back. I promise."

She sighed, certain he had no hope of getting anyone to come here and help him. But then his hands came to her hair, stroking a path from the top of her head to the back of it, and gently tipping it up. And every bit of common sense fled her mind like geese flying south for the winter. "You're one pretty woman, Emily McCain. Especially out here, like this, with the stars twinkling behind you and the—"

She narrowed her eyes, jerking away fast. "Jack McCain, are you trying to sway me with flattery?"

"Well . . . no, I mean, I was—"

"Do you think I'm some empty-headed schoolgirl who swoons when a handsome man says pretty words he doesn't even mean?"

"Aha!" he said.

"Aha, what?" she demanded, fists on her hips.

"You think I'm handsome."

"I most certainly do not."

"You just said so. Handsome man, you said. I heard it. You think I'm handsome."

She rolled her eyes, turning her back to him.

"And for your information, Emily McCain—"

"Stop calling me that."

"Why? It's your name. And for your information, *Mrs. Jack McCain,* I don't think you're empty-headed, and I *do* think you're beautiful. So there!"

She went stiff, not turning to face him. "You do?"

"Yeah. I do." He moved closer. She felt him, heard his steps, and then his hands closed on her shoulders from behind. "And if you don't know it, then maybe you ought to spend some quality time in front of a mirror. Because you are, Emily." Then he came still closer, and she felt the heat of his breath on her neck, and then the touch of his lips there. Softly, gently. A fire licked at her belly when his whiskers rasped over her sensitive skin, and she jumped. But he stopped, lifting his head away.

"Your dinner is on the table," she said. "And there's water heating for a bath. Clem . . . he always liked a hot bath after a day of plowing. It'll be ready by the time you finish eating." Her voice was trembling.

"Okay," he whispered close to her ear. "You sure do take good care of me, Emily. You're one hell of a woman. One hell of a wife."

Jack strode past her, whistling softly as he headed back inside. But he paused just inside the door, and wondered just what the hell was happening to him. Because he really had meant it when he'd told her she was beautiful. And when his lips had brushed across her nape, and she'd trembled in his arms . . .

Well, hell, it was only natural. He was a red-blooded man. He ought to be worried if he *didn't* feel some kind of response.

And it had been that. *Some kind* of response.

He sat down at the table. A second later, a tiny, warm body had snuggled up in his lap. He glanced down, and Sarah Jane glanced up with eyes as big as all outdoors.

"Get down, Sarah, and let Jack eat his dinner," Matthew said in a big-brother tone.

"But Pa used to let me sit on his lap while he ate his dinner!"

"Well Pa's not here anymore, Sarah," Matthew said, his voice softer now.

Sarah looked up at Jack, and her eyes were damp now. "Sorry, Jack," she whispered, and started to climb down.

Jack's arms snagged her little body and hauled her right back up again, almost on their own. "You sit right here, Sarah Jane," he heard himself say. "I don't mind a bit."

Her whole face lit up when she smiled. And then she leaned her head on his shoulder, and something went soft in Jack's chest. He really didn't mind. It was the oddest thing.

# Chapter 5

Emily wished to heaven she knew what Jack was up to. Part of her was afraid that when he left this morning he wasn't going to be coming back. Even now he was packing leftovers from last night's meal into a sack, as if he planned to be gone a while.

"Jack, won't you tell me how you plan to convince men to work for us when we don't have a dime to pay them?"

Jack only smiled. Lordy, he was handsome when he smiled. And when he bathed.

Emily tried to chase the shameful thought from her mind, but couldn't. She'd been unable to resist peeking in at him last night, after she'd tucked the children into bed. He'd been soaking in the big metal tub, head tipped back, so relaxed she'd thought he'd been sleeping at first. He was even more beautiful undressed. Lean and strong. And as she'd looked at him, a strange, wonderful feeling had taken hold of her body. A kind of a yearning she thought was considered sinful in a woman. But it hadn't *felt* sinful. Just . . . new. And exciting, somehow.

Shame on her.

"If it works," Jack was saying, "then I'll tell you."

"And if it doesn't?"

He shrugged. "Oh, I'm pretty sure it will. This sort of thing is my area of expertise, after all."

"But if it doesn't?" she asked again.

He studied her face for a moment. "Then I'll be back to finish that plowing." He watched her eyes, then frowned slightly. "I *am* coming back, Emily. That's it, isn't it? You're afraid I won't."

Averting her eyes, she whispered, "Of course not."

"Well you're sure worried about something. If it isn't that, then what?"

Shrugging, she turned away. "Nothing."

Jack moved forward, took her shoulders, and turned her around again. "Talk to me, Emily. Come on, what good is a husband if you can't tell him what's on your mind? Hmm?"

Her eyes burned, and that made her angry. And suddenly it all just came flooding out. "Fine. I'll talk. Yes, I'm worried. I'm worried you won't come back. I'm worried that field won't get plowed, and the crop won't get planted, and the mortgage won't get paid. I'm worried I'll lose the only home those two children have ever known, and to be honest, I'm worried that I might have made the biggest mistake of my life when I decided to depend on a man I don't even know to fix the mess my life is in right now." The tears spilled over, but she dashed them away.

When she looked at Jack again, he seemed stunned, and maybe a little bit confused as he searched her face. He swallowed hard, his Adam's apple swelling with the force of it. And he said, "Emily, I'm worried, too. About all those things, and a dozen others that you wouldn't believe if I told you." He shook his head, glancing at the porch, where the children sat on the front step watching their every move. Then he met her eyes again. "Let's take it one worry at a time, okay? I *am* coming back, and I'm gonna do my damnedest to fix the rest of this. I promise."

She stared up at him, and she knew that hope was in her eyes when she did.

"Now are you gonna disappoint young Matthew by not kissing your husband good-bye?"

She felt her eyes widen, but before she could reply, Jack's arms slid around her waist, and he pulled her close. So close her body pressed tight to his. And then he bent his head and kissed her. His mouth was soft, gentle, coaxing, and in a moment she felt the tension ease out of her with a sigh. Her hands rested on his shoulders, and he moved his mouth over hers in a caressing touch that sent liquid heat spilling through her whole body. Her mouth relaxed beneath the tender touch of his, and when he straightened away, he looked down at her, and licked his lips.

"I'll be back," he said, his voice slightly hoarse. And this time she believed him.

Something was wrong with the way this whole thing was going. Jack tried to be analytical about identifying the problem, but it wasn't the type that could be analyzed. His motives had changed. All of a sudden, getting Emily's crop planted and saving that farm for her and the kids was just as important as finding his way back to his own time. All of a sudden, he wasn't just conning her. He really wanted to help.

The change had started the previous night when he'd held little Sarah on his lap. She'd fallen asleep there, and Jack had had to carry her up the stairs and tuck her into bed. She'd looked like a little angel, sleeping there in her pretty room with her little doll beside her. He hated to think where she'd be sleeping if she lost her home. And then there was Matthew, trying so hard to be a man. He'd spent the entire dinner hour giving Jack a list of tips on farm work, and telling how his dad always did it, the pride clear in his voice. He'd loved his father, and lost him. What if he lost his home, too?

But it was that kiss this morning that had been the topper. He never should have kissed her. Damn. She tasted like honey, and he wanted more. A lot more.

He kept thinking about last night when she'd started washing the dirt away from him with her balled-up apron. Her touch had done things to him . . . things it usually took a knockout of cover-model quality, wearing a thong, to do. He liked his women lean and mean and gorgeous. He liked them hot and hungry and without an inhibition in their fluff-filled heads. He liked them young, and comfortable in the fast lane.

He had *never* liked them shy, or old-fashioned, or—God forbid—moral!

But he liked Emily. He liked her *a lot*. She was strong and smart and determined. She'd do anything for those kids, and that, for some reason, made his heart go soft. She was a grown-up. A woman who knew who she was.

Jack thought about all of that as he sat in the saloon sipping a strong, dark-colored beer, wearing Clem Hawkins's best Levi's and his black Stetson hat. This place was great. He couldn't get over it. Batwing doors and a scuffed-up, rough-cut bar top. Even a mirror behind the bar in case a riot should break out. Hey, every Western barroom brawl needed one, so some no-account scallywag could get thrown into it and smash it to bits. Old-fashioned bottles lined shelves beneath the mirror, and malodorous men smoked hand-rolled cigarettes and drank shots of red-eye.

"Hey, you," someone said, and Jack turned his head to see his pal the sheriff pushing through the batwing doors. He didn't quite have The Duke's saunter down, but he was close. "Shouldn't you be out at the Hawkins' place, manning a plow?"

Finally, the opening he'd been waiting for. "No hurry, Sheriff. I can outplow any man in this town."

Some of the talk in the saloon stopped, and several heads turned in Jack's direction.

"Oh, can you, now?" Sheriff Stonewall asked.

"Damn straight. Shoot, I've never *met* a man who could plow faster than me. I'm the best there is."

The sheriff looked around the room with a grin on his face. No doubt thinking he was about to stir up trouble for the new kid. "You all hear that? Jack here thinks he can outplow any man in town."

"Oughtta put his money where his mouth is," said one oversized brute in bib overalls.

"Well, I would, if I had any. Truth is, I'm pretty much busted. Had to trade my watch just to get this beer."

"Shame," the brute said. "So I guess all you got is big talk, then, huh?"

"Oh, hell no. I'm willing to back it up. If anyone here is man enough to take me up on it, that is?" He looked around the room.

"Now just how in Sam Hill are you gonna do that?"

Jack shrugged, scratched his head, and searched the ceiling as if for answers. Then he snapped his fingers. "I got it! A challenge! A contest!"

"Now hold on," the sheriff began.

"What sort of contest?" another man asked.

"Well now, let me think on this a minute," Jack said, pretending to mull it all over in his mind. "Suppose we stage a plowing contest out at Miss Emily's place, hmm? Then I can prove once and for all that I'm the best man in this town. I'll take on all comers. I'll—"

"Shoot, that ain't no good," the big guy interrupted. "You need a prize for any sort a contest, an' you already said you was flat busted."

"I don't see that it matters. I'm going to be the winner, and I already have the finest prize in Oklahoma."

"Oh, do you, now? And what would that be?"

Jack opened his sack on the bar and began extracting dishes of food from last night's dinner, including a hefty slice of that blueberry pie. "I married me the best cook in seven counties," he said, hoping he sounded authentic. "That woman could make a man's mouth water from a mile away. Just smell this." He lifted the pie, and several men leaned over to sniff at it as he moved it around. "Hey, I know!" he shouted as if he'd just thought of it. "My wife could cook a full-blown feast of a meal for the winner and his family. Including a blueberry pie. A man's wife would be mighty grateful to have a night off from cooking his dinner." The men around him looked at one another, considering it.

Almost had them. Jack shrugged, set the plate down on the table in front of him. "Not that it much matters, because I'll be the winner. There's not a man in this town who can man a plow like I can."

"You're on!" the burly one yelled.

"I'm in," said another.

"Whenever you're ready," said a third.

Jack smiled, and shrugged. "Well, the sun's shining and it's early in the day. How soon can you fellas meet me out at the farm?"

Men crowded around Jack, and there was so much noise he could barely hear himself think. He saw Sheriff Stonewall shaking his head. "I'd best come, too," the sheriff said, leaning close. "You'll be needin' a judge, and someone to keep order. I hope to hell you know what you're doing, son."

Jack knew *exactly* what he was doing. And it was working like a charm.

"I don't believe it," Emily said, as she stood on the front porch looking on in amazement. Men, a dozen of them at least, were lining up in her three fields, each with a set of plows and a horse, or a mule, or an ox. She took three steps forward, and stopped, as Jack came limping up the path, being helped by Marty Burleson, a local farmer who was as big as a tree. And suddenly her throat went dry, and she found herself running forward.

"What's wrong, what's happened?"

"Oh, now, Miz Emily, he'll be fine. Turned his ankle is all."

"I'm afraid I've ruined it for everyone," Jack said, looking depressed, shaking his head. Then he lifted his gaze. "But no. I made a deal and the deal stands. Guess I just won't get to show off for my wife . . . this time."

"I'd have beat you anyway, Jack. But we'll have to hash that out when the ankle's better. Right now I gotta get back there, before the sheriff fires the signal shot." Marty handed Jack off to Emily, then lumbered away at top speed.

Pulling Jack's arm around her shoulders, Emily began moving toward the house. But he stopped her, and sent her a grin. "Not that I mind your arms around me, Em, but uh, the ankle's fine."

She blinked, staring at him. "Suppose you tell me just what is going on here, Jack McCain?"

He looked so sheepish, so pleased with himself, it made her want to shake him. "Well, it's a contest. To see who's the best plowin' plantin' farmer in this whole dang town. Winner gets a home-cooked meal, courtesy of the talented Emily McCain."

Her hands went to her hips and she gaped at him. "Oh, does he, now?"

"Yeah. I realize I should have cleared that part of it with you first, but I didn't exactly have a lot of time. The marks . . . er . . . contestants were ready to bite. I had to move fast."

"I see."

He studied her face, his smile fading. "Look, Em, by suppertime the plowing will be done, and not just that north field, either, but all of it."

"You *tricked* those men. Didn't you, Jack?"

"Well . . . no. I . . . I just bragged a little about how good I was to get their dander up, and—"

"So you lied to them, too."

"It got results!"

"It's dishonest. Jack, I don't like this! Don't you think they'll realize they've been taken advantage of?"

"Not until the fields are plowed, I hope," he said. "And the only thing I took advantage of was their overblown egos."

She lowered her head, and slowly shook it. "Oh, Jack . . ."

"Look, there's no harm done. The fields are getting plowed in a single afternoon, and all for the price of one good meal." As he spoke the sheriff's gun went off, and the men and animals began moving. Soon there was such a dust being raised that Emily couldn't even see the men out there working.

All while Jack was headed for the house and a cool drink on his supposedly turned ankle. Emily followed, snapping at him. "This is wrong, Jack. It's . . . it's just wrong, and I don't like it."

"Well, it's kinda late for that now."

"I want no part of this!"

Jack mounted the bottom step, shook his head, and kept walking. "Well, I suppose you can refuse to cook the prize for the winner if you want to, but it's a prize he'll have earned. And I don't imagine he'll be too happy about not getting it."

"None of them will be too happy when they realize they've been played for fools!" She followed him into the house. "Jack, you can go your merry way when this is over, but the children and I have to *live* here."

Jack turned to face her, lifting his hands palms up, at his sides. "Dammit, Em, I don't see what you're getting so worked up about! I'm only trying to help you here!"

"I can do without that kind of help, *Mr*. McCain."

"Shoot, you need any kind of help you can get. *Mrs*. McCain."

"If you do anything like this again, I'll . . . I'll . . ."

"You'll what? Send me on up to prison?"

Inhaling deeply, she forced herself to be calm. "I wouldn't do that." She sighed. "I suppose you . . . you were only trying to help. In your way."

He was quiet for a moment. "Yeah. Well, I guess I should have cleared it with you first. Next time, I'll—"

"There won't be a next time, Jack. I'll save this farm by honest hard work, or I'll lose it. Either way, I intend to keep my honor and my pride intact."

"Honor and pride," he said, very softly. "Do they keep you warm on cold, lonely nights, Em? Are they what you hold onto instead of a man?"

She went stiff, her back to him. "They'll have to do until I find a man I can love . . . a man I can respect, Jack."

She knew those words stung him when he didn't reply. Drawing a fortifying breath, she squared her shoulders and lifted her chin. "I'd best get to cooking that meal."

# Chapter 6

*Jack* woke in the small bedroom he'd been assigned. The sun beamed down blindingly, and he had the feeling he should have been awake long before now.

Yesterday had gone perfectly. The fields had gotten plowed in a matter of a single afternoon, and by the time a winner was declared (the huge brute Emily called Marty) Emily had made a feast fit for a king and packed it all in a wicker basket for him to take home.

Perfect.

Except for her reaction to it all. She'd as much as told Jack that she didn't respect him. Must have been the turned ankle thing, he figured. He probably would have looked better to her if he'd been out there plowing with the rest of the men. But hell, he didn't know what he was doing, and only would have made a fool of himself.

Maybe that was what she wanted.

Nah.

He got up, washed up, dressed, and headed downstairs in search of breakfast. He found it just by following his nose. The oven was still warm, and a plate full of eggs and bacon and biscuits and home fries was tucked away inside, waiting just for him.

Only, nobody else was around.

Frowning, Jack headed outside and followed the sounds of voices to the north field, where he spotted the others. Emily, Sarah Jane, and Matthew were all running around with sacks of seed, iron rakes, and hoes. The children seemed to be having fun, but Emily was hard at work. Sweat already glistened on her skin. And no wonder. It must be eighty out there already, and she was wearing a long-sleeved blouse that buttoned tight at the wrists, and a dark-blue skirt that reached to her feet. For Pete's sake.

He hurried forward. "Hey, you shouldn't be doing this," he said.

She stopped what she was doing and lifted up her head to eye him. Straggles of damp auburn hair stuck to her face. "Somebody has to."

"Yeah, well, I think I can handle this, at least. It doesn't look as tough as plowing." She shrugged and kept raking.

Jack moved forward and took the rake from her hands. "You should have woke me, Em."

"Saw no need."

"No doubt you figured I wouldn't be much help anyway," he said, watching her face. Then he amended, "No, it's not that. It's that you're still mad at me for yesterday." He dropped the rake and gripped her shoulders, shaking his head as he examined her face. "You look ready to drop, Emily. Don't do this to yourself again, you hear me? I don't like it."

"I'll do just exactly what I . . ." She didn't finish. Her eyes sort of rolled back and her body went limp.

Jack caught her in his arms, his heart damn near stopping with fear as he scooped her up.

Sarah Jane began to shriek at the top of her lungs, and for a long moment it didn't seem like she'd stop. Jack shouted her name, loud and firmly, until she snapped out of it and focused on him, her eyes red, puffy, and terrified. She stared up at him as he cradled her beloved aunt in his arms. He knew what the little one was thinking. That her aunt had died just as her mother and her father had done. That she was alone. The poor thing was so traumatized, all he wanted to do was hug her, and he likely would have if it hadn't meant setting Emily down first.

"Sarah Jane," Jack said, firmly but gently. "Your Aunt Em has only fainted, is all. From the heat. She's gonna be okay, I promise."

Those big green eyes blinked up at him so trustingly that Jack felt his stomach turn over.

"He's right," Matthew said, although Jack had seen the fear in the boy's eyes as well. "She was up late cleanin' up from that dinner she had to make, and then long before dawn, milkin' the cow and makin' breakfast before she came out here. I don't even think she ate. And I heard Miss Brightwater say she wasn't taking care of herself and was gonna work till she dropped." He looked up at Jack. "Is that what she did?"

"That's what she did, but she won't be doing it again," Jack said. "She'll be fine."

"She's not gonna die like Pa and Ma did?" Sarah Jane whispered.

Jack's heart was rapidly melting into a big muddy puddle. "No, honey. I won't let that happen, I promise. Now c'mon, let's get her back to the house, where we can take proper care of her, hmm?"

The children nodded hard, and Jack hefted Emily a bit higher in his arms, realizing for the first time how slight she was. God, she ought to be heavier, a woman of her height. But she wasn't, and he suspected it was because she'd been working so damned hard for so damned long.

No more, he heard some heroic-sounding stranger whispering inside his head. And then he wondered who *that* was.

At the house, he settled Emily in her bed, then used the basin of cool water and the cloth that Sarah brought in to bathe her face and neck. Her skin was hot and sticky and he knew she had to get cooled down fast.

"Listen, I need you two to go on back outside, okay? I want you to pick your Aunt Em a nice bunch of flowers for when she wakes up."

The two seemed relieved to have been given something to do, and turned, but then Jack said, "Wait a minute." He went to them and touched each small face. They seemed okay. "Listen, it's hot outside. Get a drink of water, and look for those flowers in a shady place, okay? You don't want to get too much sun like Aunt Em did."

Nodding, they rushed off immediately. Good. Jack drew a breath and settled himself on the edge of Emily's bed. Then he told himself to keep this quick and clinical, and he began to unbutton her blouse. As he spread it open, he saw that she wore a shift underneath. It was white, with pretty lace around the neckline. Sleeveless and simple. He unfastened the heavy skirt and dragged that off her as well. He took off her shoes, and then he reached underneath the shift to peel away the ridiculous stockings. God, no wonder she'd given way to the heat.

But as his hands brushed over her thighs, her eyes slowly blinked open and then they went very wide as she said, "What in heaven's name are you *doing*?" and began kicking with both feet so that he either had to back off or risk a broken bone.

"Ow! Calm down, woman! For crying out loud, I was just—"

"Just *what*?"

At least she'd stopped kicking. Jack sighed and shook his head. "Look, you were working too hard, you got overheated, and you passed out cold."

"I have never *passed out* in my life, Mr. McCain."

"You have now, honey. And it's no wonder. My God, you were wearing more layers than—"

"I'm wearing what's appropriate," she countered.

"Not for hard work under the hot sun, Em. Come on, you're still running hot. Now just lie there and be quiet, will you? That shift covers everything important. Besides, we're married."

She glared at him. He glared back, and went right on with what he was doing. He sat down on the edge of the bed again, and when she didn't kick him off, he dipped the cloth into the cool water and brought it to her neck, dabbing it there, then moving it over her shoulders. She was stiff at first, but then she closed her eyes and sighed.

"It does feel good," she whispered.

"Sure it does. Now how's your head?"

"Throbbing."

"Um-hmm. I figured as much." He shook his head. "I have it on good authority that you haven't been taking care of yourself, Em—not at all. That's gonna end right here, right now. You're gonna lie right there in that bed today, and you're gonna let me take care of everything else."

She rolled her eyes. "Right."

"Exactly right. Now I'm gonna bring you up that plate of breakfast, and I'm gonna sprinkle a little extra salt in it because it's good for what ails you. And I want you to drink water today. All you can hold. You're dehydrated."

She frowned. "De—"

"No water and too much sweating. When you work like that you need to drink like a fish, Em. Not that you're gonna be working like that anymore. And if you try to put those ridiculous clothes back on again, I'll burn them. It's hot outside. God, where I come from, women wear short skirts or cutoff Levi's and sleeveless blouses in this kind of weather."

Her eyes went very big. "They . . . bare their arms? Their *legs*?"

"Yes, and nobody thinks anything of it."

She shook her head. "Where do you come from, Jack? You've never told me."

He looked at her for a long moment. "It's . . . probably about time we . . . er . . . talked about that. Maybe . . . maybe it'll help explain why I'm so damned useless around here."

"Oh, Jack, you're not—"

"You said so yourself, Em. But there's a reason. Look . . ." He lowered his head and slowly shook it. "Here," he said finally, reaching into his pocket and pulling out his little planning calendar. "Take a look at this."

Tilting her head slightly and frowning, she reached out and took the small booklet from him. Then she flipped pages, reading the notes he'd scrawled. It took a full minute before her eyes went wide, and she stared up at him again. "This says 1999."

"That's right."

"Well . . . well that's just ridiculous, Jack."

He sighed deeply. "Look, I know how it sounds. Why do you think it's taken me so long to tell you? Emily, I was born in 1971."

"Oh, Jack . . ."

Great, now there was worry in her eyes. Like maybe she thought he was losing his crackers. "Wait a minute. I'll be right back." He got up and headed into his room down the hall. He rummaged through the box of stuff he'd stashed under the bed, and finally just picked up the whole thing and carried it back to the bedroom. "Here," he said. "There's enough proof in here to convince anybody. Look." He pulled out a ring. "My class ring. See that?" He showed her, and she read the engraving aloud.

"Hillcrest High School, Class of 1989."

She was still blinking in shock when he stuffed a handful of crumpled bills in her hand. Tens and twenties, a few singles. "Go on, check them. This is all the cash I had on me. Look at the dates. Does that look like the money you use? And here, here's my credit card, with the expiration date, and . . ." He stopped there because she'd gone completely still, and her eyes were wide. She didn't look worried anymore . . . she looked scared.

"How can this be, Jack? What are you doing here?"

"Aw, come on, Em, don't be afraid of me. I don't know how this happened or why."

"Tell me what you do know," she said. "You're living in my house, with my children, and I—"

"And you think I'm some kind of demon or something. I know. Look, I'll tell you everything I know." He closed his eyes, sighing. "I hardly know where to begin."

"At the beginning."

He opened his eyes and nodded. "Okay. I was born not far from here. My mother died young and my father left, so I was raised by my grandmother on a farm out near the spot where we first met. But I hated farm work. All I ever thought about was getting away from it, finding an easy way to make money. Grandma always said I'd pay for it one day. I just didn't listen."

He glanced at her to see if she was still listening. She seemed riveted. "I got out young, and started pulling con games on rich locals: selling shares in nonexistent co-ops and playing phony land deals and making big money. But the cops started hassling me, and to be honest, my conscience bothered me, too. So I decided to turn over a new leaf. From then on I only swindled criminals." He shook his head. "And I was *good at it*."

"Good? How can you call cheating people good?"

"I figured they deserved it. They didn't earn their money honestly anyway."

"So that justifies you not earning yours honestly?"

He averted his eyes from her big, probing ones. "I know. You're right, I know." He sighed. "Anyway, the day that I ended up here with you, the police had picked me up. They didn't intend to arrest me at all. They really didn't care what I did as long as I didn't ply my trade on honest citizens. But I'd been involved with a major criminal, one they'd been after for years, and they decided I might have information they could use against him. So they took me in, put me in handcuffs, and told me either to tell them everything I knew, or they'd arrest me."

She tilted her head. "Why didn't they simply ask you? Surely you'd have told them if you knew anything that might have helped them stop a dangerous criminal." She looked harder at him. "You would have . . . wouldn't you, Jack?"

He shook his head. "I don't know. If I did, he'd have shot me at the first opportunity. But the chance to find out never came. The criminal and his goons had no intention of letting me get to police headquarters to make a statement. They ambushed us, shot both the cops. I ran for it, they gave chase, and I dove over what I thought was a stone wall for cover. Only it was actually a well, and, when I hit the bottom, I was here. A hundred and nine years in the past."

Her eyes were so big, so pretty and wide and curious and amazed. He'd never seen her look this childlike. "That's why you asked me about the old wishing well."

"Yeah. It . . . it's crazy, but it's the only thing I could think of. My grandmother said there was a stone on that well with an engraved verse."

"Yes . . . 'Make a wish upon this well, but wishes don't come free. Make a promise here as well, and your wish you will see,'" Emily quoted. "As you fell . . . you . . . you made a wish?"

"More like a prayer," he admitted. "I swore I'd go straight, work harder than I ever had to earn an honest living, if I only survived."

She sighed deeply. "And once you've kept your end of the bargain . . . you'll find the well again. And then you'll be able to go back."

He blinked. "Well . . . I guess so."

Emily sighed again. "I suppose I should tell you, should have told you before, when you first asked me. Jack, I . . . I saw that well once myself. Not all that long ago. But I could never find it again. For a while, I thought I must have dreamed the whole thing. But dream or not, I pitched in a penny, and made a wish of my own."

He nodded. "You wished for a way to keep this place for the kids, right? For someone to come along and help with the work."

She looked away. "Something like that."

"The well fairies must be having a hell of a laugh at both of us, then," he said. "You got stuck with a guy who knows about as much about farming as you can fit in a thimble, and I kept my end of the bargain by pulling a con to get the work done."

She smiled slightly and shook her head. "This is all so unbelievable."

"Look, you did me a huge favor by keeping me out of prison, Em. And the least I can do to pay you back is take care of you, until I find out how the hell to get back to my own time."

She looked up quickly when he said that, eyes wide, then shuddered. "How . . . long do you think that will be?"

"I have no way of knowing. But until then, you're gonna be taking a well-deserved vacation."

"But Jack, I can't—"

He covered her hand with his and she went silent, staring down at his hand and not saying a word. "Give me a chance, huh? No one ever has. I want to try to do this. Maybe if I keep my promise, actually do some work for once in my life, I'll get back where I belong. Let me try, Em. Just let me try."

Closing her eyes, she whispered, "Okay. All right."

He grinned. "Great. Now I'm bringing up that food, and then I'm going to go out and finish the planting, and I don't want any arguments."

She nodded.

The bedroom door burst open, and the kids came inside bearing fists full of weeds in full blossom.

"Ah, my little helpers are back," Jack said. "Sarah Jane, you're gonna take care of Aunt Em just like she takes care of you when you're sick. If she tries to get up or get dressed or do any work, I want you to come right out and get me, okay?"

Sarah Jane nodded hard. "I will!"

"Matt, I need you to show me just what the heck to do out there in the fields. And don't be afraid to say so if I'm doing it wrong or making stupid mistakes, okay?"

Matthew nodded. Jack clasped the boy's shoulder. Together they headed out the door.

Emily disliked this. Jack's attentiveness. His pampering. Because he seemed so sincere, and so concerned for her, and she could get used to that sort of thing. She was used to being the one doing the worrying. She was used to putting herself last. Now someone was putting her first for the first time in her life.

And he was going to disappear again just as soon as he could find a way.

She hadn't told him all of what she'd wished for out at that old wishing well, because it had been so personal and so frivolous and girlish. But she'd wished for a man to love her. To love her the way she'd always dreamed of being loved . . . the way she'd given up ever finding for herself.

But he wasn't that man. He wasn't her wish come true. He was working to fulfill his promise because it would get him away from her all the sooner. And for no other reason. She'd best remember that.

The big lug who won that supper was on his way up the trail to Emily's place when Matthew and Jack went out the front door. "What's the matter?" Jack called. "You run out of food already?"

Marty shrugged and sent a glance toward little Matthew. "I wanted a word with you, Jack. If you have a minute."

"A minute's about all I have. Matt, why don't you fetch us a jug of water to take out to the field with us, hmm?"

Matt was off like a shot, and Jack turned to Marty. "Okay. We're alone, what is it?"

Marty drew a breath. "You don't know much about farmin', do you, Jack?"

Jack felt his hackles rise, but Marty rushed on. "Look, don't take it bad, okay? But I figured out what you were up to yesterday, and to tell you the truth, I was pretty impressed with the way you pulled it off."

Jack's head came up. "Wait a minute. You knew . . . and you went ahead and plowed that field anyway?"

"Sure. Hey, a man's got his pride, you know. The thing is, Jack, I'm not the smartest fellow in town. And if I caught on, it's a sure bet the others will, too. You're not gonna be able to keep pullin' tricks like that contest all summer, and you sure as all hell can't raise and harvest the crop on your own. And if you don't, Miss Emily's gonna lose this place."

Jack sighed. "You think I don't know that?"

"So what are you gonna do about it?"

Shaking his head, Jack stood straighter. "I'm gonna learn as I go, I guess. Hell, what else can I do?"

Marty eyed him. "You can swallow your pride and let me lend a hand."

Jack's brows went up. "You want to help me?"

"Not you. Miss Emily. I can teach you all you need to know about farming, and help you out. You can give me a hand at my place. It'll all even out in the end, and if we're lucky, Miss Emily will have a healthy harvest and be able to pay off that mortgage. What do you say?"

Jack swallowed hard and kept his eyes on the ground. "There's a lot I don't know about besides just farming," he said. "You might be taking on more than you know."

"Hell, we'll go a day at a time. I'm willin' if you are."

Drawing a breath, and hating like hell to admit he needed help from the big lug, Jack told himself to buck up and do what was necessary. He thrust out a hand, and Marty shook it. "It's a deal," Jack said. "And uh . . . thanks."

Marty grinned, and when Matthew returned from the well with the water jug in hand, the three of them headed out. All day, Marty and Matthew instructed Jack in the intricacies of farm work. It was hard, hot, and exhausting. But there was something else, too. There was the way young Matthew looked up at him. The way the kid would stand just the way Jack was standing when they stopped for a break. Or if they sat down to take five in the shade, the way Matt would sit just as close beside Jack as he could manage. It touched something in Jack.

He figured that was par for the course. This whole damned family was managing to get to him, somehow. He was starting to think he'd miss them like crazy when he found his way back to his own time. All of them. Especially Emily.

# Chapter 7

The summer sun burned hot, but Jack didn't mind. He sat on a blanket munching fried chicken and watching the kids splash in the stream. Emily sat beside him, leaning back against the wide trunk of an old oak tree. Above her, nestled in the branches, was the tree house Jack and Matthew had started building. It wasn't going to make *Architectural Digest*, but Jack thought it was shaping up nicely. And the hours he and the kids had spent there working on it together were—and this was odd—some of the best times Jack had ever had.

Emily looked better. Jack had been taking on more and more of the chores around the place, and she had more color in her cheeks. He just wished the worry he saw whenever he looked into her eyes would ease up.

"The crop looks good," he said, wanting to draw her out of her thoughts, or else crawl into them with her. He'd been growing more and more intrigued by and drawn to Emily with every day that passed. But she was like a closed book to him. It was as if her skin were a hard shell that covered everything underneath. And though he'd tried, he hadn't been able to break through that barrier.

"You've outdone yourself, Jack." She looked at him, finally, and shook her head. "I can hardly believe you're the same man who didn't even know how to plow a field a couple of months ago."

"It's true, I've learned a lot. You know what surprises me most?"

"What?" she asked. The wind toyed with a runaway wisp of red.

"I . . . I'm kinda starting to like it. Oh, not the work part. But seeing the results, you know? I look out there at that sorghum standing tall, and I feel . . . I don't know . . ."

"Pride," she said, nodding. "You should be proud, you know. It's a feeling you can take with you . . . when you go back."

When he went back. It seemed that every time they talked she found a way to bring that into the conversation. Like she was reminding him . . . or maybe reminding herself.

"You know if you went and checked, that old wishing well might be there waiting for you even now. You've certainly kept your promise to work harder than you ever have."

"I haven't done what I came here to do yet, Em. I don't want to see the well again before I'm finished."

She nodded, licking her lips. "Have you spoken to the children about that yet?" she asked.

"About what? My leaving?" She nodded, and Jack shrugged. "I don't see the point. I mean, who knows if I'll ever find a way to get back to my own time. Why worry them for nothing?"

She lifted her chin. "They're getting awfully fond of you, Jack. It's not fair to keep it from them. You're going to leave us . . . them, I mean . . . either way. It's not as if you plan to stay married to a woman you don't love even if you can't find your way back where you belong."

"Hell, Emily—"

"Well, it's true, isn't it?"

He looked into her eyes, and felt something deep in his belly, something that scared the hell out of him. "Do we have to talk about this now? You're always worrying about things that haven't even happened yet, Em. Why don't we just put this off and deal with it when the time comes?"

"Because they need to know, Jack. They can't go getting their hopes up only to have their hearts broken in the end."

"They need to know?" he said, suddenly seeing something he hadn't seen before in her eyes. "Or maybe it's that you need to know."

She looked away quickly.

"Emily . . . have you ever tried to stop worrying about the future and just enjoy the present?" She shook her head, still not facing him, but he took her chin in two fingers and turned her head toward him. "I'm here, right now, today. At this very moment, I'm your husband . . . and you're my wife."

"But . . . it's not real." She had that scared look again. That doe-in-the-headlights look that made him just want to wrap her up in his arms and hold her there until it went away.

"Then let's make it real," he said, and he leaned closer, sliding his hand to the back of her head and threading his fingers in her hair. He held her still for his kiss, and pressed his mouth to hers. And for just an instant, she let him. She relaxed her lips apart, and let him trace them with his tongue, let him kiss her deeply, thoroughly, let him taste her . . . and he thought it was like tasting heaven.

And then she flattened her hands to his chest and pushed him away.

"Damn," he said, and he was breathless, aroused, hungry for more of her. "Emily McCain, you're gonna wish you'd made the most of this when I'm gone." He touched her hair, then closed his eyes. "I know I sure as hell am."

She shook her head in denial, parted her lips to speak, then closed them again. And instead of blurting out whatever she'd been about to say, she said, very calmly, "There's no future for us,

Jack. Anything we have now is temporary . . . it's a fantasy, and we both know it. I've never been the sort of woman who could exist on fantasies."

He licked his lips, tasting her on them. "It's no fantasy, Em. I want you. And I think you want me, too. That's solid reality, lady."

"It's fleeting reality," she said. "It's a dream that ends the minute we open our eyes."

"Haven't you ever heard of living in the moment?"

She faced him, and he almost gasped aloud when he saw the tears brimming in her eyes. Tears! But why? "I can't live in the moment, Jack. Not when I know that moment will end. I don't want to spend the rest of my life wishing I could go back and live it again. I can't live that way."

My God. Could she . . . could she actually be starting to . . . to *feel* something for him? She got to her feet, turning away, but Jack leaped up too, catching her arm and turning her back again. "So you think you're better off if you never know what you're missing?"

"If I never know it, I can't very well miss it, now can I?"

He shook his head, frustrated. " 'Tis better to have loved and lost, than never to have loved,' " he quoted.

"Pretty words, Jack. But the wrong words. Lust is what you're talking about, not love. And I'm too old a woman to confuse the two."

He blinked and stared at her. "Did you just admit to feeling lust? For me? The prim and proper Emily Hawkins McCain? I can't believe it."

Her eyes narrowed and she glared at him. "Proper I may be, Jack McCain, but still a woman."

He tried to touch her hair, but she pulled away. "Hey, come on. I was just being sarcastic, Em." She turned her back to him, and . . . God, she was trembling. "Emily, I'm sorry," he said, and he slid his hands over her shoulders.

"I'm weak where you're concerned," she whispered, and the way she said it made it sound like some dark confession.

"You're supposed to be. We're *married*, Emily. There's no shame in what you're feeling. To tell you the truth it . . . it's kind of humbling."

She made a noise of disbelief. "I should think you'd be proud to have reduced me to such an admission."

"No," he said, very softly. "Not proud. Humbled, Emily. To think a woman like you could . . . could feel that way toward a man like me. When I know damn well I'm nowhere near good enough for you."

"You're right," she whispered. "You're not."

He said nothing. Let her beat up on him if it made her feel better.

"The man good enough for me"—she went on, her voice strained, her body still shaking—"will be a man who's willing to stay. To make a life here on this farm, and to be a father, a *permanent* one, to Matthew and Sarah Jane." He thought she was crying, but couldn't see her face, and knew she wouldn't want him seeing her tears anyway.

"And what about passion, Emily?" he asked slowly. "What about desire?"

"Those things are unimportant."

"That's bull and you know it."

She turned, and he saw he'd been right. Her cheeks glistened with the kiss of her tears. "I've lived without those things for a long time, Jack. And I was perfectly happy to go on without them until . . ." She bit her lip to stop her words.

"Until I came along," he finished for her. She didn't answer, but just stood there facing him with strands of her burnished hair framing her face and dancing in the breeze. Her cheeks flushed with color and her eyes were gleaming and damp. Her dress hugged her little waistline, hiding everything else, making Jack want to take it off her. Maybe . . . maybe he didn't have to leave her. Maybe . . . he could be the kind of man she wanted.

"What if—"

"No," she said before he could complete the sentence. "Don't even say it, Jack."

He searched her pretty face, her luminous eyes. "Why not?"

"Because I know you're very good at making people believe what you want them to. And because if you make me believe . . . you'll destroy me, Jack."

He wouldn't . . . or maybe he would. Because he didn't know if he *could* be the kind of man she needed. The kind who would stay. He didn't know. . . .

But maybe it was high time he found out.

# Chapter 8

"You plannin' to take Miss Emily to the harvest dance, Jack?"

Jack glanced up at the oversized Marty as they worked a row apart with hoes, chopping down weeds. He sure had come full circle, hadn't he? Jack remembered once vowing he'd never pull another weed in his life. He almost smiled as he wiped his brow with the back of his hand, and leaned on the hoe handle.

"Harvest dance? Hell, Marty, we haven't even begun to harvest this stuff yet."

"Well, you got your crop planted a mite later than most."

"So everyone else is already bringing it in?"

"Yeah. Most are done already. The dance is Saturday night at the Perkins' barn."

Jack nodded, eyeing the tallish, reed-type crop he'd grown. He'd worked harder than he'd ever worked in his life since he'd come here. And damned if he didn't get out of bed every morning looking forward to it, and fall into bed at night satisfied with what he'd managed to accomplish that day. And with the respect he saw in Emily's eyes when she looked at him now. That meant more to him than he ever would have believed possible.

He slept better here, and ate better, too. God, the way Emily cooked, he'd half expected to develop a spare tire by the time this summer ended. Oh, he'd grown bigger, all right. But none of it was spare anything. When he took off his shirt and looked in the mirror, he liked what he saw. He liked it a lot.

He'd made every effort to give Emily a peek at his newly muscular chest and flat abs and washboard pecs. Okay, not quite washboard, but they were getting there. And at his hardened biceps and all that. In fact, he'd paraded past her several times, stripped bare from the waist up.

All she ever did was turn her head and politely ask him to put some clothes on.

Hell. The woman was . . . the woman was . . .

He glanced back toward the house. That was the fourth pail of water she'd carried in from the well outside. She was overdoing it again. And even now that the sun wasn't quite as brutal and the nights were cool, it was still too warm for her to be working so hard. The kids were out by the barn, playing some kind of game that involved hopping, jumping, and shouting with laughter.

A reluctant smile tugged at Jack's lips as he watched them.

"So?" Marty prodded. "About the dance?"

"Well, I can ask her, Marty," he said slowly, still sending worried gazes back toward the house every few moments. "But I don't know if she'll want to go with me." What was she doing with all that water? Scrubbing floors? Washing clothes?

"She ought to."

Something about the tone of Marty's voice made Jack look at him and pay attention. "Why's that?"

" 'Cause . . . Well, Jack, folks have been speculatin' about . . . about the two of you, and . . ."

*"And . . . ?"*

With a big sigh, Marty shook his head. "Most are of the opinion that you'll only be around long enough to harvest the crop. And that Miss Emily will be a free woman again before October."

"Oh, they are, are they?"

"Yeah. A lot of the single men are hopin' you'll be gone sooner. Like by Saturday night. They watch every day to see if you've started bringin' in the sorghum yet."

Jack went very still. "Are you saying they're all just waiting for me to leave so they can move in on my wife?"

Marty nodded solemnly. "Yup. That's exactly what I'm saying."

"Why those dirty, two-faced little . . ." His head came up. "Does she know about this?"

"Well, she's always known. I mean, there was no shortage of suitors at the door once ol' Clem was buried. But Miss Emily . . ." Marty shook his head and grinned crookedly. "She opined that they were only after this 'ere farm. Can you imagine?"

Oh, he could well imagine that. The woman had chosen him because she thought he'd never be interested in her. And hell, he'd been burning up for her ever since.

But to know that other men might be as well . . . well, now, that put things in a whole different light. What if she decided that one of them would make her a better husband than smilin' Jack McCain, con man extraordinaire? What if that was why she kept reminding him that he planned to leave as soon as the harvest was in?

Dammit, she didn't *want* any of them. She wanted *him*!

But she'd told him herself that desire was low on her list of priorities. What she needed was a dependable man, one who was in it for the long haul. A father for the kids. This thought drew his gaze their way again, and then made his throat close off. Sarah Jane's pigtails were crooked. He'd braided her hair for her this morning, insisting it was about time he learn how, and the little monster had giggled and wriggled the whole time. Emily had wanted to redo his handiwork when she'd seen the results, but Sarah Jane wouldn't let her. She said she liked her hair just the way Uncle Jack had fixed it, crooked or not.

A tear welled up in Jack's eye—a hot one that had no business being there. And all of a sudden he threw the hoe down to the ground and stomped toward the house.

"Jack?" Marty called. "What're you doin'?"

"I'll tell you what I'm *not* doing, Marty. I'm *not* stepping aside to let some other son-of-a-gun move in on my family!"

He thought he heard a deep chuckle as he marched from the field to the house, but he ignored it. He wasn't sure what he was feeling right now, and he didn't bother trying to analyze it. He was too stirred up to think straight. He just knew he had to tell her . . . tell her . . . *something*.

He'd surged through the door, scanned the kitchen, and headed up the stairs, still running on pure emotion. But when he burst into her bedroom, he forgot everything.

Everything.

Because she was sitting in that big metal tub, leaning back against it, head tilted up, eyes closed. The water was only up to her waist, and she was completely naked, and utterly . . . utterly . . .

"Beautiful," he whispered.

Her eyes blinked open. Then she looked up at him, and they widened. "Jack, get out!"

He stayed right where he was with his hat in his hands, and reached back to close the door behind him even as he shook his head from side to side. "I couldn't walk out of here now if I tried, Em."

Her arms were crossed over her breasts now, head lowered, cheeks hot. Jack moved closer to the tub. When she didn't scream bloody murder, as he half expected her to, he moved still closer, until he could kneel down beside it. Then he reached up to take her hands in his. Very gently, he moved them away and lowered them to her sides, so he could look at her. She was blushing all over, with her hair loose and tumbling in burnished curls over her shoulders, its ends damp and dragging in the water.

"My God, Emily, I've never seen anything so beautiful in my life. I mean . . . I mean all this time, I've been living under the same roof with you, and I knew you were beautiful, but . . . but I didn't know the half of it."

"Stop it," she whispered.

Her arms were so long and slender; her skin milky, untouched by the sun; her breasts perfect, plump, and soft. He'd never seen anything look more . . . more feminine. Woman. She was just the soul of woman. A goddess. An angel. A woman.

"Jesus, Em, if I could paint, I'd paint you just like this."

"Jack . . ."

"Look at you," he went on. "How could you ever think I wouldn't want you?" Finally he lifted his gaze to meet her eyes. "Hmm?" Then he trailed the backs of his fingers over her breasts. She caught her breath as his knuckles skimmed her nipples. "I'd die to have you in my arms right now," he said, staring hard at her.

She looked right back at him. Her gaze was probing and deep; her voice, raspy and hoarse. "Are you saying what you think I want to hear, Jack? So you can get what you want?"

He shook his head slowly. "I'm saying the truth, Emily. And it's what we both want. But I'll turn around and walk out of here right now if you tell me to."

She licked her lips and said nothing. So Jack got to his feet, and unbuttoned his shirt, and then shrugged it off. She sat still, just staring at him. And she looked scared, but she also looked aroused. And in need.

"Jack . . . I've never . . . been with a man."

He was so hard he ached. "I won't hurt you, Emily. I swear to Christ, I won't."

She closed her eyes. "Yes, you will, Jack," she whispered. "But not today, at least. Not today." She rose to her feet very slowly.

Water ran in gentle rivulets down her skin. She held out a hand. Jack couldn't move for a long moment as his eyes devoured her. And when he could, he managed to get free of his jeans, boots, and socks almost all in one effort. And then he took the hands she offered, and he stepped into the tub with her.

# Chapter 9

He was so tender, so careful with her. His touches, his kisses nearly brought tears to her eyes. Emily had never been so brazen. And yet she felt no shame in this. She was thirty-five years old, and married, and she'd spent her entire life taking care of other people. Her sister, and then Clem and the children. Just this once, she was going to take care of herself.

She'd wanted Jack all along. She knew that. Oh, she'd denied it for a time, even to herself, but the feeling had been there, burning inside her, growing stronger all the time. She couldn't keep fighting it. She didn't want to.

Even knowing it didn't mean anything. Even knowing he'd be gone long before winter set in, leaving her alone again.

He sank into the water, his hands at her waist, and he pulled her down with him, cradling her in his arms. He kissed her . . . first her lips, and then everywhere. He kissed her eyes, her neck, her breasts . . . and Emily felt the fire burn like none she'd ever imagined. His hands moved over her with a touch that made her heart pound, and her breaths came short and fast. He touched her most private places, and when she shied away he whispered gently to her, coaxing her and calming her, and touching her until she couldn't resist or refuse. Her mind seemed to have melted into a pool of utter longing. A need gnawed at her belly and made her ache for some foreign kind of fulfillment.

Finally he pulled her legs around his waist and settled her atop him, and very, very slowly, he pressed himself inside her. Filling her. Stretching her. She gasped, impatient now because this yearning was going to explode soon if he didn't . . . didn't do something. She moved herself lower, then cried out in a sudden sharp pain. "Jack!"

He went utterly still. "All right," he whispered. "All right. It's okay now. Easy, Em. Trust me, my beautiful Emily." He stroked her, one hand toying with her breast while the other moved between them to tease her at the spot where they were joined. His mouth found hers, and in seconds, that fire was spreading through her again. And Jack began to move with her, slowly at first, but then faster, and harder, driving her closer and closer to something she'd never felt.

And then it happened. The sky exploded, and she cried his name, and her entire body was seized in the grip of utter sensation, and release, and pleasure so intense it made her shudder all over.

He held her close, bent to kiss her neck, and then whispered, "My God, Emily, it's never been like this for me before. Never."

She lifted her head, met his eyes. Breathlessly, she whispered, "Are you . . . can we . . ."

"Again?" he asked with a tender smile.

Emily nodded. And Jack got out of the tub, and bent over it to scoop her into his arms. He carried her to the bed and they did it again. Emily thought her body would shatter with the sensations he brought to her. She thought her skin would melt from the heat. But there was more. There was the emotion that flooded her heart for this man. And that was when she realized that she'd made a terrible mistake.

She'd fallen in love with him. She loved Jack McCain, this stranger from another time. This man who had to leave her in the end. She loved him, and when he went away, it was going to break her heart.

Lordy, but her heart felt as if it were already breaking!

He held her gently when it was over, tight to his chest, his arms almost possessive. She kept her face low so he wouldn't see her tears. Her body was sated, flushed with satisfaction. She felt like a woman for the first time in her life. But her heart was left yearning for more. So much more.

"Em?" he asked. "Honey? Are you okay?"

She only nodded. "It was . . . it was wonderful, Jack."

She heard the breath sigh out of his hard chest in relief. "I thought it was pretty wonderful myself," he told her.

She said nothing, just snuggled closer to him. She didn't want this to end. But she knew it had to.

"We . . . we should talk," Jack said.

Of course he'd want to talk. He'd want to remind her that this little interlude didn't change anything. That he still had to go back to his own time. Back where he belonged. And she still had to stay here and make a life for the children. Nothing had changed.

"It's all right, Jack," she whispered. "You don't have to say anything. I know."

He stroked her hair. "Do you?"

"Of course. I'm not a child. I understand that men have . . . have needs. I realize that's all this was."

He seemed to stiffen beside her. "Is that what you think?"

"It's what I know."

"But, Emily, I—" He stopped then, because the sound of rattling wheels and the clip-clop steps of a horse and carriage came clearly through the slightly opened window.

"Lordy, someone's come calling!" Emily hurried out of bed,

taking the sheet with her and gathering up her clothes as she went. She peeked outside. "Goodness, it's Mr. Sheldon!"

"Who?" Jack sat up and began to dress at a more leisurely pace. Too leisurely, she thought.

"The banker! He's determined to take this farm from me and has been from the start! Hurry up, Jack!"

"Oh." Jack sighed. He was unwilling to let Emily go one more minute with her mixed-up notions about what he was thinking and feeling, but figured he had no choice. He figured she'd die of embarrassment if the jerk outside caught them naked in bed. So he finished dressing and headed downstairs just in time for the banker to rap on the front door. When he opened it, he saw Marty hurrying up the steps, too, obviously curious about what the man wanted.

The fellow eyed Jack up and down, a look of disdain crossing his pinched face as he stepped inside. He quickly dismissed Jack and searched for Emily. "I need to speak with Miss Hawkins," he said.

"That's Mrs. McCain," Jack told him. "And she'll be with you in a minute. But since I'm here, why don't you tell me what it is you're here about?"

Sheldon offered a fake smile. "It's business. Private business between Emily and myself."

"Is that right?"

He nodded. "So if you don't mind, I'll wait for her."

"I'm right here."

Both men looked up to see Emily descending the stairs, her skirts in place and her hair pinned up. Only Jack could see that her eyes still sparkled and her cheeks still glowed with the aftereffects of lovemaking. God, he wanted her again already. But there was something else in those green eyes, too. A certain heartache he was beginning to think he understood.

"Good," Mr. Sheldon said. "Now if you *gentlemen* will excuse us—"

"Mr. Sheldon, Jack is my husband. Any business you have with me, you also have with him. Is that understood?"

The man's head pulled back a bit, and he stiffened as if surprised. "Come now, Emily. Everyone in town knows this farce is more a business arrangement than a marriage. McCain's only interest in you and this farm is that it's keeping him out of jail. And your only interest in him is as a free hand."

Jack had picked up Sheldon by his starched lapels before he knew he was going to move, and he lifted him right off his feet. Marty quickly gripped Jack's shoulders and pulled him back. Jack had the satisfaction of seeing the guy's eyes bulge before he set him back on the floor again. "State your business and leave, mister, before I decide to use you for fertilizer."

Sheldon brushed at his shirtfront and smoothed his jacket. "Well. It's obvious you haven't changed your criminal ways, McCain."

"What do you want, Mr. Sheldon?" Emily asked firmly.

The man sighed. "Fine, have it your way. I only came to deliver a friendly bit of advice, Emily."

"That being?"

"The grain auction is being held this Saturday."

Emily literally staggered two steps backward, her face paling so suddenly that Jack thought she was going to pass out cold. He rushed to her side and eased her into a chair. "I don't get it," he said. "What does that mean?"

"We . . . we have a steady market for the crops we grow. Every September the farmers gather in town to meet the buyers, who come to negotiate a fair price for the grain. They're mostly cattle ranchers from farther south—from certain counties in Texas and Arizona where there's too little rain to grow the quality of sorghum we can produce here. They pay cash and haul the grain back with them."

Emily explained it all slowly and clearly, but even then Jack could see her lower lip trembling and her eyes darting around in what looked like panic before they finally landed on the banker again. "But we never hold the grain auction until the end of September. They shouldn't be here for three weeks yet."

"Well, I sent a few telegrams, letting them know that all the locals would have their harvest in by the day after tomorrow, and that the date had been moved up accordingly. I thought it rather nice to hold the auction on the same day as the harvest dance for a change."

Emily's eyes narrowed and she rose to her feet. "You did this deliberately. You *know* I can't possibly get this crop harvested by the day after tomorrow!"

He shrugged. "Oh? You can't? Well, then I suppose you might as well deal with me now, as later." He reached into his coat and pulled out a folded paper. "Sign this, Emily. The farm will belong to me, and your debt will be forgiven. I've been very generous, even put in a clause allowing you and the children to remain living in the house . . . providing you get rid of this so-called husband of yours. I won't house a convict."

Emily looked up at Jack. Her eyes were watering. Jack saw those eyes. Big and round, and damp. And he reached out, took the papers from Sheldon's hand, and easily tore them in half, then in half again, and again, and then he tossed the pieces over the guy's head like confetti.

"The crop will be in on time. The debt will be paid in full. And this *convict* isn't going anywhere. You got that?"

Emily blinked, looking stunned and slightly unsure.

"If you don't agree to my terms now," Sheldon said, "then my generosity ends. I'll take the farm anyway, and toss you *and* those orphans out. Not a roof over their heads, Emily. Is that the way you want to raise them? Is that what you promised your sister on her deathbed?"

"That's it," Jack said, and he grabbed Sheldon by one arm, twisted it and tossed the jerk right over his shoulder. "You wanna get the door, Marty? I need to take out the trash."

Marty grinned and opened the door, and Jack stepped through it and hurled the sputtering, shouting banker right off the porch and onto the dusty ground. "Don't let me catch you on this property again, or I'll have the sheriff arrest you for trespassing."

The man got up, brushed at his clothes, and shouted threats all the way to his buckboard. Jack stood on the porch with his arms folded over his chest until Sheldon rattled out of sight. Then a soft voice made him turn.

"It's impossible," Emily whispered from beyond the screen door. "It's just impossible. Jack, we only have two days until the auction, and we haven't even begun. It would take a dozen men to harvest the crop in that short a time. There's just no way . . ."

Jack went to her, and saw Marty standing behind her shaking his head as if he agreed with every word. Jack put his hands on Emily's shoulders. "I'll find a way. Trust me, Emily. I swear, I'll make this work."

She closed her eyes and lowered her head. "I know you'll try," she said, then turned and walked back into the house.

Jack watched her go.

Marty came out and walked beside him, back out toward the fields. "She's right, you know," the big lug said. "Jack, the two of us working dawn to dusk might . . . *might* be able to harvest half the sorghum in this field on time. But there'd be another half to go, and then two other fields. There's no way we can do it. Not if we could work day and night nonstop from now till Saturday. There's just no way."

Jack stopped halfway between the house and the fields, and stood looking out at the crops. "You sure?"

"I been doing this all my life, Jack. Yeah. I'm sure."

"Okay, then. Okay. I guess there's only one way. And Emily's not going to like it . . . but I don't see as we have a choice."

Marty stared at him, frowning. Then the frown eased and his brows rose. "Not another contest? Jack, Miss Emily'd have liked to skin you alive the last time! And she said if you ever did anything like that again she'd—"

"I know. I know." He gripped Marty's arm and steered him past the field, and toward the road into town instead. "So what do you think for a prize this time, Marty? Another feast? Or maybe we could offer cash . . . you know, payable once we sell the crop."

Marty just lowered his head and shook it. "Miss Emily's gonna be madder than a wet hen when she finds out," he muttered.

$\mathcal{I}$t didn't go exactly the way Jack had planned it. Oh, he altered his approach a bit. This time he didn't use boasting or bragging to lure the local men into an ego-fest. He tried being humble for a change.

With his back to the bar and a beer in his hand, he said, "Guys, I have to swallow my pride here and admit that I can't get my grain harvested in time for that auction on Saturday. Not alone, anyway."

"Gee," someone said. "What a surprise."

"No, no surprise. I suppose I should have seen this coming. But you know, it wasn't exactly fair of Sheldon to move the date up like that."

A few men muttered in agreement to that point, at least.

"So what you gonna do, Jack," someone said. "Stage another contest?" Laughter built up around him.

"Yeah," said another. "Fool us into harvesting your crop for you for free while you nurse a twisted ankle again?"

"All for the chance to win a meal!" The third speaker shook his head as the laughter grew louder. "We ain't gonna fall for the same trick twice, McCain."

"It wasn't a trick," Jack denied, putting on his most innocent face. "Okay, I'll admit, I didn't know what I was doing. And I did need the plowing done, but it was an honest contest. The winner got exactly what he was promised. Didn't you, Marty?"

Marty nodded. "That meal of Miss Emily's was worth every minute of plowing I done," he said, nodding hard to emphasize every word.

"So what do you say, guys? You want to do it again? You all compete and the guy who harvests the most grain by Saturday gets a feast, prepared and delivered, the very next day?"

The men in the saloon muttered and shook their head. "We been harvestin' sorghum for weeks now, Jack," one called. "You're gonna have to do better than that."

Jack gnawed his lower lip. "All right," he said slowly. "How about cash? I'll give a cash prize as well, just as soon as we get paid for the crop."

Again there was muttering and shaking of heads. "No man here would take cash from Miss Emily," one said. "It'd be like takin' food from those little uns' mouths."

Frustrated, Jack slammed his glass down onto the bar. "Well, what then? Name it, guys. I'm in a desperate situation here."

Finally, one guy, young and lean and good looking, sauntered up to the bar. "Well, I can think of one thing that might entice some of these men to take you up on this harvest contest idea, Jack. The single ones, anyway."

Jack felt a tingle up his spine. "What are you getting at?"

"The harvest dance, Saturday night. The winner gets to escort Miss Emily to the dance."

Jack blinked, searched the room, and saw many smiles and nodding heads. His throat went dry. He searched his mind. Searched his heart, too, and knew what he had to do. And then he heard himself say, "You're on."

There was a soft gasp from just beyond those batwing doors, and when Jack looked up, he glimpsed Mary Brightwater looking in at him, shaking her ringlets in disapproval.

# Chapter 10

"*You* . . . you . . . you did *what*?" Emily stood on the front porch watching hordes of men assemble in her fields. She'd known the moment she'd seen them descending that Jack had pulled another trick on them, had conned them with some phony contest just like before.

But she'd never dreamed he would have promised *her* as the prize!

"Look, there's nothing to worry about."

"Nothing to worry about!" She stared up at him, so shocked . . . so . . . so *hurt* that she could feel her entire body trembling with rage. "How could you, Jack? You bartered me as if I were some light-skirted saloon girl! Or is that what you think of me now? Is it? Just because I gave myself to you do you think I'm . . ."

"*No!*" he denied. "No, Emily, it's nothing *like* that. I mean, I have a plan. Trust me."

"Trust you? Trust *you*?" She drew back her hand and slapped him so hard the impact nearly freed her shoulder from its socket.

Jack just looked at her as his face turned red.

"I will *never* forgive you for this, Jack. Never!" She felt the tears brimming, so she turned her back to him.

She heard his frustrated sigh. "I want to explain," he said to her back. "But I don't have time now. I have to go. Just know you're all wrong about this, Em. But you'll see that. You'll see." Then his booted feet stomped away, across the porch and down the steps.

Emily walked into the house, her feet dragging. But she had barely heard the door slam behind her when a cheerful voice called, "Isn't this the most romantic thing you've ever heard of?"

Emily stiffened and tried to remember that Mary Brightwater was a friend. It wasn't her fault that this insane idea of hers had backfired so miserably. She'd only been trying to help.

"Romantic?" Emily asked. "He's bartering with me as if I'm a prize heifer at a county fair!"

"Surely two dances with one of the local boys isn't too high a price to pay for getting your harvest in, Emily."

Emily turned, brows lifting. "Two dances?"

"Well, yes. It was one of the conditions Jack set. Didn't he tell you?"

Tipping her head to one side, Emily said, "No. He didn't."

Mary smiled and hurried into the kitchen, lifting the tin pot to check its weight, then nodding and pouring the still-warm brew into two cups. "Sit down, Emily. You really ought to know the details."

"Yes, I suppose I should. Since I *am* the prize in question."

Mary shrugged and set the cups on the table, taking a chair. Emily sat opposite her. "Jack only agreed to let the winner have two dances with you. Any two dances he wishes, except the waltz, and the last dance of the night."

Blinking in surprise, Emily sipped her coffee and refrained from commenting.

"Jack further said that he would bring you to the dance himself, and that only he would be allowed to take you home. And he informed the men that he would be keeping a close eye on the one who wins those two dances. At the first sign of impropriety, the deal is off."

"Really?" Emily asked, but her voice had become a croak by now.

"And then he informed them that it wasn't going to matter at any rate, because he intended to win this contest himself."

Emily sniffed. "He told them the same thing last time, and then faked a twisted ankle to get out of having to live up to the claim."

Mary glanced toward the front door, through which the fields were visible. "Not this time," she said with a nod.

Emily looked outside just as the sheriff fired a pistol shot into the air to signal the start of the contest. Jack was there, at the nearest end of the field, sickle in hand, and when that shot rang out, he sprang into motion. Emily blinked and shook her head. "I don't . . . I don't understand. Why would he bother? The crop will get harvested whether he participates in this madness or not."

Mary stared at Emily with her jaw gaping. "I declare, Emily, why do you think *any* of them are bothering?"

Emily look down at the floor. "Men are a mystery to me. I suppose it's something to do with the male ego."

"It's something to do with *you*. Emily, you're a beautiful, capable, intelligent woman. Every unmarried male in this town is enamored with you."

"I'm a thirty-five-year-old widow with two children," Emily corrected her.

"You're a prize that men would fight for, and that crowd out in your field is proof of it." She sighed. "Look at them, Emily. Look at Jack. I vow, he's fighting harder than any of them!"

Emily swallowed the sudden dryness in her throat.

"Let's go out and watch," Mary said, jumping to her feet and

snatching Emily's hand. And before Emily could argue she was being dragged through the house and across the lawn to the north
field.

Jack worked like a man possessed. Emily watched as he swung
the sickle again and again. In a short while, he had to pause to peel
his shirt from his sweat-dampened skin, and then he dove right back
into the grain again. Emily stood mesmerized, her eyes on him and
him alone. The steady flex and release of his corded muscles. The
way his hair stuck to his face as it grew damp with sweat. In no time
at all he'd pulled far ahead of his competitors. And to think he was
a man who'd admitted that he'd spent his life avoiding physical la-
bor. A man she was convinced felt nothing for her beyond sexual
desire.

What if she'd been wrong?

*A* hand on his shoulder made Jack pause in swinging the sickle,
which had been getting heavier with every arc. He turned, irritated
at the interruption. He'd been totally focused on the rhythm of his
movements. But when he saw who stood there, his irritation fled.
"Emily . . ."

"I . . . brought you a cool drink. Lemonade."

He saw the dewy glass in her hand and took it, gulped the con-
tents gratefully, then swiped his mouth with the back of his hand.
"Thanks. I needed that."

She nodded and took the glass back. "The others have stopped
at least long enough to snatch a bite to eat."

"Good," he said. "That'll give me a better lead on them." He
sent her a wink and started to turn away.

"At least have a biscuit, and another drink. You'll . . . you'll de-
hydrate if you don't." She was using his own word, but he didn't
mind when she pulled the biscuit from her apron pocket and

poured more lemonade into the glass from the tin pitcher she carried in her free hand.

He didn't argue. He wolfed the biscuit down so fast he barely bothered to chew, and then he gulped more liquid.

As he did, Emily said, "Jack . . . I judged you too quickly before. I . . . Mary explained the conditions you set, and I want you to know it's all right."

He swallowed, licked his lips, and stared at her. "It is?"

"Yes," she said. "I . . . I won't mind so much dancing with one of these men. I mean, it's only two dances, after all, and it's little enough to ask in return for getting the harvest in."

"Really." He said it flatly, watching her face.

"Yes, really. So you needn't kill yourself trying to win. I won't be angry with you."

He smiled very slightly. He was exhausted, and the day was only half over. And yet there remained a little cockiness in him. "You may not mind dancing with one of those rednecks, Em. But I'd mind it. I'd mind it a whole lot. So rest assured, it's not gonna happen."

"It's . . . not?"

"I want you all to myself Saturday night."

"You . . . do?"

"I wouldn't have pulled this scam if I thought there was any doubt I could win. Even though I knew it was the only way to get the crop in, Em, I wouldn't have done it. Not if I wasn't sure."

She looked so damned bewildered that it was clear she still wasn't getting it. So he jerked her into his arms, pulled her tight against him, and kissed her hard and deep.

But when he lifted his head, she still looked bewildered. And now she was blushing to boot.

"Honey," he said, "I don't know how you expect me to carry out my plan to win this thing with you out here distracting me this way." He smiled at her, and she seemed totally at a loss.

"Well . . . I'll . . . go then."

"Pick out something pretty for Saturday night," he called as she turned and began hurrying away. " 'Cause I plan to claim every single dance with you. That's a promise, Emily McCain."

She looked back and her lips pulled into a tremulous, uncertain smile.

"Damn," Jack muttered when she finally turned away again. "What a woman." He shook his head and lifted his sickle.

"We have a winner!" the sheriff called, and he held Jack's fisted hand up high above his head. They stood on a slight rise among a crowd of tired, dirty, sweaty men, silhouetted in the twilight of dusk. Around them the field lay flat, nothing standing beyond uneven stubble and an occasional missed stalk, bent or broken.

Jack was coated in sweat and dirt and bits of sorghum. His hair was wet, his chest was bare, and his knees were wobbly. He didn't look as if he could stand up much longer. But he was grinning crookedly, all the same.

Emily's entire crop had been harvested. She saw Mr. Sheldon from the corner of her eye as he slammed his hat onto his head and stomped away. He must realize he'd lost. It was over. He was beaten.

But she stopped thinking about that when Jack sank to his knees in the dust. The men around him dissipated, shaking their heads in begrudging admiration and muttering that maybe he wasn't such a tinhorn after all. Even the sheriff gave Jack a friendly slap on the shoulder.

Emily went to Jack and dragged one of his arms around her shoulders, helping him to his feet.

"I did it," he muttered, looking up at her as he limped toward the house. "I won."

"Yes, you did. But if you don't get some rest you won't be capable of dancing with me on Saturday night."

He sighed blissfully. "No chance of that, Em. No chance at all." He managed to move his feet every now and then as she helped him into the house.

# Chapter 11

*Jack* opened his eyes. He was wet. Cool. Oh, yeah, he was soaking in a lukewarm bath in that big ol' tin tub. And he was languishing under the gentle touch of hands that were as strong and capable as they were soft and erotic.

"Emily," he muttered.

"Who else?" She rinsed the soap off his chest. "Think you can stand up long enough to get into bed?"

"Hey, didn't I just prove I'm the manliest man out here?"

She smiled at him, but there was a sadness behind her eyes, even now. "Come on then." She gripped his arm to help him, steadied him as he stepped out, buck naked, and then briskly began to towel him off. She drew him toward the bed and yanked the covers back. "In you go."

He gripped her arm. "Not alone, I'm not." When he fell into the bed he pulled her in with him, and in a heartbeat his arms locked around her waist and his mouth found hers. God, it felt good to kiss

her. And this time he felt like he'd earned her kiss. Like maybe he
was worthy of her after all.

But then, why was she pulling herself free?

He let go, and she got out of the bed fast, jerking the covers
back up over him, and shaking her head. "I . . . can't, Jack."

"But—"

"No buts. This . . . this thing between us . . . well, it's gone as
far as it can, we both know that."

"Wha—"

Her eyes bored into him as she quoted the verse he'd seen carved
on that well: the words he'd heard his grandmother repeat in her
singsong voice so many times he knew them by heart.

"Make a wish upon this well, but wishes don't come free.
Make a promise here as well, and your wish you will see.
A voyage will you take then, your promise to fulfill.
And when you've kept your vow, shall I appear here on this
　　hill.
With one more wish to grant you, one more gift to bestow.
Any wish you care to make; to stay, perhaps, or go."

"Emily, that's—"

"It's what brought you here. And now . . . now, well, you've
done what you came here to do, Jack. You saw the crop harvested
and even loaded the wagons and put them in the barn for the night
in case of rain. You've done what you promised and then some. So I
have no doubt you'll find that well right where you last saw it.
You'll be able to . . . to go back."

He lowered his head and shook it. He wasn't even sure why, but
the thought made his heart ache.

"Go to sleep now, Jack," Em whispered. "Matthew volunteered
to milk Bessie for you tonight, and Sarah Jane is feeding the hens.

They're already out in the barn getting started, so you just rest, and in the morning, we'll go find that well."

He drew a breath, lifted his chin, and saw something in her eyes. Heartache. Longing. And a dancing reflection of . . . light. Red light.

He turned fast, and then sprang from the bed when he saw the tongues of flame licking up from the barn. "Fire! Oh, Jesus, the kids!" He was on his feet and pulling on his pants before Emily got out of the room and raced after him.

Fire leaped from every opening in the rough-hewn, weathered boards. The shingles seemed to melt before his eyes. Jack raced around the building seeking a way in, realizing that the crop, the entire crop, was being destroyed right before his eyes, and that as hard as he'd worked for it, it didn't matter. Nothing mattered except those kids.

Something emerged from the burning building—a large form, flames dancing from its back. "Marty!" Jack yelled, and he plowed into the big man, knocking him down and rolling him in the dirt.

"The children!" Marty cried. "I didn't know . . . and then I heard them and I went back, but they . . ."

"I'll get them."

Emily was on her feet, running toward the burning barn, but Jack caught her, turned her. "I'll get them, Emily. I swear to Christ, I will. Please, stay out here, safe. Trust me." He leaned in, kissed her hard and fast, then turned and, covering his face with one arm, ran through the flames.

"I do trust you, Jack!" she called after him.

Jack burst through a gap between walls of fire and into the darkness of the barn. He couldn't see. He couldn't breathe. Smoke filled the place, and the heat was so intense it was like a furnace. A roar filled his ears and he wasn't sure he could have heard the kids if they had shouted at him. But he had to try. He wasn't leaving this damned barn without them!

"Matt! Sarah!" He moved forward, knowing a search would prove useless. He was blind. So he simply moved toward where he thought they'd be. Near the cow. Matt had been milking, right?

As he drew closer, Bessie's thrashing and frantic bellowing overwhelmed the roar of fire in his ears, and Jack followed the sound, found her in the thick smoke, and untied her. "You're on your own, girl." He pointed her toward escape and slapped her rump hard. The bovine bolted, bellowing to the heavens.

Jack knelt and felt around, discovering the toppled milk pail and the spilled milk. The little stool was still there. A sob tore through his chest. Cupping his hands like a megaphone he yelled again. "Matthew! Answer me!"

A long, wailing word he thought might have been "help" came from farther inside, and Jack ran, banged into a post, shook himself, and ran again.

"I'm right here! Talk to me so I can find you," he repeated. "Talk to me!"

"R-right here! Jack!"

He followed the frightened little girl's voice, and wound up on the floor where she'd been crouching, terrified, in a corner. Small arms twisted so tight around his neck that he couldn't even breathe the smoke-laden air. And he didn't care. He held that tiny body close and tried to calm her trembling. "Where's your brother, Sarah? Where's Matt?"

"I-I-I think he's dead!" she cried, and then started coughing and sobbing alternately.

Jack knelt down and felt the boy's limp body. He leaned close and felt the touch of Matt's breath on his cheek. Then he gripped Sarah's shoulders. "He's not dead. Do you hear me, Sarah?"

Her arms snagged him around the neck in answer, and tears smeared his shoulder as little Sarah buried her head there. She wouldn't let go, terror made her cling to him. And he couldn't ask her to let go. "Sarah, climb onto my back," he shouted over the ever-growing roar. "Wrap your legs around my waist, and your arms around my neck. That's it. Tighter now."

She did as he told her, and as soon as she clung in place, he knelt to scoop Matt up into his arms. "Hold on tight, Sarah," Jack called. "Don't let go." He felt her nod, but didn't hear her answer. Her face was pressed to the back of his shirt, and he figured that was just as well. Maybe it would filter some of the smoke the poor child was breathing. But not enough. God, she was coughing with every breath, and a few steps more and he was, as well.

Matthew wasn't, but Jack almost wished he would.

Finally, Jack felt air on his face and stumbled forward, through an opening, into the night, the burst of fresh, cool air hitting him full in the face.

"Jack! Matthew!" Emily cried. She rushed forward and took the boy from Jack's arms. Jack sank to his knees and felt a weight lifted from his back. Looking up, he saw Marty, his face sooty but soft as he eased little Sarah off Jack's back and set her on her feet.

Sarah's arms instantly clamped around Jack's neck again. "I knew you'd come!" she cried. "I knew it. I love you, Jack."

"I love you, too, Sarah," he heard himself whisper hoarsely, the words so natural and honest that he didn't even have to think about them before he said them.

He glanced up to see Emily kneeling, clutching Matthew, and sobbing. "Emily?" Jack got to his feet.

"He's . . . not breathing, Jack. God, please . . . he's not breathing. . . ."

Tears streamed over Em's cheeks, glistening in the fireglow. Jack was there in an instant, easing Matt from her arms. "I can't lose him," he said, as if the child were his to lose. But it felt as if he were. He recalled Matt's miniature imitation of the man of the house. The way he was so protective of Sarah and Emily. The smile on his face when he hauled that fish out of the stream. The front tooth just about ready to fall out.

"No dammit, I can't lose him!" Jack stretched the still child on the ground, pinched his nose, and leaned close, covering Matt's mouth with his own. Breathing into tiny lungs, he paused, repeated it, paused, and counted. He didn't even realize he was counting out loud. When he got to fifteen, he straightened and positioned his hands over Matt's sternum, depressed, released, depressed again. Back to breathing.

"Jack? Jack, what are you . . . ?"

"He's putting Matthew's air back, Aunt Emily," Sarah said, interpreting what she was seeing as best she could. "Uncle Jack will make Matthew all right again. I know he will."

*God, let me live up to her innocent faith. I don't want to let that angel down.*

Breaths again, compressions again, and over and over, for how long, Jack didn't know. He only knew that he'd have likely gone on all night long, but for one thing.

Matthew coughed.

Emily cried out. Marty gasped aloud. Sarah crowded in to hug her brother.

"Easy, easy," Jack said to everyone, including himself, as he watched Matthew blink him into focus, saw the color returning to his face in the glow of the fire.

Emily sank to the ground and gathered both children close to her. Her skirts were like a safe nest, a haven to them, and the children huddled close. She held them, but her eyes, gleaming with tears, were on Jack. The picture that the three of them made there, together, safe, made his chest swell with something that felt a lot like pride. But he'd failed, all the same.

"We . . . lost the crop, Em. I'm sorry."

"I don't care. Jack, I don't care if we lose every shingle on this place and the place with them. You saved my babies. I have them. I have *them*." She closed her eyes. "You are a hero, Jack. Our hero."

Jack's throat swelled, and he moved closer, knelt down, and put his arms around the three of them. Matthew could barely talk. His voice was coarse, gravelly. "I saw someone, Jack. That man, Mr. Sheldon, from the bank."

Jack went still. "He was in the barn before the fire?"

Matthew nodded. "He didn't see me, though. I ducked," he rasped.

"I seen him, too," Marty said. Jack rose again, turning. He'd forgotten Marty was even here. "I was comin' over to see if you needed any help with chores tonight, seein' as how you about killed yourself winning that contest today. And I passed him on the road, goin' the other way, back toward town. Then I seen the smoke."

"So you rushed out here to try to fight the fire."

Marty shook his head. "To save the sorghum. If I'd known those two younguns was in there, I'd have let it burn, but I didn't hear 'em yellin' until after I'd pulled the wagons out. I went back in, but . . ."

"Wait a minute," Jack said. "You pulled the wagons out?"

Marty nodded, then lifted a beefy arm and pointed. Off in the distance, five wagons heaped with freshly cut sorghum stood in a crooked row, perfectly safe from the fire. Bessie the cow, her rump singed in places, was nibbling a bit of the harvested crop.

Jack looked at Emily. She stared back at him and slowly, her face lit up in a smile.

Emily's happy mood dissipated Saturday morning. Oh, it had lasted through the bidding, and the collecting of a lovely price for her crop. And it had lasted through her visit with Sheriff Stonewall, and the pleasure of watching Mr. Sheldon be arrested and put in a jail cell to await the circuit judge's next visit. It lasted through the picnic lunch by the stream when Jack took Matthew and Sarah fishing, swimming, and tree-climbing.

It should have lasted all day. Because she had her farm, minus one replacable barn. And she had her precious angels, safe and happy, all thanks to Jack.

But now, as they sat watching the children play by the water's edge, Jack said the words that eliminated her good mood . . . maybe forever.

"Let's go up the hill and see if that well's decided to make itself visible to me yet."

Emily's throat went dry. Her heart seemed to shatter. She'd thought . . . well, that he'd at least stay with her until after the harvest dance tonight. He'd said . . .

Oh, but what did it matter? He'd saved her children and her farm, and the least she could do in return was let him go. Without guilt or repercussions or tears. But it was hard to be noble. Because she loved him. She loved him so incredibly much.

But she only said, "All right," and called to the children, "Take the picnic basket back to the house for me, darlings. Uncle Jack and I will be . . . I mean . . . I'll be there in a few minutes, all right?"

Sarah nodded and smiled. Matthew tilted his head, as if detecting something wrong with her voice or her words, but not quite able to figure out what. He hefted the basket, and the two ran off toward the house.

She turned, and when Jack offered his arm, she took it. They walked together around the bend in the river, to the narrow, dusty road beyond it, and along that road for a good distance. Then they veered off it, went up the slight hill, and parted some brush in the spot where the well was supposed to have been.

And it stood there, solid and real, as if it had been there all along. The words were still chiseled into its stone. And Jack drew a breath and sighed. "So I guess I should do this by the traditional method, huh?" he asked, and he fished a coin from his pocket.

"I guess so." Emily averted her face to hide her tears, bit her lip, and vowed not to cry until he was gone. "I'll . . . I'll explain to the children. I'll make them understand."

He only nodded. "Would uh . . . I be out of line if I asked for a kiss? For luck?"

Her smile, she knew, was shaky, but she shook her head, and stood on tiptoe and pressed her lips to his. He kissed her, then kissed her again. And then he swept her into his arms and bent her backward and kissed her as if his very life depended on it.

And finally, he straightened away. "Well," he said. "Here goes nothing."

Emily braced herself, wondering how it would happen. Would he simply vanish? Dissolve into some kind of magic mist and evaporate? It didn't matter. He'd be gone, out of her life forever.

"I'll never forget you, Jack," she whispered.

"Well, I should hope not," he replied, and then he tossed his coin into the well and cleared his throat, and held her hand tight. "I wish with all my heart that Emily Hawkins McCain would let me be her husband." She looked up fast, and he took both her hands and stared deeply into her eyes. "Her *real* husband," he said. "And a father to Matthew and Sarah. And I wish that she could love me. Because if she could, then I'd never have need to wish for anything else, ever again."

Emily just stood there, blinking at him, her heart swelling until she thought it would burst as his words sank in. "Jack?" she whispered.

"I love you, Emily," he told her. "I swear I do. I don't want to go back to the future. I want to stay here, with you and the kids. If . . . if you'll have me."

Her lips trembling, she smiled. "If I tell you no . . . then I'll have no escort to the harvest dance tonight," she managed to blurt out, feeling giddy and silly and insanely, madly in love. Like a young girl! "So I guess I have no choice."

"Guess not," he said, but he still looked a bit uncertain.

"I love you too, Jack. I tried not to. I was afraid to let myself feel this . . . because I didn't think you'd ever feel it, too. And I thought you'd leave me in the end, and I didn't want my heart broken. But all my fighting didn't stop it. I love you, and I think I have from the second I saw you in your silly twentieth-century clothes in that crowd of convicts."

"Oh yeah?"

She nodded. Jack's smile faded slowly, and he pulled her close. "I want to spend the rest of my life making you happy, Emily. And we'll start tonight, at that dance. I . . . er, don't suppose you know the Macarena?"

She gave him a frown, then shook her head and snuggled close to his chest, relishing the embrace of his strong arms around her, knowing this was where she belonged, where they both belonged. They stood like that for a long moment, surrounded by brambles, caressed by the breeze, and cradled by the hillside. And behind them the old well shimmered for just a moment, and then faded away.

1/06